For a few insane moments, he'd forgotten that Leigh believed he was dead.

He'd forgotten that, due to plastic surgery, he had a face she'd never seen. He'd expected her to fling herself at him, weeping, in an act of recognition and reunion. Instead, her first reaction had seemed to be one of...fear.

John shook his head, trying to exorcize the memory of the straight-to-the-gut jolt of electricity he'd experienced when his gaze had connected with Leigh's for the first time in five and a half years.

Leigh was the only woman he'd ever loved. And, as he'd just discovered, she was also the mother of his only child.

John expelled a breath he hadn't realized he'd been holding. Leigh and Andy. The partner he thought he'd lost forever. The son he'd never had a chance to know.

They were *his*. Come hell or high water, he'd never let them go again.

Dear Reader,

Holiday greetings from all of us at Silhouette Books to all of you. And along with my best wishes, I wanted to give you a present, so I put together six of the best books ever as your holiday surprise. Emilie Richards starts things off with *Woman Without a Name*. I don't want to give away a single one of the fabulous twists and turns packed into this book, but I *can* say this: You've come to expect incredible emotion, riveting characters and compelling storytelling from this award-winning writer, and this book will not disappoint a single one of your high expectations.

And in keeping with the season, here's the next of our HOLIDAY HONEYMOONS, a miniseries shared with Desire and written by Carole Buck and Merline Lovelace. *A Bride for Saint Nick* is Carole's first Intimate Moments novel, but you'll join me in wishing for many more once you've read this tale of a man who thinks he has no hope of love, only to discover—just in time for Christmas—that a wife and a ready-made family are his for the asking.

As for the rest of the month, what could be better than new books from Sally Tyler Hayes and Anita Meyer, along with the contemporary debuts of historical authors Elizabeth Mayne and Cheryl St.John? So sit back, pick up a book and start to enjoy the holiday season. And don't forget to come back next month for some Happy New Year reading right here at Silhouette Intimate Moments, where the best is always waiting to be unwrapped.

Yours,

Leslie Wainger

Leslie Wainger
Senior Editor and Editorial Coordinator

Please address questions and book requests to:
Silhouette Reader Service
U.S.: 3010 Walden Ave., P.O. Box 1325, Buffalo, NY 14269
Canadian: P.O. Box 609, Fort Erie, Ont. L2A 5X3

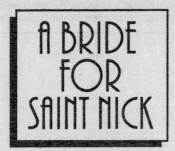

A BRIDE FOR SAINT NICK

CAROLE BUCK

Published by Silhouette Books

America's Publisher of Contemporary Romance

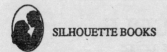 SILHOUETTE BOOKS

ISBN 0-373-07752-1

A BRIDE FOR SAINT NICK

Books by Carole Buck

Silhouette Intimate Moments

†*A Bride for Saint Nick* #752

Silhouette Desire

Time Enough for Love #565
Paradise Remembered #614
White Lace Promises #644
Red-Hot Satin #677
Knight and Day #699
Blue Sky Guy #750
Sparks #808
Dark Intentions #899
Annie Says I Do #934
Peachy's Proposal #976
Zoe and the Best Man #989

Silhouette Romance

Make-believe Marriage #752

Silhouette Books

Silhouette Summer Sizzlers 1993
"Hot Copy"

†Holiday Honeymoons
*Wedding Belles

CAROLE BUCK

is a television news writer and movie reviewer who lives in Atlanta. She is single, and her hobbies include cake decorating, ballet and traveling. She collects frogs, but does not kiss them. Carole says she's in love with life; she hopes the books she writes reflect this.

Prologue

The photos arrived via courier at noon on the day before Thanksgiving, but the former Justice Department operative to whom they'd been sent didn't get around to looking at them until late that evening.

There was nothing unusual about this. In the five and a half years since the reported death of his onetime alter ego, Nicholas "Saint Nick" Marchand, John Gulliver had embraced the night. He'd sought sanctuary under cover of darkness, away from inquiring eyes and awkward questions. Although he had not eschewed the daylight completely, the hours between dusk and dawn were the ones he'd come to prefer.

He'd chosen to be alone. To separate from so-called "ordinary life" as much as possible. Settling into an essentially nocturnal existence had made the achievement of this self-imposed isolation easier.

It also served to intimidate his employees. Not a lot. Just enough to make a point about his priorities. He knew that the time codes on the faxes and E-mail messages by which he generally communicated alerted people to the fact that he was up and operating while they were slacking off or sleeping. The transmissions tended to create the impression that he was

committed to doing business twenty-four hours a day, seven
days a week, fifty-two weeks a year.

By inclination and training, John Gulliver was a man who
calculated the odds and elbowed for advantage in every situation. He therefore relished the edge this always-on-the-job image inevitably gave him. It kept the folks who worked for him
on their toes. He might be an absentee boss in the sense of sel-
dom being on the scene, but he emphatically was not an oblivious employer.

There were those who objected to his modus operandi, of
course. They didn't last. Those who adjusted to his methods—
who earned his professional trust—were well rewarded for their
pains. He picked the best people he could find and paid them
every penny they were worth. If they eventually developed an
itch for entrepreneurial independence, he was prepared to offer them advice and investment capital.

The dispatcher of the photographs that arrived at John's
home on the fourth Wednesday in November was a woman
named Lucy Falco. She was the office manager of Gulliver's
Travels, the Atlanta-based travel agency he owned. He'd hired
her a little over three years ago. While her résumé credentials
had been somewhat less impressive than those of the other
candidates who'd applied for the position, there had been
something about her frank and feisty attitude that had intrigued him. He'd gone with his gut and awarded her the job.
He'd never regretted the decision.

Well, no. Not *never*. Because although Ms. Falco had "adjusted" to his methods in record time, she'd never fully accepted them. She seemed particularly determined to personally
acquaint him with travel-agency clients whom he preferred to
consider only in bottom-line terms.

Hence, her practice of forwarding the "Having a wonderful
time!" postcards she received from Gulliver's customers while
they were on their agency-arranged trips as well as the effusive
letters of appreciation they often wrote once they returned
home. Ditto, her passing along of the souvenir photographs
that frequently accompanied these gushingly grateful mis-
sives.

For a long time, he'd simply chucked such stuff into a
wastebasket and forgotten about it. Recently, however, he'd

found himself feeling a curious need to spend a few minutes skimming the notes and scanning the pictures before disposing of them.

John Gulliver had tried not to analyze the source of this disconcerting impulse too deeply. Instead, he'd reminded himself that assessing customer feedback was a time-honored business technique.

Expelling a restive sigh, he tore open the courier pack that contained Lucy Falco's latest offering and spilled out the contents. There were a dozen-or-so color photographs, several letters, two newspaper clippings and a note penned on the travel agency's distinctive stationery. He picked up the last item and started to read.

"Dear Mr. Gulliver," the handwritten communiqué began. Although he'd made it clear that he had no objection to her using his given name, his office manager inexplicably insisted on using the formal mode of address in all their dealings. "Just in case you missed it, I'm enclosing an article from Monday's *New York Times* on the prosecution of the people involved in our recent problem cruise."

John felt one corner of his mouth kick up at the uncharacteristically understated choice of adjectives. The cruise in question, which Gulliver's Travels had donated as a prize for a Halloween charity ball in Atlanta, had turned out to be a front for a drug-smuggling operation. The newlyweds who'd won it had been plunged into a modern-day pirate drama. To describe what had happened to them as a "problem" was akin to calling the hijacking of a plane to Havana an "unscheduled course adjustment."

The note went on, referring to the groom who'd been entangled in the high-seas misadventure.

Josh Keegan has already approached the agency about planning a *second* honeymoon trip for him and his wife, Cari. His only stipulation: *No boats!*

On another subject: Abigail Davis's decorating job at Gulliver's Travels continues to draw raves from everyone who walks in. What a talent she has! You really should come and check her work out for yourself.

"Such subtlety, Ms. Falco," John murmured sardonically, then continued reading.

The photos I include are from a terrific couple—Marcy-Anne and Maxwell Gregg—who celebrated their fiftieth anniversary with a leaf-peeping expedition to New England. They've used Gulliver's Travels many times in the past, so we tried to do something very special for them. I think we succeeded. Marcy-Anne says they had a fabulous time, seeing all kinds of gorgeous fall foliage and making some new friends along the way.

Fifty years of holy wedlock. That's something to be proud of, don't you think? My one and only marriage lasted barely fifty weeks!

But never mind about that.

I hope you have a very happy Thanksgiving. Planning on going anywhere?

Yours sincerely,
Lucy Falco

John Gulliver set aside the note, then reached slowly for the Greggs' photos. The hand with which he reached—his right—had been scarred by fire and was missing part of its little finger. The disfigurement was one of a number of legacies from the incendiary car crash in which Nicholas "Saint Nick" Marchand allegedly had been killed.

Although obviously not what it had once been, the injured hand seemed profoundly familiar to him. Not so, the facial features that had been painstakingly reconstructed from shattered bone and ruined skin after his accident. Try as he might, they were still very difficult to accept as his own.

This was not to say that the image that now confronted him when he glanced in a mirror was repulsive. It wasn't. Imperfect, yes, but by no means terrible to gaze upon. Indeed, he'd overheard his new visage described as "compelling looking" more than once. His ability to attract women—on those rare occasions during the past few years when he'd chosen to test it—seemed as potent as ever. Perhaps even more so.

And yet . . .

It wasn't *his* face. And there were moments when he seriously doubted that he would ever feel as though it was. He'd lost count of the occasions when he'd accidentally caught sight of his reflection and wondered—with an almost visceral rush of alarm—at whom he was looking. Even when recognition finally kicked in, the sense of alienation lingered like a toxic residue.

Taking a steadying breath, John began shuffling methodically through the Greggs' snapshots. The autumnal scenery they'd photographed left him unmoved. He knew the glorious reds and golds were transitory. The leaves that blazed so vibrantly on film had long since withered into lifeless brown and fallen to the ground . . . forgotten.

He hesitated for a few seconds when he came to a picture of what he assumed must be the happy couple. They were standing in front of what appeared to be a small bookstore, holding hands.

Marcy-Anne was short, silver-haired and projected an aura of belle-of-the-ball coquettishness. Maxwell was a balding old bull of a man who beamed down at the daintily-made woman beside him with the ardor of a husband who'd said "I do" half a minute—rather than half a century—ago.

Fifty years, John mused, suddenly conscious of the rhythmic thudding of his pulse. The simply furnished room in which he was sitting was very, very quiet. Only the faint hum from the top-of-the-line electronic equipment that connected him to the outside world disturbed the silence. *What must it be like to share that much?*

He shoved aside the question before his brain had a chance to complete it and shifted the photo to the bottom of the stack. He briefly considered consigning the rest of the pictures to the trash, but decided he should finish what he'd started.

Next, a photo of more foliage.

A close-up of Marcy-Anne, solo, flirting with the camera.

Maxwell, alone, posing in a pumpkin patch.

More foliage.

And then . . .

John Gulliver's heart lurched, slamming against the inside of his rib cage with sledgehammer force. His breath clotted at the top of his throat. The circuits of his nervous system surged toward overload. He started to shake.

"God," he somehow managed to whisper. The crash that had cost him his face had impacted his vocal chords, too. His voice was lower and less smooth than it had been. "Dear . . . God.

For nearly five and a half years, he'd wondered. Riven by guilt and grief, he'd lived with agonizing uncertainties and awful speculations. To have the questions that had tormented him for so long answered like this, purely by chance—

He stiffened, chilled to the marrow of his bones by a terrible truth: Had this photograph been sent to him a few months ago, he would have thrown it away without looking at it.

His vision blurred. He blinked several times, then focused again on the soul-shattering picture his final shuffle of the stack had revealed.

It was another snapshot of Marcy-Anne and Maxwell. This one showed them flanking a willowy blonde whose smile, although undeniably appealing, didn't quite reach her wide-set blue eyes. She was in her late twenties. Young enough to be the Greggs' granddaughter.

Only John Gulliver knew she wasn't. The Greggs' granddaughter, that is. He knew this because he knew the woman in the photograph had no living relatives. Her lack of family ties was clearly spelled out in government intelligence files. She'd also confided her solitary status to him on a moonlit walk nearly six years ago.

Or, rather, she'd confided it to Nicholas Marchand, the man she'd believed him to be.

That man—a convicted criminal, an alleged killer—had been someone every instinct she had must have shrieked at her to avoid. Yet she'd come to him like a moth to a flame. She'd come, offering her untouched body and innocent heart without reservation.

And he'd taken them. *Him.* Not Nicholas Marchand. Because Nicholas Marchand had been a role, not a real man. He'd taken her body and heart, knowing that it was utterly wrong— unethical, immoral, downright dangerous—to do so.

He hadn't been able to stop himself.

He'd seduced her with lies. Big lies. Little lies. Lies deliberately thought out. Lies improvised on the spur of the moment. He'd held on to her in the same duplicitous manner. And in the bitterest of ironies, he'd found that the only way he could begin to atone for the deceptions he'd practiced was to become an active participant in what some might call the ultimate fraud.

John touched the tip of one finger to the image of the woman standing between Marcy-Anne and Maxwell Gregg. The passage of time appeared to have wrought very few physical changes in her, he observed with a pang. She seemed slightly more curvaceous than he remembered, although the clothing she had on made it difficult to accurately assess her shape. Her flaxen hair, which had once tumbled halfway down her supple back, now barely brushed her slim shoulders. The girlish freshness that had softened her features even in the throes of sexual ecstasy was gone, heightening her fine-boned beauty in a way, yet also rendering it more austere—less accessible—than it had been.

All in all, however, she looked very much as she had the last time they'd been together.

Unlike him.

"Suzanne," he finally said, uttering the name he hadn't pronounced aloud since the day he'd acquiesced to his former supervisor's contention that it was best if the woman for whom he had broken every rule, betrayed every code of righteous conduct, was allowed to go on believing that he'd been Nicholas Marchand and that Nicholas Marchand was dead, buried and most likely burning in hell. "Sweet . . . Suzanne Whitney."

Suzanne Whitney had said she loved the man nicknamed "Saint Nick." Had she mourned his passing? Did she mourn him still?

John stared down at the photograph he gripped in his scarred right hand. Who had she become? he wondered, his throat tight and aching. He was aware that the government had given her a new identity in much the same way it had given him a new face. Had she accepted this precipitous change of circumstances with more grace than he'd accepted his radically altered appearance? Had she sought help in adjusting, or had she held the world at arm's length as he had chosen to do?

He inhaled on a shudder.

Whoever she now was...

Whatever kind of life she'd made for herself...

How would she react to a stranger named John Gulliver? How would she respond to a man she'd never really met, yet who knew her intimately?

It was madness to contemplate the possibility of seeking her out, of course. He recognized that. No good could come of exhuming the past and trying to explain it away.

Still...

Discovering Suzanne Whitney's new name and current whereabouts would be child's play for him, he reflected. A few seconds at his computer keyboard would grant him full access to the New England itinerary Gulliver's Travels had arranged for the Greggs. And if that didn't give him the information he needed, he could interrogate Lucy Falco. She would be so thrilled by his unprecedented show of interest that she would never think to ask why he was inquiring about a fiftieth-anniversary trip taken by a septuagenarian couple he didn't know.

He simply wanted to make certain that Suzanne was all right, he told himself. To know that she'd survived her involvement with Nicholas Marchand reasonably intact, if not wholly unscathed. He had no intention of approaching her. *None!*

Yes...he might watch over her from a distance. And yes, he might try to find some anonymous way of expiating the sins he'd committed against her. But he would never, ever attempt to reawaken her emotions or to renew their physical union.

Unless...

No!

Never.

Ever.

How long John Gulliver sat studying the face of the woman who'd given herself to the man he'd once pretended to be, he was never able to calculate. Nor could he ever be sure at what minute of what hour he decided on a course of action. The length of time it took him to compose—and recompose, and compose yet again—a three-sentence computer message to Lucy Falco was similarly impossible to gauge.

However, when he finally dispatched the E-mail request for information into cyberspace and happened to glance toward one of the windows in the room in which he was sitting, he realized that the sun was beginning to come up.

Federal Prisoner No. 00394756—aka Anthony Stone—didn't give a damn about day or night, light or dark. For him, the traditional tick-tock of seconds, minutes and hours had little meaning.

To many of those incarcerated in the maximum-security facility that had been his home for nearly five years, the passage of time was an adversary. A twisted few regarded it as an ally. For him, it was simply something to be endured—ignored, when possible—until that inevitable moment when he chose to exert his power.

How much power could a convicted felon facing life-plus-ten-years in a concrete cell have at his disposal? Federal Prisoner No. 00394756 laughed softly. *That* would be telling, he thought. Suffice to say, it was more than enough to set him free whenever and however he chose.

An almost-voluptuous sense of anticipation stirred within him.

"Soon," he murmured. "Very, very soon."

The time of deliverance was coming. *His* time. *His* deliverance. He was willing to wait for it. To savor the implications of its inexorable approach. And while he did that...

Let the so-called "authorities"—the fools who thought they'd brought him down, because he was *allowing* them to keep him behind bars—slip deeper into their bureaucratic complacency.

Let those who owed him grow more acutely aware of their debts, more fearful of how he would demand repayment.

Let his enemy, Nicholas "Saint Nick" Marchand—the man he'd hated above all others—go on rotting in an unwept-over grave, feeding worms and maggots.

And let the woman he'd claimed for himself five and a half years ago continue as she was. Chastely faithful to his memory. Vigilantly protective of what they'd created together. Not within his grasp, exactly, but definitely under his thumb.

Federal Prisoner 00394756 closed his eyes.

"I'm coming, Suzanne," he whispered hoarsely, his mind filling with the image of a fair-haired, sky-eyed woman. His body pulsed with the memory of the May night they'd finally joined as one. "For you . . . and for my son."

Chapter 1

Andy McKay had Christmas on his mind and he obviously wanted his mother to know it.

"Twenny-*two*," he declared loudly, smacking his left index finger against the calendar that hung at kid's-eye level on the door of the refrigerator in the McKays' cream-and-yellow kitchen. "Twenny-*three*. Twenny-*four*." His fingertip landed on a square decorated with a crayoned-in wreath. He glanced over his shoulder, apparently checking to be sure that his audience was paying sufficient attention to his recitation. After a moment he announced, "Just *twenny-four* days 'til Christmas, Mommy."

"Uh-huh." Leigh McKay swallowed the final mouthful of her breakfast tea, then deposited the daisy-decorated mug in the sink. "That's one day less than it was yesterday."

Like that of most youngsters his age, Andy's grasp of the concept of time was still a bit iffy, so it took him a few seconds to absorb the meaning of this last statement. Leigh watched as he thought through the implications of her words. The intensity of his concentration furrowed his smooth, fair-skinned forehead and narrowed his usually wide and sparkling blue-gray eyes. For an instant, he looked much older than his four years and nine months. For an instant, she thought she caught a hint of the darkly compelling man she prayed was his—

No!

Stop it, Leigh ordered herself, fighting to keep her expression neutral. *You'll drive yourself crazy looking for similarities, trying to match what you think you see today with memories that are nearly six years old. Andy is Andy and he's your son. It doesn't matter who his father is. Or isn't. The past is over and done with. You have to leave it alone.*

"One day less—" Andy echoed, looking back at the calendar. Then, suddenly, he gave a triumphant yelp and whirled around to face his mother.

"Yes!" he exulted, all little-boy innocence once again. His eyes danced. His dimples flashed as he turned on a grin. "And tomorrow it will be *another* day less, right, Mommy?"

Leigh nodded, summoning up a quick—and what felt like a rather crooked—smile. "That's right, Andy," she affirmed in as light a tone as she could manage. "Tomorrow there will be twenty-three days 'til Christmas."

Her son gave a gleeful giggle, apparently oblivious to her momentary upset. For this she was profoundly grateful. Deep in her heart, she knew that the issue of Andy's paternity was something she and her son would have to confront and come to terms with sometime in the future. She just prayed that the inevitable moment of reckoning would not arrive too soon...nor impact too destructively.

"Tomorrow after tomorrow will be twenny-*two* days 'til Christmas," Andy proclaimed, seizing the opportunity to expand upon his chosen subject. "And tomorrow after tomorrow after tomorrow will be twenny-one days 'til Christmas. And tomorrow after tomorrow after tomorrow after tomorrow—"

"It will be the tomorrow after *New Year's* before we get out of here if you don't get a move on, young man," Leigh interrupted. She glanced at her wristwatch, commanding herself to focus on the here and now. Obsessing about what had been—and what might be because of it—was dangerous. The people who'd helped her build her present life had stressed that, over and over again. "Which could be a problem. Didn't I hear you say something the other day about planning to tell Santa that you'd been especially good about not dawdling in the mornings this past year?''

"I wasn't dawdling!" The protest was huffy, but there was a hint of anxiety lurking just beneath the indignation. Being able to claim the distinction of having been "especially good" was very important at this time of year. Little boys who couldn't do so ran a serious risk of being disappointed on Christmas morning.

Or so Leigh knew one very special little boy wholeheartedly believed.

"No?" She lifted an eyebrow, trying to quell a pang of guilt over having resorted to using an implied threat to get her son going. A working mom had to do what a working mom had to do to keep things on schedule, she reminded herself. And heaven knew, her calendar was especially crammed today.

Still...stooping to using seasonal blackmail on a preschooler wasn't a very nice thing to do. And even if she accepted the premise that there were times when doing a "not nice" thing was absolutely necessary, she couldn't help but feel that it was a wee bit early in the holiday period for her to start utilizing Santa Claus as a behavior-modification tool. The jolly old elf was a very heavy weapon in a parent's disciplinary arsenal. He deserved to be held in reserve for those moments when nothing short of his mediating influence would do.

"I was just tryin' to tell you how long 'til Christmas." Andy gazed up at her limpidly, appealing for absolution. "Like...on the TV news. So, like, you could know how many days you have for shoppin' and stuff."

A sudden impulse toward laughter tickled the back of Leigh's throat—part nerves, part genuine amusement. She swallowed it, knowing her status as the adult-in-charge would be compromised if she didn't. Still, she had to give her son credit for concocting a very ingenious rationalization for what he'd been up to.

"I certainly appreciate that, Andy," she assured him gravely. "But I'd appreciate it even more if you got your teeth brushed and put on your jacket and mittens."

For a moment, her son seemed to consider renewing his Christmas-is-coming pitch. Then something—perhaps the realization that he had "twenny-three" more days to press home the importance of the approaching holiday—made him change his mind.

"Okay, Mommy!" he cheerfully concurred and dashed away to do as he'd been bidden. His small, boot-clad feet thudded against the floor, making it possible to track his path away from the kitchen, up the stairs and into his second-floor bedroom.

It was remarkable how much noise one little boy could generate, Leigh reflected as she marshaled her thoughts toward the workday ahead.

Even more remarkable—miraculous, some might say—was how great a difference that same small child had made to his mother's violence-shattered life.

"Here we are," Leigh said about twenty-five minutes later as she pulled up in front of the small preschool Andy attended. Bringing her aging station wagon to a halt, she shifted into Park and turned to her son. "Now, remember. I'm driving to Brattleboro today for business, so Nonna P. will pick you up this afternoon instead of me."

Nonna P. was Andy's nickname for Donatella Pietra. A soft-spoken widow in her late fifties, Nonna was the answer to a single parent's child-care prayers. She'd moved to Vermont from Newark, New Jersey, a little more than two years ago and begun baby-sitting for Andy shortly after her arrival. He adored her unconditionally and she reciprocated his affection without reserve. "I love him like my own," she'd declared on more than one occasion.

"I'll remember," Andy promised, tugging clumsily at his safety harness with mittened fingers. Leigh knew better than to offer a helping hand. Unsolicited assistance, she'd learned, would offend her son's burgeoning male ego. After a brief struggle between boy and seat-belt buckle, the fastener released with a metallic *snick*.

"Kiss?" she asked, initiating what had become something of a morning ritual for them. She tried not to wonder how long this ritual would endure. Her son was growing up so quickly! All too soon, there would come a day when he would decide he was too old for public displays of maternal affection. When he would groan "Ah, jeez, Ma" if she attempted any physical contact more intimate than a handshake.

But until that day arrived ...

"Hug," Andy countered decisively, scooting toward her.

She encircled his small but solid body with her arms, holding him close for a few precious seconds. "Love you, sweetie," she whispered, brushing her lips against his silky, toffee-brown hair.

His response was a squeeze, followed by a brief but unmistakable snuggle; then, very softly, "Love you, too, Mommy."

A moment later, Andy started to wriggle free of her embrace, obviously eager to reassert himself as an independent, almost-five-year-old. Leigh McKay did what she knew she must.

After breathing a swift, silent prayer for her son's continued well-being, she let him go.

A postcard, John Gulliver thought with a strange surge of emotion as he drove slowly along the snow-lined main street of what could only be called a "picturesque" New England village. *The guys from the Witness Security Program stuck Suzanne in the middle of a postcard!*

He wasn't certain why his reaction to the setting was so acute. Having been to this part of Vermont a couple of times during his youth, he'd had a pretty good idea what to expect. But even had he not had memories of previous visits to draw upon, he'd gotten a detailed description of the place from Marcy-Anne Gregg when he'd spoken to her by phone yesterday evening.

"Mah husband and Ah positively fell in love with that little town, Mr. Gulliver," she'd confided in a molasses-and-magnolia drawl during the course of what had turned out to be a protracted conversation. "Maxwell is particularly fond of the Federal style of architecture and the village green is surrounded by some perfectly preserved buildin's from that period. Ah, personally, was quite taken with the covered bridges.. There's three of them right there in the area, you know. *Much* prettier than the one in that Clint Eastwood movie about Madison County, if you ask me. And then, to find out Ah was in a place that's home to no fewer than *four* church bells that may have been made by Mr. Paul Revere himself—why, Ah was thrilled beyond words. Which is exactly what Ah told dear Tiffany Toulouse when Ah spoke to her after our return. By the

way, did Ah mention what a *wonderful* job Tiffany did in ar-
rangin' our anniversary trip? Well, even if Ah did, let me mention it again. And that darlin' Lucy Falco was just the soul of
consideration toward us, too. Why a sweet girl like that isn't
married is beyond me. Although, Ah do believe Ah recall her
sayin' somethin' about havin' had a husband at one time. Before she came to work for you at Gulliver's Travels, Ah gather.
Ah hope he didn't die on her or somethin' heartbreakin' like
that. Which isn't to say that havin' a husband pass on to his
reward might not be easier to endure than havin' a live one walk
out the door because he'd fallen in love with another woman.
Or with another *man*. Ah saw a talk show about that very subject just the other day, you know. Ah was shocked. Just
shocked. Ah had to watch the whole thing to make sure Ah
truly was seein' and hearin' what Ah thought Ah was seein' and
hearin'. In any case— Oh. Oh, dear. Ah seem to have gotten
mahself off the track. What was Ah sayin'—?''

"That you were thrilled beyond words at finding yourself in
a place that boasts four church bells supposedly made by Paul
Revere," he'd responded dryly. Listening patiently to little old
ladies babbling on about seemingly irrelevant subjects was not
his forte. Still, the interrogator's instincts he'd honed during his
years as a federal agent had warned him that Marcy-Anne
Gregg would yield up the information he was seeking in her
own discursively chatty fashion or not at all. And since obtaining that information was crucial to the success of his quest
to find Suzanne...

Learning her current location through the computer—to say
nothing of uncovering the details of her new identity—had
proved impossible. Yes, he'd been able to access the itinerary
Gulliver's Travels had arranged for the Greggs. The problem
was, said itinerary stretched over a period of three weeks and
included ten stops in four states. There was no way for him to
determine when during those three weeks or in which of those
four states the photograph of Suzanne had been taken.

Which wasn't to say he hadn't tried. He'd spent much of
Thanksgiving Day staring at the fateful snapshot, searching in
vain for visual clues. He'd digitalized it, loaded it onto his
computer, enhanced it electronically and gone over the image,
pixel by pixel.

Nothing. Absolutely nothing.

Questioning Lucy Falco via phone the day after Thanksgiving had been equally frustrating. It had been more than a little unsettling, as well.

As he'd expected, his travel-agency office manager had been delighted by his show of interest in the Greggs' trip. She'd plainly thought that her long-running effort to increase his personal involvement in the business was finally starting to pay off. But after her first rush of surprised pleasure had dissipated, she'd begun to sound curious about why *he* was so curious about Marcy-Anne and Maxwell's golden-anniversary expedition.

Finding himself oddly reluctant to lie, yet utterly unwilling to offer any hint of the truth, he'd shifted conversational gears. While Lucy had followed his cue without missing a beat, he'd had the feeling that she'd gone on speculating about the reason for his previous inquiries. He hadn't liked that feeling. He hadn't liked the sense of potential vulnerability that had accompanied it, either.

Following his fruitless call to the all-too-perceptive Ms. Falco, he'd seriously considered reestablishing contact with some of his former colleagues in the Justice Department and pressuring them for information. But after assessing the pros and cons, he'd decided to hold this option in reserve. If all else failed . . .

For much of the final weekend of November, he'd thought that this might be the case. That all else *would* fail and he would be forced to turn to the very people who'd made the decision to leave Suzanne Whitney ignorant of the truth about Nicholas Marchand. Using the telephone number he'd gotten from Gulliver's Travels' files, he'd called the Greggs' home in Marietta, Georgia, over and over again. Over and over again, he'd gotten no answer.

Finally, at 6:45 p.m. on Sunday, Marcy-Anne had picked up.

At 7:02 p.m., he'd hit pay dirt.

"Why, of *course* Ah remember that photograph," the older woman had cheerfully assured him. She'd then proceeded to prove her assertion—at length. Eventually she'd concluded, "Such a lovely girl, don't you think? One of mah best friends has an unmarried grandson who'd just eat her up with a spoon if he ever met her. And she's so clever, too. Ah just *adored* that little bookshop of hers...."

A scant ten hours later, John Gulliver had been winging his way toward the Burlington International Airport. Once there, he'd picked up a rental car and headed southeast along I-89.

Braking at an intersection, he glanced around, still oddly affected by what he was seeing. He could easily envision Suzanne settling down in a place like this. Despite her involvement with the fast-living Saint Nick Marchand, she hadn't been a bright-lights, big-city kind of girl. Her tastes had been simple. Her values, traditional.

Could he envision *himself* settling down in a place like this? John wondered uncomfortably, checking the rearview mirror. Not bloody likely. Maybe there'd been a period, a long time ago, when he might have had the grace to fit into this pristine peacefulness. But not now. Not... anymore.

After a moment or two, he shifted his foot from the brake to the gas and drove on. His hands tightened on the steering wheel. If the information Marcy-Anne Gregg had given him was correct, Suzanne's bookshop should be coming up in just a few—

John sucked in his breath. Yes. Oh, God. Yes. There it was. On the right.

Don't stop, he told himself.

He did.

All right. He backpedaled, his heart starting to race. *Stop and look. Just don't get out of the car.*

He did that, too.

Okay! Okay! He acquiesced, narrowing his eyes against the bright sunlight and filling his lungs with cold, crisp air. *Get out of the car. There's no harm in that. There's no harm in standing around like a tourist for a minute or so. But you cannot go into that store....*

The silvery jingle of a pair of bells announced John Gulliver's entrance into Suzanne's small-business establishment. He knew the sound was meant to be welcoming, but something inside him heard it as a warning to turn on his heel and go.

He couldn't.

He could recite chapter and verse why he should leave, but he simply *could not* make himself walk out. Not yet.

He had to see her again.

To hear her speak, one more time.

To touch—

"Is there something I can help you with, sir?"

The voice was female but unfamiliar. John pivoted away from the rack of regional guidebooks he'd been pretending to peruse and came face-to-face with a bone-thin redhead in her early twenties. She was dressed in a plaid flannel shirt, a long, drooping skirt and clunky brown boots.

John Gulliver had spent a lot of years making split-second assessments of people. He was good at it. He'd had to be. He never would have survived his time undercover otherwise.

His split-second assessment of the redhead was that she was trouble. What kind, how much and exactly for whom, he couldn't tell. But there was something . . . *off* . . . about her and his instincts warned him to tread carefully because of it.

It was more than the fact that she was a naturally pretty female working very hard at being plain, he decided, trying to analyze the reasons for his negative gut reaction. The key was that her eyes were way too old for her milk-pale face. This was a woman who had lost her illusions about life a long, long time ago, and lost them hard.

Whoever she was, whatever she'd done or had done to her in the past, she definitely was out of place in this quiet little town.

And she sensed the same incongruity about him, he realized with an inward jolt, picking up a slight stiffening of her posture as their gazes met. She sensed it . . . and it unnerved her.

The man who had lived and nearly died as Saint Nick Marchand had become accustomed to making people uneasy. He knew that the burn marks on the left side of his neck, the scarring on his left temple and the disfigurement of his right hand hinted at an unpleasant personal history. They tended to make others wary or worse. But in this case . . .

Whatever it was about him that the redhead was reacting to, John thought grimly, it ran more than skin-deep.

"Sir?" she asked again, her eyes flicking back and forth. There was an edgy quality to her gaze, which suggested that she, too, was used to making snap judgments about people.

John moderated his stance, reminding himself that he apparently was dealing with someone employed by Suzanne. The last thing he wanted was to have her badmouthing him to her boss. If truth be told, he wasn't sure whether he wanted to have her mentioning him to her boss at all.

"I'm just looking, thank you," he said. "Is that all right? My browsing?"

"All right?" The redhead gestured nervously. "Oh, uh, of course. I mean, that's what we're here for. The shop, that is. For...browsing."

"And buying." He ventured a carefully calibrated smile. *You can trust me,* it was intended to communicate. *I'm a harmless out-of-towner who just happened to stop by.*

The woman blinked several times, obviously affected by his shift in manner. "Well, yeah," she affirmed after a moment, some of the tension seeping out of her skinny body. The corners of her thin lips curved upward a couple of centimeters. "That, too."

John made a show of glancing around the shop. It had a cozy, old-fashioned feel. In addition to shelf upon shelf of books, there was a colorful selection of postcards and stationery supplies, plus a display of what looked like local handicrafts.

A poster tacked to the wall behind the cash register announced that Story Hour was scheduled for 3:00 to 4:00 p.m. on Thursday. A small footnote alerted prospective attendees that refreshments would be served.

There were a few reminders of the coming holiday season scattered around—a ribboned holly wreath on the door; a whimsical papier-mâché Santa Claus sitting on a table stacked with books marked Good for Giving. The effect was charming, not commercialized Christmas overkill.

"Great place you have here," he commented, catching the tempting scent of freshly brewed coffee drifting out from somewhere in the back. While his admiration was sincere, it was not without calculation. Experience had taught him that there were few things more effective than using a compliment for bait when angling for information.

"Don't I *wish.*"

John glanced back at the redhead, startled by the fervor of her response. He'd expected some pro forma correction of his assumption about the ownership of the store, which he could then use as an opening to ask a few questions about Suzanne. Instead he'd gotten . . . what?

An admission of envy? he speculated, replaying the remark in his mind. *Yes. Maybe.* But the covetousness had been tempered by something he couldn't quite get a line on. It had sounded a lot like sadness.

"I beg your pardon?" he asked after a second or two.

His companion hunched her shoulders and dipped her head, apparently regretting her previous reply. "The store doesn't belong to me," she told him hastily, plucking at her skirt. "The woman who owns it isn't here right now. She's in Brattleboro on business."

What John Gulliver felt then was impossible to describe. It was too powerful. Too painful. It was so excruciatingly far beyond disappointment that it wasn't even in the same emotional universe.

"So . . . you're in charge," he finally managed to remark.

It was an innocuous, throwaway line, uttered only because he felt he had to offer some reaction to the information he'd been given. But even in the midst of his own tumult, John could tell that it had struck a nerve in the redhead. She drew herself up, plainly construing his words as a challenge to her competence and/or character.

"Yes, sir," she stated, cocking her chin. "*I'm* in charge. My name's Deirdre Bleeker and I've been working for Ms.—"

The bells on the front door jingled. John stiffened at the sound and pivoted, conscious that he'd left himself very exposed. Nicholas Marchand would never, *ever,* have stood with his back to an unlocked door.

A wiry man clad in grease-stained jeans and a well-worn khaki parka entered the shop on a blast of wintry air. He appeared to be in his early thirties and exuded an air of Norman Rockwell-esque solidity.

"Mornin', Dee," he said, his Yankee accent turning the *or* in morning into an elongated *aww.* "Came by to see if that book I ordered got in yet."

The redhead flushed. The sudden rush of color into her cheeks could have been anger. Or embarrassment. Or a combination of the two.

"W-Wes," she stammered, meeting the newcomer's gaze for a moment, then glancing away. "The b-book you ordered?" She moistened her lips. "I . . . uh . . . yes. I *think* it's here. But I'm not sure. If you'll just, uh, give me a minute to look in the back . . ." She paused, slanting an uneasy glance up at John.

"No problem, Ms. Bleeker," he said courteously. "Thank you for your time."

"Oh . . . sure." The formality of his manner seemed to discomfort her. Or perhaps she'd just realized that although she'd been forthcoming with her name, he'd refrained from offering his.

"Dee?"

Deirdre darted another look at the parka-clad man, the color in her face still feverishly high. "I'll check about the book, Wes," she said tightly, then scurried away.

After surveying the shop one more time, John headed toward the door.

"New here?" Wes questioned, pronouncing the second word *hee-yuh*. "Haven't seen you 'round before."

John checked his step and met the other man's eyes. He saw a combination of assessment and uncertainty in their hazel depths. And a hint of masculine territoriality, too. Somewhere in the back of his mind John recognized that Wes—unlike himself, unlike Deirdre Bleeker—seemed to "fit" in this post-card-perfect New England town. The notion did nothing for his mood.

"Maybe you haven't been looking," he suggested evenly, then exited to the ting-a-ling of bells.

He drove around for a time after that, considering his next move. Although he had the address, he decided against cruising by Suzanne's house. Scoping out her business was one thing. Not a wise thing, to be sure, but he could justify it to himself to a certain degree. The bookshop was open to the public, after all. Suzanne's home, on the other hand, was private. A supposed sanctuary. As much as he might want to do so, he could not bring himself to go snooping around there. It smacked of . . . violation.

Besides, he had no way of knowing how tight a watch the people who administered the Witness Security Program were keeping on Suzanne. Had this been early in her relocation process, he would have figured that the inspector assigned to the case was maintaining close and regular contact. More than five years in? Some easing in the level of vigilance seemed likely. But he couldn't be sure.

The bottom line: he wasn't about to run the risk of attracting the attention of the U.S. Marshals Service. If that agency thought a protected witness's past was intruding on his or her new life, that witness was likely to be uprooted and resettled in a new place with *another* new identity. And if that happened with Suzanne...

He was going to have to find a place to stay, John decided. Concerns about tipping off some federal law-enforcement officer notwithstanding, he couldn't—all right, *wouldn't*—leave until he'd had a chance to see his former lover again.

He also felt compelled to do some discreet digging about Deirdre Bleeker. And Wes Whatever-His-Last-Name-Was, the book-orderer, too. This wasn't to imply a lack of confidence in the Marshals Service's competence. Indeed, as far as he was aware, no witness who'd adhered to the agency's security guidelines had ever been harmed. Still. Even the most professional of professionals occasionally slipped up.

John brought his rental car to a halt across from what appeared to be a school playground. A dozen or so bundled-up little kids were romping around in the snow under the supervision of a pair of women. It was a charmingly bucolic scene except for what appeared to be the beginning of an argument over a swing.

He set the brake, turned off the engine and released his seat belt. Reaching to the right, he popped open the sedan's glove compartment and extracted a guidebook he'd picked up at the Burlington airport. He could hear the children yelping exuberantly and calling back and forth to each other.

He wasn't going to stick around long, he told himself firmly as he thumbed through the book's index. He simply wanted to find out whether Suzanne was okay. Whether she was...happy.

And he would know—one way or the other—as soon as he laid eyes on her. He truly believed that. Because while he'd lied to her about nearly everything and had essentially gotten away with it, she'd been transparent as glass to him. What she'd said, she'd meant. What she'd felt, she'd showed.

John Gulliver closed his eyes for a moment, conjuring up the image of the woman in the photograph Lucy Falco had sent him.

"Suzanne..."

Did her mouth still taste like wild strawberries? he wondered, his blood beginning to thrum. Did her skin still feel like sun-warmed silk? Was she still shy about her body and slow to be stirred, yet unstintingly generous at the peak of—

A child screamed.

John opened his eyes, his gaze slewing toward the playground. A moment later, he was out of the car and dashing across the street.

The incipient argument at the swing set had erupted into something serious. As John drew near, he saw a little boy in a bulky, electric-blue jacket sprawled in the snow. The child wasn't moving. Crimson blood flowed from a gash on the right side of his head.

"T.J. and M-Mark were f-f-fighting!" one little girl stammered at him, tears pouring down her cheeks.

"Mark swinged the swing at T.J.!" another sobbed.

"Only *Andy* got hitted instead!" a pasty-faced boy concluded shrilly.

One of the women John had noted earlier was kneeling by the injured youngster, apparently trying to determine how badly he was hurt. The other was standing a few feet away, wringing her hands, clearly overwhelmed. She looked as though she might pass out at any second.

"Is Andy *dead?*" one of the children demanded. "Did the swing *kill* him?"

"No!" John raised his voice and infused it with every ounce of authority he possessed. He maneuvered his way through the mob of semihysterical munchkins and hunkered down beside the kneeling woman. "Andy's *not* dead," he stressed, sliding his hand inside the turned-up collar of the unconscious boy's jacket and checking for a pulse. After several hideous seconds—God, the kid was so pale, so still!—he found what he was seeking. Relief washed through him like a cleansing tide. "Andy's *alive.*"

"But he's *bweeding!*" a little girl wailed.

"His brains are coming out!" It was the same child who'd inquired about the possibility of Andy's demise.

"Brains are gray," John snapped. "Do you see anything gray?"

"Are you a doctor?" the kneeling woman asked shakily, looking at him with a pleadingly hopeful expression.

"No." He shook his head. "But I've got a car right across the street and I'm ready to drive you and this little guy to the nearest ER."

"M-Mommy," Andy whimpered, tears clouding his blue-gray eyes. Although he'd regained some color in his face, the light sprinkling of freckles on his cheeks and nose was starkly evident. "I w-want...my *mommy.*"

"I know, buddy," John answered, masking his anger at the woman under discussion. Where the hell was she? he asked himself. Didn't she care that her son had nearly had his skull cracked open? "She's going to be here any minute."

"I want her—" the child gave a choky sob "—n-now."

They were in an examining room in a small medical clinic not far from the playground where Andy had been injured. John was seated in a straight-backed chair, the little boy was in his lap. The doctor who'd departed about ten minutes ago had suggested that his young patient might be more comfortable lying down while he awaited his mother's arrival. Andy had cried out against the idea, clutching at John, seemingly terrified of losing contact with him. The physician had quickly backed off, but warned of the need to keep things calm and quiet.

John stroked a hand down Andy's back, shaken by the sense of protectiveness he was experiencing. Was there something about this specific child that had triggered it? he wondered. Or was it a by-product of the emotional roller coaster he'd been riding since he'd seen the photograph of Suzanne?

He had no idea.

Neither did he know how long it had been since the kneeling woman—Thalia Jenkins, her name had turned out to be—had assented to his offer to transport her and Andy to the nearest medical facility. He was too jacked up on adrenaline to have a reliable sense of the passage of time.

The drive to the clinic had been nightmarish. Despite Thalia Jenkins's efforts to stanch the flow, there'd been blood all over the place. The coppery smell of it brought back some of the worst of John's postaccident memories.

A few minutes into the trip, Andy had regained full consciousness and started crying wildly. He'd obviously been frightened out of his wits. His teacher's frantic efforts to comfort him had only increased his agitation. Astonishingly, he'd responded when John had spoken his name several times in quick succession and told him—in no uncertain terms—that he was going to be "all right."

It had been John who'd carried Andy into the clinic. It had been John who'd stayed with him through all that followed, including a lengthy stitching-up process. At one point, he'd tried to step back and let Thalia Jenkins take over. She was better equipped to dispense TLC than he was, he'd reasoned, acutely aware that displays of compassion had never been one of his strong points. Besides, the little boy *knew* her.

This "knowing" argument had cut no ice with Andy. Against all reason, he'd wanted John—a stranger—and only John. So John had remained by his side. Thalia Jenkins had been relegated to filling out paperwork and trying to locate Andy's errant mother.

"You should be really proud of yourself, you know," he commented softly. "You've been very, very brave."

Andy shifted, snuffled pathetically and muttered something under his breath. Only one word—"cried"—was intelligible.

John grimaced. Shortly after their arrival, one of the clinic staffers had attempted to get Andy to stop sobbing by admonishing him to act like a "big boy" rather than a "baby." Infuriated, John had come perilously close to slugging the guy. He'd settled for telling him to shut the hell up and behave like an adult rather than an idiot.

"It's okay to cry, Andy," he said.

Andy snuffled again, then lifted his head. His light brown lashes were spangled with tears and his nose was running. "D-did you ever?"

"Did I ever...what? Cry?"

"Y-Yeah."

John hesitated. If truth be told, he'd almost broken down while the doctor had been suturing Andy's head wound. He'd been helping to hold the boy still during the procedure. It didn't matter that his doing so had saved Andy the indignity of being strapped down. He'd still felt like the worst kind of traitor. A peculiar sense of shame—and a desperate wish that it could be himself on the table, not a blameless little child—had pushed him to the emotional edge.

Andy dragged the back of his right hand under his nose. "Like, did you cry when you got your owwies?"

It took John a moment to figure out to what this last word referred. Then he realized that Andy was studying the scars on his neck and temple. The child seemed intrigued rather than repulsed by them.

"Yes," he finally replied. The answer was stark, a distillation of the ordeal he'd endured after the accident in which his alter ego—the sham man to whom Suzanne Whitney had given herself—supposedly had been killed. "I cried when I got my owwies."

"Were you little?"

"No. I was a grown-up."

Andy was silent for several seconds, apparently needing some time to absorb the idea of an adult male shedding tears. Eventually he volunteered in a close-to-conversational tone, "I'm almost five."

"Oh?" John was grateful for the change of subject, to say nothing of his young charge's calmed-down mood. "When's your birthday?"

"Febber-rary eleven. My mommy marked it with a stick-on star on the 'frigerator calendar at my house. I'm not sure how many days 'til then, though. I haven't counted up yet."

"February eleventh, huh? Have you given much thought to what kind of presents you'd like?"

"Not really. I wanna wait and see what Santa brings me."

"Smart move. Still, I'll bet you have a few ideas in the back of your head."

"Well, yeah. One."

"And what's that?"

"A baby."

John nearly choked. He'd expected Andy to say he wanted a truck. Or some toy soldiers. Maybe even a computer. Whatever it was that little kids were hot on these days. But a *baby?*

"You want a . . . baby?" he finally managed.

"Uh-huh. A *boy* baby. I could help take care of him, you know? 'Cept for the poopy diaper stuff. Baby poop really stinks. I could teach him things, too. *And* be the boss, cuz I'd be bigger. That'd be really cool. Only I don't think it's gonna work out. There has to be a daddy to plant the baby seed, see, and I don't have one. I asked Mommy if we could do it by ourselves but she said no. I think she was kind of upset."

"Well . . . I can understand why she might be." John considered asking about the man who'd "planted" Andy himself, but quickly discarded the idea. It really was none of his business. Then his thoughts shifted. For one singularly ill-advised moment, he contemplated the notion of the child he and Suzanne Whitney might have had, had they met and come together under different circumstances. A could-have-been, should-have-been sense of regret seared through him.

"Are you a daddy, Mr. Gullible?" Andy asked, sniffing.

John cleared his throat, shaken by the depth of the yearning he'd just felt. He'd never seen himself as a candidate for fatherhood. To discover that he had the urge to—

"Mr. Gullible?" his young companion pressed.

"No," he responded, managing to blunt the edge of the word before it left his tongue. He let the mispronunciation of his last name pass. It wasn't important. "No, Andy. I'm not a daddy."

"Are you married?"

"No."

Andy sniveled loudly and wiped his nose. "How old are you?"

Still a bit off-balance, John had to take a second to think. "I was thirty-eight in November."

"Thirty-eight?" It was difficult to tell whether the little boy was impressed or appalled. Maybe a little of both. "Wow! That's a lot more years than me, isn't it?"

"It certainly is."

There was a pause. Andy heaved a sigh and leaned his head against John's chest. After a moment he asked in a curious voice, "Will my owwie be on me forever? Like yours?"

"You mean, will you have a scar?" He began rubbing the boy's back again. It occurred to him that he couldn't recall the last time he'd held a child, much less tended to an upset and hurting one. He was acting on instincts he'd had no idea he possessed. He just hoped that he was doing what he should, the way he should.

"Yeah."

"Well—"

"I have a mark on me from when I was borned. Mommy says an angel kissed me."

"That's not really...uh..." John grimaced, uncertain how he should respond. Just because a child seemed sanguine about someone else having scars didn't mean he was going to take kindly to hearing that he would likely have one of his own. This was something for a *parent* to handle, dammit!

"Bryan at school has a scar on his belly." There was a hint of envy in this statement. "His 'pendix blew up or something. He shows people all the time. 'Cept Miss Jenkins says it's bad manners. 'Specially at lunch."

"Well...you may have a scar, too, Andy," John said carefully. "Not like mine, though. Or, uh, Bryan's. And once your hair grows back, people probably won't notice it very much."

The little boy shifted and looked up at him quizzically. "What if I got bald? Would people notice my scar then?"

"If you got...bald?" Good grief. Where had the kid come up with such a scenario? "I suppose. Yes. People probably would notice your scar if you were bald."

"And then I'd have to tell how it came from a dumb swing, huh. Like, if somebody asked about it. They'd think I was a weenie."

"You could always make up a more interesting story."

"You mean, *lie?*"

The boy sounded genuinely shocked. John winced inwardly, realizing that he'd stepped over an ethical line without even thinking about it. "Forget that," he quickly retracted. "I think you should stick with the truth."

"That's what Mommy says," Andy responded forthrightly. Then he frowned, his expression growing thoughtful. "But sometimes...a made-up story can be just for fun, right? 'Stead of bein' a bad lie. So, what if I said my scar came from a...uh...uh...Indian? Yeah! From an *Indian* who tried to *scalp* me! And I could tell how I fought him—"

"Andy—"

"I'll take care of those insurance forms later!" a female voice declared from the other side of the examining-room door. "Right now I'm going to see my son!"

Something in the fierce, brooking-no-argument tone of this assertion compelled John to his feet. He stood, lifting Andy as he rose.

"Mommy!" the little boy cried shrilly, squirming around. *"Mommy!"*

The door to the examining room swung open. A woman rushed in, her shoulder-skimming blond hair flying, her blue eyes wild with anxiety.

The woman was Suzanne Whitney.

Chapter 2

"Andy," Leigh McKay whispered as she kissed and cuddled her beloved son. "Oh... Andy."

"M-Mommy." Andy gulped convulsively, burrowing his forehead against her shoulder. "I was w-waiting and waiting and you didn't c-c-come!"

Guilt struck like a stiletto blade, slicing to the very core of Leigh's soul. She tightened her embrace, reliving the abject terror she'd experienced during her mad-dash drive back from Brattleboro following a panicked telephone call from Dee Bleeker. Although she'd taken the precaution of leaving her assistant a contact number for every single stop she'd planned to make on her business rounds, Leigh doubted that she would ever be able to forgive herself for being out of town on this day. Andy had needed her and she hadn't been there!

"I know, sweetie," she responded throatily. Her vision wavered. She blinked hard, telling herself she could not give way to tears. "I know. And I'm so, so sorry. But Mommy's here with you now, Andy. Mommy's here... and everything's going to be all right."

Her son began to cry. Leigh let him weep, recognizing that he needed the release after all he'd endured. Holding him close against her heart, she rocked back and forth in a gentle rhythm.

"There, there," she crooned, massaging Andy's heaving shoulders with tender fingers. No matter that earlier in the day her thoughts had focused on how swiftly he was growing up and how soon he might be pulling away from her. At this moment, he was her baby. Soothing his hurts and making him feel secure again were the only things that mattered to her.

"M-M-Mommy..."

"Mommy's here," she repeated, wincing as she looked at the section of his scalp that had been shaved for stitching. The doctor had said that Andy was going to be fine. He'd also said that her son had been extraordinarily lucky. "Mommy's with you. Shh. Yes. Yes. Everything's okay. I know what happened was very scary. And your head must be hurting you a lot right now. But it's going to be all right, Andy. Shh. Shh. Oh, honey. You've been so good. So brave. Just the best boy who ever was."

The tear storm only lasted a few minutes. As wrenching sobs moderated into sloppy sniffles and intermittent hiccups, Leigh shifted a portion of her attention to the man from whose arms she'd more or less snatched her son when she'd burst into the examining room.

He was standing a few feet away, his eyes fixed on her and Andy. Tall, with a leanly powerful physique, he exuded an aura of tautly leashed energy. His dark hair was disheveled and heavily threaded with silver. His coarse-skinned face was harshly angular, its features cast in an uncompromising and less-than-symmetrical mold. Scarring on the left side of his neck and left temple shocked at first glance, then somehow integrated into a very compelling whole.

He could have been downright ugly—physically revolting, even—for all it would have mattered to Leigh. She'd heard, very briefly from Thalia Jenkins, what this man had done for her only child. She knew that her mother's heart would have taught her to see him as a hero, no matter how unattractive he might have appeared to the rest of the world.

The intensity of his silent, unblinking scrutiny was unnerving. Even more disturbing was the shock of connection she experienced when his eyes met hers. Her pulse scrambled in response to the dark, deliberate look. Her breath shortened. Her palms grew moist while her mouth went bone-dry. Had she been standing rather than sitting, her legs probably would have given way beneath her.

He was a stranger, she thought dizzily. A man she'd never seen before in her life. Yet for one mind-blowing moment, she would have sworn that she knew him. And that he knew her.

Intimately. Absolutely.

In ways she scarcely knew herself.

Which was *insane*. There was only one man who'd ever tapped into the secrets of her heart and soul.

Only one man who'd shown her that she possessed a capacity for passion of which she'd never dreamed.

That man, Nicholas "Saint Nick" Marchand, was dead.

She'd wept for him—and for the irreparable changes loving him had wrought in her life—more times than she could count. What she'd felt for him, because of him, she never expected to feel again.

"Wh-who—?" she faltered.

The stranger took a step toward her, a slight hitch in his stride marring the fluency of the movement. Leigh had the impression that he intended to make some kind of physical contact with her. She shrank back in her seat. The man stiffened, obviously picking up on her involuntary withdrawal. An expression she couldn't interpret streaked across his distinctive face. Although she sensed that he wanted to do otherwise, he remained where he was.

"I'm John Gulliver." The low, faintly raspy sound of his voice sandpapered Leigh's already badly abraded nerves. There was nothing familiar about the way he spoke. She would have taken an oath on that in court. Nonetheless, something inside her seemed to quiver in recognition.

Leigh drew a deep breath, fighting for control. The emotional equilibrium she'd struggled so hard to recover after the devastation she'd suffered five and a half years ago seemed to be unraveling into chaos. The news of her son's accident had rocked her badly, of course. But what she was feeling now—

"Go home, Mommy?" Andy suddenly pleaded, sounding very, very young.

The door to the examining room swung open. "Ms. McKay?" someone questioned. "Is everything all right?"

Her heart pounding like a tom-tom, Leigh glanced distractedly from her son to the person at the door and back to the disturbing stranger. She bit her lower lip, abruptly realizing that she'd forgotten his name. She knew he'd identified himself to her just a few moments ago, but she couldn't remember what he'd said.

"M-Mommy?"

"Take care of your son, Ms. McKay," Andy's dark-haired savior counseled softly, his gaze dropping briefly to the child in her arms before returning to her face. His eyes bore deeply into hers. "He's a very special boy."

Again, Leigh had the unsettling impression that the man wanted to reach out and touch her. But he didn't. Instead, he paused for a beat after he finished speaking, then turned on his heel and walked out.

John Gulliver took a deep drink of Scotch, trying to come to terms with the life-altering implications of the discovery he'd made scarcely three hours ago.

God save him, he had a son.

Or, rather... Nicholas "Saint Nick" Marchand had a son.

The evidence was indisputable, he told himself as he knocked back another mouthful of liquor. The last time he and Suzanne had made love—

Leigh, he corrected sharply, giving himself a swift mental kick. *She's Leigh McKay now. Remember that.*

Although he'd been aware of Suzanne Whitney's new identity, thanks to his protracted conversation with Marcy-Anne Gregg, he'd persisted in thinking of her by her "real" name. He knew that he was going to have to stop doing so or risk making a potentially irreparable mistake the next time he saw her.

And there *was* going to be a next time. No matter his previous resolutions about trying to maintain a discreet distance from his—Saint Nick's—former lover. It was now impossible for him to stay away. The revelation of young Andy McKay's existence had changed everything.

The last time he and "Leigh" had made love had been a little more than five and a half years ago, on the night of May tenth. Her four-going-on-five-year-old son had been born on February eleventh.

Nine months later. Almost to the day.

He *had* to be the boy's father! Forget prophylactics. No form of protection—and he'd always made it a point to practice so-called "safe" sex—was one-hundred-percent effective.

More to the point: Suzanne—*Leigh, dammit!*—had been a sexual innocent when she'd yielded herself to the man she knew as Nicholas Marchand. There'd been no other lovers in her virginal life. He'd practically had to teach her how to kiss, for heaven's sake! And although she'd eventually evolved into an exquisitely satisfying bed partner, she'd retained an astonishing degree of modesty throughout their affair. While he'd been able to coax her into baring her body in front of him once or twice, he seriously doubted that she'd ever seen him totally nude.

Though undeniably provocative, her reticence had frustrated him at times. He believed that lovemaking should be reciprocal. A balancing of erotic give-and-take between two people. He'd never been able to persuade Suz— All right, all right! He would remember! Her name was *Leigh*. He'd never been able to persuade *Leigh* that her pleasure was as important to him as his own.

John shifted, acutely conscious of a sudden tightening in his groin. He drained his glass and set it down. Raking his disfigured right hand through his already mussed-up hair, he steeled himself against a potent rush of sexual hunger. Searching for distraction, he glanced restlessly around what he'd been informed was probably the last available hotel room in the area.

That he'd secured the accommodation—in a small inn on the outskirts of town—had been a rare stroke of luck. According to the proprietor of the lodging, there'd been a cancelation just moments before he'd phoned.

Asked how long he intended to stay, John had hesitated. He hadn't thought things through that far. In point of fact, he hadn't thought things through at all. He was lurching from moment to moment, still reeling from the shocking events of the past few hours.

Then, suddenly, he'd recalled Andy's artless comment about waiting to see what Santa brought before coming up with a list of potential birthday gifts. Impulsively, he'd inquired about the possibility of remaining at the inn through Christmas.

No problem, had been the pleasant reply.

He'd detected a hint of suspicion when he'd shown up at the front desk to register for a three-week-plus stay carrying nothing more than a small overnight bag and a personal computer. An offhand allusion to luggage problems and the presentation of his "platinum preferred" credit card had seemed to ameliorate most of the doubts about his desirability as a guest.

Any lingering uncertainties had been decisively dispelled when he'd thought to offer his Gulliver's Travels business card. The proprietor had not only recognized the name, he'd also begun talking about the wonderful old couple the agency had arranged to stay at his inn a few months back during the height of the fall-foliage season.

John clenched and unclenched his hands. The garrulous Marcy-Anne Gregg had said nothing to him about Leigh McKay's having a son. Of course, he hadn't thought to inquire about the possibility. Why should he? He'd inferred from a number of the older woman's comments—including the one hinting at matchmaking aspirations involving her best friend's unmarried grandson—that Leigh was still unattached. The notion that she might be a single mother had never entered his mind. If it had...

If it had, he damned sure would have done more cyber-sleuthing than he had before departing for Vermont! He'd limited his electronic intelligence-gathering to obtaining the basics—Leigh McKay's business address and phone number, her home address and unlisted home phone number, her motor-vehicle registration—for several reasons. Chief among them was a concern that hacking into supposedly secure data bases might trip an alarm or two. The woman who'd once been known as Suzanne Whitney was under government protection, after all. It had seemed logical to assume that someone in the Justice Department would have made provisions to detect unauthorized efforts to access information about her.

Someone in the Justice Department...

A wave of anger sluiced through John. He surged to his feet, the impulse to lash out running murderously strong within him. He began to pace around the room.

Damn them, he thought savagely. *Damn them straight to hell.*

He didn't doubt for an instant that his controller in the "Saint Nick" case—an eighteen-month-long operation that had flushed a major crime syndicate down the toilet and, co-incidentally, had put a psychotic slimeball named Anthony Stone in a cage where he belonged—knew about Andy McKay's existence. Hell. Odds were, Drake Nordling had been aware that Suzanne Whitney was pregnant the day he'd enlisted him in the conspiracy to keep her ignorant of the truth about Nicholas Marchand.

Nordling had never said a word, John reflected bitterly. Never dropped a hint. He'd pretended to offer a choice, but it actually had been a fait accompli.

He remembered the scene with awful clarity. It had taken place six weeks after Nicholas Marchand supposedly had died. For nearly four of those six weeks, he'd been in a coma. For much of the rest of the time, he'd drifted in and out of consciousness—zonked on painkillers and suffering from what doctors told him was short-term, trauma-induced memory loss.

Concern for Suzanne had dominated his thoughts during those intermittent periods when he'd been lucid. He'd finally managed to croak out the first syllable of her name one evening while Nordling was visiting in his hospital room.

"She's okay, Gulliver," his superior had told him. "Don't worry. We're talking care of her."

This assurance had been sufficient to calm him—for a while. Eventually, however, John had felt an overwhelming need to push the issue again. He'd understood the reasons that might mitigate against Suzanne coming to the hospital to see him. What he hadn't understood was why she'd apparently made no attempt to get in touch. And so...

"Suzanne Whitney's gone," Nordling had responded after he'd finally marshaled the energy to ask where she was and what she was doing.

"Go-ne?" His voice had been weak, its shredded timbre unfamiliar to his ears.

"We've had her in a neutral site since we started to roll up the Saint Nick operation, and we're in the process of relocating her." Nordling's reply had been matter-of-fact. His eyes had

had the cold, steely glint of a pair of ball bearings. "She's been very cooperative. Of course, the information she's given us is basically small potatoes. She was only a secretary at the front corporation that was helping to launder the syndicate's money, after all. She had no idea what was going on. Still, she's smart. She saw things. Heard things. Maybe she didn't understand their significance, but she remembered them. As a result, she's been able to clear up a couple of questions about how the company did business. Even though we're probably not going to use her on the stand at trial, I feel we owe her some accommodation and protection . . . all things considered."

A terrible wave of dizziness had broken over John at that point. For a few galling moments, he'd thought he might lose consciousness again. But he'd battled back the darkness.

"Can't . . ." he'd finally managed to force out. Yet, even as he'd spoken, he'd known he was wrong. His boss—and his boss's bosses within the United States Attorney's Organized Crime Strike Force Unit—could do just about anything they damn well pleased in a case like this, and he was in no condition to stop them.

Then Nordling had delivered the hammer blow.

"We decided it was wiser not to tell her about John Gulliver," he'd said. "As far as Suzanne Whitney's concerned, you're still Nicholas Marchand. And Nicholas Marchand was killed in a car crash six weeks ago, on the evening of May eleventh."

John had uttered an inarticulate sound of protest. There'd been a warning *beep-beep-beep* from one of the machines to which he was hooked up. Almost simultaneously, the door to his room had swung open. A handsome African-American woman—a nurse—had entered at a quick-march pace.

"Problem?" she'd asked.

"Not at all, nurse," Nordling had immediately declared, his manner dismissive. "Everything's just fine."

"You got a medical degree since I saw you last?" the woman had countered as she crossed swiftly to John's bedside. The tone of the question had suggested that unless he had—and probably not even then—his opinion carried zero weight with her.

Nordling, uncharacteristically, had not attempted to exert his authority. The nurse had briskly checked John's monitors, then leaned over so she could look into his eyes and he into hers. The bandages on his face and neck had severely restricted his peripheral vision and made it difficult for him to turn his head. He'd been grateful for her consideration.

"You shouldn't get yourself excited, Mr. Gulliver," she'd said quietly, then flicked a disdainful glance across the bed at Nordling. "You want me to pull the plug on this visitor of yours?"

"No," he'd refused following a brief, energy-gathering pause. "I'm . . . okay."

After letting a few seconds tick by, the nurse had nodded. Straightening, she'd cast another dark look at Nordling. "Five minutes more and you're out of here," she'd declared, then had pivoted and stalked out.

As soon as the door had shut behind her, Nordling had moved closer to John's bed and placed a hand on his plaster-encased left forearm. If the contact had been intended to be comforting, it had failed miserably.

"Think the situation through," he'd said. "You'll see it's for the best. You and I both know you broke a lot of rules by getting involved with Suzanne Whitney. Issues of morality aside, it was *dangerous*. You turned her into a potential target. Saint Nick made more than a few enemies. There's a chance his fatal accident wasn't so accidental, although I don't know that we'll ever have the evidence to prove it. The local police did a poor job of preserving the crash site. In any case, now that Saint Nick's gone, there may be some people inclined toward taking out their residual hostilities on his lady friend. And if word should get around that Nicholas Marchand is alive and actually a federal agent named John Gulliver . . ."

Nordling had paused, not bothering to spell out the potential consequences of the turn of events he'd just suggested. He hadn't needed to. John had been more than capable of conjuring up ugly scenarios on his own.

"She's obviously got feelings for you," Nordling had resumed in an even tone after a short, sharp silence. "Or maybe I should say, for Marchand. That comment I made about her being very cooperative doesn't apply to the subject of Saint

Nick. About him, she's given us nothing. Nada. According to her, he was a perfect gentleman. A Boy Scout. If she found out the truth... Well, let's assume she could get over the fact that you lied to her. She'd probably want to help nurse you back to health. And that could put *both* of you in the cross fire."

John had muttered a curse.

"Exactly," the other man had concurred without missing a beat. "There's also the matter of what kind of recovery you're going to make. Now, I have a lot of confidence in you, Gulliver. And in your doctors. But let's be straight, here. You've got some tough times ahead. Multiple surgeries. Months of physical therapy. With no guarantees at the end. Would you really want to suck Suzanne into that kind of mess? I don't know. Maybe you think she could handle it. I realize she's mature for her age. Considering that she's been making her own way in the world since her folks died—when she was what? Eighteen?— she'd have to be. Even so. She's barely twenty-three...."

There had been another pause. John had found himself focusing on the pattern of his respiration. It had suddenly seemed vitally important to keep it slow and steady. To prove to himself that there was *something* over which he could still exert at least a modicum of control.

Breathe in.

Breathe out.

"The government's going to give her a new identity," Nordling had finally said. "Settle her into a nice, clean life. Get her free of all the crap she's fallen into. And if you truly care about her..."

John had shut his eyes. For a single, brutal second, he'd actually regretted that he'd survived the crash in which Nicholas Marchand supposedly had died.

"I...know," he'd eventually replied, his chest feeling as though it had been strapped with slowly tightening bands of steel. "If I truly care...I'll let her go."

And so he had. Although it had felt as though he was slicing out his heart by doing so, he'd relinquished his dreams of making a future with Suzanne Whitney. He'd told himself that he wished her nothing but happiness in her new, government-engineered existence.

As for what he'd wished for himself...

John Gulliver came to a halt in the middle of his elegantly comfortable hotel room. His temples were pounding. Headaches—infrequent but blindingly fierce—were another legacy of Nick Marchand's "fatal" accident. Like the scarring. And the faint limp that sometimes manifested itself when he was extremely tired or under great stress.

He had medication, but he didn't want to resort to it. He believed that it was better to try to manage pain than to mask it with some drug. He'd come out of the hospital after his initial postcrash stay feeling uncomfortably dependent on pills. Although he'd kicked the habit before it had become deeply rooted, an awareness of how easy it would be to slip into addiction had remained.

Inhaling through his nostrils, John filled his lungs to capacity, then expelled the air slowly through his mouth. He repeated the routine several times. The throbbing in his head eased a little, but not all that much.

He headed toward the bathroom, telling himself a hot shower might help. He was also vaguely aware that after all he'd been through since his usual morning ablutions, he was starting to smell a bit ripe.

He began to strip, pausing when he noticed several dried splotches on the dark turtleneck he'd just peeled off. It took him a moment to figure out that the stains must be Andy's blood. His stomach roiled at the realization, the threat of nausea uncoiling in the pit of his belly like a snake. A brackish taste invaded his mouth.

His mind's eye filled with the image of a little boy in a bright blue jacket lying motionless in the snow, bleeding. He remembered vividly how it had felt to scoop that little boy up and carry him in his arms. He remembered, too, how it had felt to hear him crying out with pain and sobbing that he wanted his mommy.

The image in John's brain changed to the pale, panicked face of a desperately frightened woman. The shock of recognition he'd experienced when he'd seen that face still resonated within him. Five and a half years' worth of emotional defenses—defenses already weakened by the impact of a single photograph—had shattered.

He'd almost lost it. For a few lunatic instants in the examining room, he'd forgotten that Suza—*Leigh*, dammit, *Leigh!*—believed he—or rather, Nicholas Marchand—was dead. He'd forgotten that he had a face she'd never seen. He'd expected her to fling herself at him, weeping, in an act of recognition and reunion.

Instead, she'd been so intent on reclaiming and comforting her child that she'd barely glanced his way. And when her maternal frenzy had abated to the point where she was able to focus on him, her first reaction had seemed to be one of . . . well, not fear, precisely, but something disturbingly close to it.

He'd recollected his radically altered appearance—his *scars*— a heartbeat after Leigh had looked up at him. He'd recollected a lot of other things when her eyes had met his.

John shook his head, trying to exorcise the memory of the straight-to-the-gut jolt of electricity he'd experienced when his gaze had connected with Suzanne Whitney's for the first time in five and a half years. Given the pain in his temples, the movement wasn't wise. But it seemed to work. At least for the moment.

After rapidly shedding the rest of his clothes, he turned toward the shower. As he did so, he caught sight of his back in the full-length mirror hung on the bathroom door. The scarring on his well-muscled shoulders he was indifferent to. But the crescent-shaped birthmark located to the right of the base of his spine seemed to pop out at him.

The mark had been listed in his confidential personnel file at the Justice Department and on the rap sheet that had been created for Nicholas Marchand. John dimly recalled Nordling telling him that police had used it to establish his identity in the immediate aftermath of the crash that had put an end to Saint Nick's existence.

Nordling, he thought, his temper spiking anew. That bastard. He'd known about Andy. He must have!

"If you truly care about her . . ."

Nordling had also known precisely which psychological buttons to push with him and how hard to push them.

"If you truly care . . ."

Care?

Suzanne Whitney was the only woman he'd ever loved.

She was also the mother of his only child.

John Gulliver expelled a breath he hadn't realized he'd been holding.

Leigh and Andy McKay. The partner he thought he'd lost forever. The son he'd never had a chance to know.

They were *his*.

Come hell, high water or Drake Nordling, he would never let them go.

Leigh McKay kept watch over Andy throughout that night. Although the doctor at the clinic had assured her that he was going to be all right, she needed to be by his side...just in case. She'd failed her son once. She had no intention of failing him again.

"Oh, Andy," she whispered, feathering her fingertips against his warm, tender-skinned cheek. "Oh, sweetie."

Her little boy was fast asleep, his slumber apparently peaceful. Although he'd pretty much given up the habit in recent months, his left thumb was plugged between his lips like a pacifier. Leigh understood the impetus behind this retreat to what Andy sometimes described as "baby" behavior. She also understood why he'd been so insistent that she check—and re-check, then re-recheck—inside his closet and toy chest and beneath his bed for monsters after she'd tucked him in.

Her son wanted to feel safe again. Really, truly safe.

She prayed to heaven that he would. She prayed with all her heart that the trauma of this day would fade, leaving no emotional scars.

As for lasting physical injuries...

Leigh stared at the stitched-up wound on the side of Andy's head, a how-much-worse-it-might-have-been chill slithering up her spine like a poisonous serpent. Her son had talked a bit about having a "forever owwie" before he'd drifted off to sleep. Although the idea had been upsetting to her, he'd acted rather gratified by the prospect. He'd also made a drowsy comment about being scalped, which she assumed was a reference to having had some of his hair shaved off.

A yawn snuck up on her. She smothered it with the back of her right hand, willing herself to stay awake.

He hadn't seemed self-conscious about being scarred, she thought suddenly, her stomach fluttering. The disconcerting stranger who'd been so kind to her son had made no effort to hide the marks on his face and neck. He hadn't flaunted his disfigurement, exactly—if *disfigurement* was the right word. But he'd seemed almost...unaware of it.

She still couldn't remember the name he'd told her during their brief conversation. Where he'd come from was a complete question mark. Why he'd felt compelled to help a child he didn't know endure an ordeal some parents would flinch from was a mystery, as well.

As for the issue of whether she would ever have an opportunity to see him again—

"Umph-muh...*hunn*," Andy muttered, wriggling around beneath the bedclothes as though trying to get comfortable.

Leigh's heart skipped a beat. Her entire body tightened.

"Andy?" she asked anxiously, leaning closer. She'd been maintaining her vigil perched on the side of his bed. Now she wondered whether it might not be better to lie down and cradle him as she'd done when he was little.

"Hunna...*kumfz*." This unintelligible response was followed by several seconds of noisy sucking. Finally Andy gave a long sigh and settled down. Although his thumb remained firmly planted in his mouth, the corners of his lips curled up slightly as though he were smiling. A silvery thread of drool glistened on the curve of his chin.

"Andy?" Leigh tried a third time, seeking and finding the pulse point on the side of his neck. The slow but steady thud-thud-thud she felt reassured her. Likewise, the unruffled sound of his breathing.

She slipped to the floor and leaned against the edge of the bed, resting her cheek on the mattress. The scent of clean sheets and Andy's skin tantalized her nostrils. Her mind drifted back to the days when she'd felt almost addicted to the way her little boy smelled. She would hold him close, nuzzle her nose against his neck and breathe in the sweet fragrance of his innocent baby flesh until she was dizzy with it.

That she could love her son without reservation still seemed miraculous to Leigh. If truth be told, she'd been horrified when she'd learned that she was pregnant. She'd been nearly three months along at the time. Although hardly ignorant of the facts of life, her emotional state had been such that she'd utterly refused to face up to what was happening inside her body until forced to do so by a physician.

The possibility of abortion had been seriously discussed. But in the end, she'd elected to carry the baby to term.

She'd planned to give up the child—*the* child, not *hers*—for adoption. Had Andy not been placed in her arms only minutes after his delivery, she almost certainly would have.

Exhausted both physically and psychologically, she'd gazed down at the scrunched-up face of the little boy to whom she had just given birth. In the space of a single heartbeat, every detail of his appearance had been imprinted on her soul. If his features had offered clues to the identity of his father, she hadn't been able to see them. Her baby had been ... unique. He'd looked like himself and no one else.

Mine, something deep within her had declared. A serene certitude—the antithesis of the distressed confusion that had eaten away at her for every waking moment of the previous nine months—had enveloped her. *This is my son.*

To say that the question of her baby's paternity had ceased to matter in that poignant moment of bonding was to overstate the case. But it definitely had faded in importance. The anguished memory of the night of his possible conception had lost some of its power to hurt her, too.

"Hello, sweetie," she'd greeted her child, stroking lightly beneath his chin. There had been a lilt in her voice she'd never heard before. "Aren't you a *good* little boy? Yes. Oh, yes, you *are.* Do you know me? I'm your *mommy.*"

Leigh sighed. Keeping Andy had saved her life. There was no doubt in her mind about that. Oh, she would have survived physically had she given him up as she'd intended, but her existence would have been a hollow one.

She sighed again. Her eyelids fluttered down. She felt so ... tired.

Eventually, the woman who'd been born Suzanne Whitney slept. And as she did, she dreamed of a dark-eyed man with silver-threaded hair and a harshly compelling face whose name

she couldn't recall . . . but whose essence seemed wholly famili-
iar.

In her dreams, this intimate stranger said he loved her.

He also promised that nothing would ever hurt her, or her
son, again.

Chapter 3

"**G**ullible?" Leigh repeated, eyeing Andy dubiously. "The man who helped you told you his name was... *Gullible?*"

"Hunh-huh," her son cheerfully affirmed through a mouthful of fruit-filled cookie. The homemade pastry was from a basket of get-well treats Donatella Pietra had delivered several hours ago. The older woman had been extremely distraught about Andy's accident. Although Leigh had assured her repeatedly that a complete recovery was in the cards, Nonna P. had seemed unpersuaded. She'd kept asking about the possibility of concussion. She'd also seemed inexplicably inclined to hold herself responsible for what had happened.

Leigh frowned, searching her memory. Gullible. Gullible. That had to be wrong. And yet—

"He's Mr. Gullible, Mommy," Andy asserted again. Dressed in his favorite pajamas and floppy-eared bunny slippers, he was ensconced on the living-room sofa like a pint-size pasha. Although he was still a bit paler than Leigh would have wished, he looked one-thousand-percent better than he had the night before. He was also clearly intent on milking his invalid status for all it was worth. "*You* know. Like on that TV show you said was made from a really famous book. 'Member? The one about the guy who went to the place filled with little people. And the little people captured him and tied him up, but he escaped. Then he went to another place that was filled with giant people. And the giant people sort of captured him, too. They picked him up—''

"Gulliver?" Comprehension dawned. "The man's name is *Gulliver?*"

Andy rolled his eyes and plucked another cookie from the plate of goodies balanced on the left arm of the sofa. "I telled you it was."

Gulliver, Leigh thought, testing the name. *Yes! That was it. And his first name was—what? James? No. Joe? Mmm... close. But it wasn't quite—*

John!

The memory of Andy's rescuer introducing himself in the examining room at the clinic surfaced and slotted smoothly into place.

"I'm John Gulliver," he'd told her in his raspily distinctive voice.

A strange tingle of reaction—unsettling, but not wholly unpleasant—danced up her spine. She recalled again the potent sense of connection she'd experienced the first time John Gulliver's gaze had met hers.

Her knees wobbled suddenly. She took a not-quite-steady step to her right and sank down into the chair she'd positioned next to the sofa an hour or so ago when Andy had tired of watching TV and asked her to read him a story.

Why? Leigh demanded of herself. Why had she felt such an instant affinity with a man she'd just met?

If she could have chalked her reaction up to a rush of appreciation for what he'd done for Andy, she would have. But there had been more than gratitude at work in the examining room, and she knew it.

Her response to John Gulliver had been visceral. Almost... sexual.

Leigh gnawed on her lower lip, her hands fisting at her sides. She wanted to be free of the fears that had tormented her for so long. To finally be healed and whole again. But after five and a half years—

"Mommy!"

This irritated-sounding exclamation jerked Leigh out of her disturbing reverie. "What is it, honey?" she quickly asked, then flashed a smile meant to assure her son that he had her full attention.

Andy cocked his head, gazing at her with winsome eyes. He was up to something. After a moment he wheedled, "Can we have pancakes for lunch?"

"Pancakes?" Leigh was relieved by the innocuousness of the request. Given his expression, she'd expected to be asked for something much more outrageous. Like a dog. Or—heaven forbid—a little brother. Andy had been on a want-a-baby kick for more than a month. Exactly what had sparked this yearning for a sibling, she wasn't sure. But he'd mentioned that he planned to plead his case when she took him to see Santa Claus later in the month. "We had pancakes for breakfast, Andy."

"So? Pancakes are one of my most favoritest foods in the whole world. 'Sides. This is my day to re-cooper-tate from my hurt head, right? You said that when you talked to Miss Bleeker on the telephone and telled her you were gonna stay home and take care of me. I heard you. You telled Nonna P., too, when she came to visit. Only I'm not sure she b'lieved you. Like, I think maybe she's a-scared I have that cun—uh—cuncushing thing she kept askin' you about. Anyways. I'm *re-cooper-tating*. And that means I should get stuff I really, really like so I'll eat it all up and get feeling better very fast."

She had to laugh. "You've got this all figured out, haven't you, Mr. Smarty-Pants."

"Uh-huh." Andy turned on a dimple-displaying grin, clearly convinced that he'd maneuvered his mother into a position where she had no choice but to acquiesce to his gustatory desires. "Can we have pancakes? Please?"

"Will you eat them without maple syrup?"

"Huh?"

"Don't you remember? You used up the syrup at breakfast."

"Oh." Andy wrinkled his nose. "Yeah. Now I do. I didn't mean to, you know. It just poured out really fast."

"Yes, well, maybe next time you'll remember to tilt the bottle, not turn it upside down. What do you say to pancakes with powdered sugar?"

"Yuck!"

"Is that a no?"

"Sugar doesn't go good with pancakes. And that powder sticks on my tongue and feels funny."

"Heavens. We can't have that." Leigh took a moment to mentally review the contents of the McKay larder, then asked, "How about pizza?"

"With pepperonis?" Her son was extremely particular about his pizza toppings.

"Unless you'd rather have it with anchovies and black olives."

Andy made a gagging sound, just as his mother had expected he would.

"How about some delicious grape jelly, then?" she teased.

"Grape jelly?" The words were inflected with astonished disbelief and punctuated by a fizzy laugh. "You're so silly, Mommy. Nobody has pizza with grape jel—"

At that point, the front doorbell rang.

"Who's there?" Andy instantly demanded.

"I don't know." Leigh rose from her chair, smoothing the front of the loose-fitting gray sweatshirt she'd pulled on earlier along with a pair of wash-faded jeans. She wondered fleetingly whether Nonna P. might have decided to pay another call. Perhaps a second visit would persuade the older woman that Andy truly was going to be all right. "I guess I'll have to go and find out."

Which she did.

"Oh!" she exclaimed on a startled exhalation once she'd opened the door and saw who their caller was. Although the air rushing in from the outside was frigid, her body seemed to suffuse with heat. "Mr.... Mr. G-Gulliver."

"Good morning, Ms. McKay," he returned quietly, inclining his head. He was wearing an expensive-looking tan raincoat and carried a tissue-wrapped package in his left hand. Although his manner was diffident, there was something very determined in his eyes. "I hope I'm not catching you at a bad time."

"Oh, no. Not at all." She gestured him inside and shut the front door, conscious of an abrupt acceleration in her pulse. She also realized that her hands were trembling. "I'm very glad to see you again. I wasn't sure I would. See you again, I mean. And I . . . I wanted to.''

John Gulliver lifted his left eyebrow, causing the scarred skin on his temple to pucker. ''You did?''

''Of course.'' Leigh was taken aback by his seeming skepticism. ''I was terribly upset yesterday at the clinic and I'm afraid my behavior toward you was...well, if not actually rude, then definitely lacking. I didn't even thank you for the help you gave Andy. What you did—the way you stepped in—'' She paused, swallowing hard as emotion threatened to clog her throat. ''And for a little b-boy you d-didn't know—''

An expression she couldn't put a name to moved across her visitor's angularly irregular features.

''Your behavior at the clinic was completely understandable,'' he replied after a few seconds. ''Andy was your first and only concern. Anything I was able to do for him—'' He stopped abruptly, his gaze flicking away from hers to connect with something behind her. She saw him stiffen. She also thought she heard him catch his breath.

Then, excitedly, ''Mr. Gullible! You came to see me!''

''Hi . . . Andy,'' the man who'd been addressed returned, a curious break in his voice. The weathered skin that lay tautly over his prominent cheekbones darkened with a rush of blood. ''You're looking much better.''

Leigh turned. Her ''re-cooper-tating'' young son was shuffling toward the front door, tugging up the elasticized waistband of his pajama pants with his left hand. His face was alight with a delighted grin.

''His name is *Gulliver,* honey,'' she corrected, disconcerted by his obvious euphoria. Although Andy was a naturally warm and outgoing little boy, she'd never seen him react this enthusiastically toward anyone, let alone a man he'd met just twenty-four hours ago.

''He's welcome to call me John, Ms. McKay,'' the individual in question said. ''Gulliver is a bit of a mouthful.''

''Wow! Yeah!'' Andy cried, clearly bowled over by the suggestion. ''Can I, Mommy? Can I?''

Leigh hesitated. She resented the response John Gulliver was eliciting from her son, she realized with a shock. No, more than resented. She was *jealous* of it. It seemed to underscore the

anxieties she harbored about the lack of a strong male authority figure in Andy's life. Although she worked very hard to be
the best parent she knew how to be, she was acutely aware of
her limitations as a single mother. She worried that those limitations would become more and more obvious as Andy grew
older.

"*Ple-e-ease,* Mommy?"

"All right." Her consent was reluctant, given mainly to avoid
the tantrum she suspected a refusal might provoke. "You can
call Mr. Gulliver John. But only because he specifically in-
vited you to. I don't want you to get the idea that this means
you have automatic permission to call every grown-up you meet
by their first name."

"I won't," her son promised fervently, yanking at his pajama bottoms again.

"I'd be pleased if you'd call me John as well, Ms. McKay."

Their guest's voice dropped a note or two as he spoke, acquiring an insinuating—almost intimate—edge. Leigh's breath
snagged at the top of her throat. She suddenly found herself
regretting her casual clothes, barely brushed hair and unmade-
up face. This shook her. It had been a long time since she'd experienced even the slightest desire to make herself attractive for
a man.

A *very* long time, she thought with a pang. And the man
who'd provoked the desire was gone forever, the central character in a past she'd been forced to shut away to preserve her
sanity and protect her son.

She met John's dark gaze for an instant, then glanced away.
Lifting her right hand, she began fluffing at her fine, shoulder-skimming hair. A moment or two later she registered the
implications of this unthinking act of preening and jerked her
hand back down to her side.

What's happening to me? she wondered, feeling herself start
to blush. And why was whatever it was happening *now,* with
this particular—

"Mommy?"

"Ms. McKay?"

Leigh started. "S-sorry," she stammered, her gaze moving
from John Gulliver to her son and back again. "I, uh, didn't
get much sleep last night and I seem to be a bit, uh, discom-

bobulated. John it is, Mr. Gulliver—if that's what you'd like."
Drawing a steadying breath, she summoned up what she hoped
looked like a cordial smile. "And please, call me Leigh."

"Thank you...Leigh."

"Take off your coat, John," Andy commanded, stepping
into the role of host. "Then come in and have a visit."

"Oh, yes." Leigh struggled against a welter of contradic-
tory emotions as she seconded the invitation. The gratitude she
felt toward John Gulliver because of his aid to Andy was beyond words. Still. She wasn't certain she wanted this man in her
home. "Please. Do. Unless you're in a hurry—"

"Not at all." The unequivocal tone of John's response suggested that her ambivalence had not gone unnoticed. This
prompted the level of Leigh's uneasiness to rachet up another
notch. Although she'd once found it extremely difficult to dis-
semble in any way, for any reason, she'd thought that the past
five and a half years had taught her to hide her feelings very
effectively. It was unsettling to have this self-perception called
into question. "I have all the time in the world."

"Well, then..." She gestured toward the coatrack that stood
in the corner to the right of the front door. Then she glanced at
Andy and said, "I think you've been up long enough. Go and
lie down on the sofa again. Mr. Gulliver and I will be in in a
minute."

"John," her son corrected, not budging an inch.

"What?"

"You're s'posed to call him *John*, Mommy."

"All right. Fine. I'll call him John. Now, scoot. Boys who
get to stay home from preschool to 're-cooper-tate' are supposed to rest, not run around the house."

Andy made a face, plainly wanting to remain with their
guest. Leigh gave him a don't-argue-with-me-young-man look
and pointed toward the living room.

"Okay," he acquiesced with a put-upon sigh, then turned
and shuffled away.

" 'Re-cooper-tate'?" John asked in a curious undertone as
he finished hanging up his coat.

Leigh pivoted back to face him, short-circuiting an instinctive urge to retreat as he took a step toward her. While Andy's
rescuer was not a huge man—perhaps six-one to her own five-

eight—he had a very formidable presence. The dark turtleneck and dark, snug-fitting jeans he was wearing underscored
the sleek, coiled-spring power of his body. He looked...
dangerous.

Yet her impulse to back away from him was not prompted by
fear. Rather, it was a reaction to the unnerving realization that
some part of her wanted John Gulliver to move closer. After
five and a half years of holding herself aloof from every member of the opposite sex except her son, she suddenly found
herself tempted to invite an obviously strong and emphatically
virile stranger into her personal space.

There had been a period, not all that long ago, when the idea
of encouraging a man—even a man she knew very well—to
come within touching distance would have been unthinkable for
her. Although she'd gotten beyond this point, she was still extremely wary about leaving herself open to anything but the
most impersonal kind of hands-on contact.

That she was physically vulnerable was a brutal truth the
woman who'd lived her first twenty-three years as Suzanne
Whitney could not refute. Although a key component of her
transformation into Leigh McKay had been taking steps to
ameliorate this vulnerability, there was no escaping the fact that
she was smaller and weaker than most men.

She could cope with this reality and the anxieties it engen-
dered. Much more difficult to handle was the sudden discovery that she was *psychologically* vulnerable, too. To find herself
face-to-face with someone who seemed capable of breaching
the emotional defenses she'd worked so hard to—

"Leigh?"

She blinked, appalled to find that she'd once again gotten
lost in a maze of thoughts. *Get a grip!* she commanded herself.

"Sorry." Her voice was a bit more breathless than it had been
the first time she'd apologized for her distractedness. She
scrambled to pick up the thread of their conversation.
"Uh...you asked me about 're-cooper-tate,' right? That's
Andy-speak for 'recuperate.' He's a real sponge when it comes
to picking up big words. But he sometimes has trouble getting
his tongue around them."

"Like Gullible for Gulliver?" John suggested with a fleeting smile.

"Exactly."

"He seems like a very smart little boy."

Leigh had heard compliments about Andy's intelligence before, of course. Even as a baby, he'd prompted people to comment on how bright-eyed and alert he was. But there was something about the tone of John Gulliver's observation....

He'd sounded *proud*, she realized. Which made no sense at all. Why should this man take pride in the gifts of a child he'd only met a day ago?

"I think Andy's pretty exceptional," she confessed, fiddling with the hem of her sweatshirt. "But then, I'm not exactly an impartial judge."

"Mommy? John?"

"He's definitely got an exceptional pair of lungs."

The flash of deadpan humor caught Leigh by surprise. Her heart gave a curious hop-skip-jump. The mental wall she'd built around her past cracked slightly, allowing a memory to slip through. Nick Marchand had also had a sneak-up-on-you kind of wit, she recalled. A keen observer of the human condition, he'd been given to offering quirky, offhand quips about—

Stop it!

Leigh shoved the memory back behind the wall and patched the crack as best she could. *Forget him*, she told herself fiercely. *You have to forget him!*

"Oh, that's nothing," she said after a moment, hoping the laugh she manufactured didn't sound as brittle to her companion as it did to her. "If they ever decide to make yelling an Olympic event—"

"Are you coming yet?" In addition to increasing in volume, Andy's voice had taken on a distinctly whiny edge.

"I think the invalid is getting impatient," John observed, glancing toward the living room. If he thought her behavior peculiar, he gave no sign of it.

"I think you're right."

Leigh led the way into the living room, her body prickling with awareness of the man who followed a step or so behind her.

"Sit here, John," Andy instructed as they entered the living room. He beamed up at his guest, patting the sofa cushion next to him.

"Thanks," John replied, accepting the invitation.

Leigh reclaimed her previous seat, trying to ignore a resurgence of the jealousy she'd felt earlier. It wasn't easy. Her son's attention was riveted on John Gulliver to the exclusion of everything else. The expression in his blue-gray eyes as he looked at the older man was...was...

It was beyond admiring, she decided, clasping her hands together. It was downright worshipful. Andy McKay had obviously found himself a hero. And for the moment, this hero apparently outranked all the other people in his little boy's universe—including the mother he'd wanted with such weepy desperation just the day before.

"This is for you, Andy," John said after a fractional pause, extending the tissue-wrapped package he'd brought with him. He slanted an uncertain look at Leigh. "I hope you don't object."

As if an objection by her would make any difference at this point, she fumed inwardly as she watched the way her son latched on to the offering. Assuming she'd been foolish enough to attempt it, it would have taken a crowbar to pry his fingers from the gift.

"No, of course not," she replied.

"What is it?" Andy lifted the package to his ear and gave it a vigorous shake. "What is it?"

"Why don't you open it up and find out?" John suggested. A beat later, he glanced at Leigh once again. "If...that's all right with you?"

The man *was* making an effort not to undermine her parental authority, she told herself, trying to be fair. A remarkably clumsy effort, to be sure, but still...an effort.

"Go ahead, Andy," she said.

Her son needed no further urging. Ripping off the tissue paper with more speed than finesse, he quickly revealed his prize. "Oh, *wow!*"

Leigh frowned. What the—?

And then she identified the object. It was a tomahawk. A lightweight plastic tomahawk decorated with several strings of yellow, red and orange beads and a trio of equally garish feathers. While it wasn't the tackiest thing she'd ever seen, it could hardly be classified as a tribute to good taste.

"This is so *cool!*" Andy squealed excitedly. He brandished the toy weapon back and forth, then looked at his benefactor with shining eyes. A moment later he flung his arms around the older male and gave him a hug. "Thanks, John!" he exclaimed after ending the impulsive embrace. "Really, truly, thanks. I can't b'lieve you 'membered what I said!"

"I remember every word, Andy."

The tone of this assertion was soft but intense and triggered an odd jitter within Leigh. It reminded her of the note of pride she'd thought she'd heard in John's earlier observation about Andy's intelligence. It wasn't... appropriate.

"What are you talking about?" she asked her son. "What did you say?"

Andy turned toward her, clearly eager to tell the tale. "It was in the doctor's, when I was waitin' for you after my owwie got fixed. Me and John talked. I told him I didn't want people to know that a swing hitted me cuz it would sound dumb. Then he told me that I should make up a better story—"

"I wasn't encouraging him to lie, Leigh," John interrupted quickly, causing her to shift her gaze back to him. He grimaced as their eyes met, plainly embarrassed. "Well, actually...I suppose I was. But I don't want you to get the impression—I mean, I didn't intend—"

"I understand," she replied, unexpectedly affected by his awkward attempt to clarify why he'd said whatever it was he'd said to her son. John Gulliver hadn't struck her as the type of man who set much store by other people's assessments of him. Yet he obviously wanted to retain her good opinion. Why this should be, she didn't know. But it touched her.

"Yeah," Andy chimed in. "He wasn't 'couragin' me to lie, Mommy. He even said tellin' the truth is the best thing. And *I* said that's what *you* always say, too. And then I told him that made-up stories aren't the same as bad lies and that maybe it would be okay if I said I got my head owwie from a fight with an Indian 'stead of a dopey old swing."

"I...see."

"The Indian was gonna be tryin' to scalp me." Andy used his new toy to underscore the drama of his words. "And *that's* how come John gave me this." He looked at his fellow sofa-sitter. "That's right, isn't it?"

"That's right." Leigh noticed that John looked her son squarely in the eye as he spoke. She liked that. She also liked the fact that he didn't seem inclined to condescend. Andy hated to be talked down to. "I just hope you'll be careful with your tomahawk. I wouldn't like to hear that you've started clobbering people with it."

"Don't worry," Andy assured him. "I won't. And I won't let anybody else clobber people with it, either. I'm gonna take my tommy-hawk to show-and-tell when I go back to pre-school, then I'm gonna put it away in a really safe place in my room. It'll be like how Mommy keeps her gun."

Like how Mommy keeps her gun...

There was a volatile silence. Leigh sat rigidly in her chair. She knew John was staring at her. She could feel the penetrating power of his gaze. Finally, steeling herself, she turned her eyes toward his.

"You have a firearm in the house, Leigh?" His inflection was difficult to interpret. Likewise, his expression.

"It's legal." She told herself she had no reason to feel defensive. She also reminded herself that this man had no right to question anything she did. "And I've been trained how to use it."

"It's in a box with a lock in a drawer in her bedroom," Andy confided. "I'm not s'posed to open the drawer, though. Or the box. And I can never, *ever* touch it. 'Cuz a gun isn't a toy. Even if I think one might not have any bullets in it, I have to leave it alone. That's the absolute rule."

John scrutinized Leigh for a moment longer, his reaction to what he was hearing still impossible to gauge. Then he glanced at Andy.

"You're always going to obey that absolute rule, aren't you, buddy?" he asked in a quietly compelling tone.

After a brief hesitation, the little boy bobbed his head. "Yeah," he pledged in a small, solemn voice, clearly awed by the older male's ultraserious manner. "Always. Cross my heart." He made an *X* on his pajama-covered chest. Then he leaned forward, his eyes wide and curious. "Do you know any rules about guns, John?"

"*Andy—*" Leigh was desperate to get off this subject and stay off it. Her status as a gun owner was something she preferred to keep to herself as much as possible. Her relocation inspector knew about it, of course. And, given the amount of time Nonna P. spent in the house, she'd felt compelled to inform the older woman about it, too. But aside from that ...

Her son's awareness that she had a gun dated back to a rainy Sunday afternoon about six months ago when he'd taken it into his head to "help" by cleaning out her bedroom drawers. She'd panicked when she'd walked in and found him rattling the gray metal lockbox in which she kept her weapon.

Once she'd recovered her composure, she'd realized there would be no fobbing Andy off with the assertion that what was inside the box was not for little boys and therefore none of his business. She'd made too great a fuss to get away with that parental ploy. So she'd unlocked the box, removed and unloaded the handgun, and shown it to her son. After he'd had a chance to study it from every angle, she'd laid down the "absolute rule" about leaving it alone.

She supposed she should be thankful that her lecture had made such an impression, she reflected. Too bad she hadn't thought to include a prohibition against blabbing about the contents of the lockbox to strangers!

"Yes, Andy," John replied evenly. "I know some rules about guns. But since your mom's obviously made sure you know all the important ones, why don't we talk about something else?"

Andy fiddled with his tomahawk for several seconds, clearly not pleased with the prospect of moving on to another topic. But he also seemed wary of trying to buck John's authority.

"Like what?" he eventually questioned.

"Like—uh—uh—"

"Like whether our guest would like some refreshments," Leigh quickly suggested, responding to the SOS she saw in John's eyes.

"Huh?" Andy gave her a blank look.

She nodded toward the plate he'd been snacking from earlier, figuring that food was one of the few subjects that might—

just might—interest him more than firearms. It took a couple of seconds, but her son finally picked up the cue.

"Oh!" he exclaimed. "Yeah. 'Freshments!" He selected a cookie and extended it to his sofa mate. "Here, John. Eat this. You'll really like it."

"Thank you." The older man accepted the treat with alacrity and took a bite. "Mmm. Very good."

"Nonna P. made them."

"Nonna P.?" The inquiry was quick. Very quick.

"She's this really nice lady who take cares of me sometimes." Andy chose a small, fruit-studded pastry for himself. "Only not today. Today it's *Mommy.*"

A wide smile accompanied the last word. The sight of it warmed Leigh like spring sunshine. The jealousy she'd felt toward John Gulliver suddenly seemed very foolish.

"Sounds like a good deal."

"Uh-huh. Totally good. It's part of my re-cooper-tating." Andy nibbled at his home-baked treat, then gestured toward the plate of goodies. "You want more 'freshments?"

"I'm fine for now, thanks."

"Mommy? You want a cookie?"

"No, thank you, sweetie."

There was a pause. It was somewhat longer than the one that had followed Andy's handgun revelation, but infinitely less charged.

"So, John," Leigh eventually said, feeling it was incumbent upon her to pick up the conversational ball and run with it. She also saw an opportunity to get answers to a few of the many questions she had about their guest. "What brings you to Vermont? I mean—you're not from around here, are you?"

"I'm based in northern Georgia."

"Ah." He didn't have a Southern drawl, she noted. But that signified nothing. She lived in Vermont and she didn't have a New England accent. "So you're—what? Up here visiting someone?"

"'Course, Mommy." A giggle. "He's visiting *us.*"

John's features seemed to tighten at this smart-alecky interpolation. He shifted his position, his gaze moving from her to Andy and back again.

"I guess you could say I'm on a working vacation," he finally replied, appearing to consider his words very carefully before he spoke them. "I own a travel agency in Atlanta—"

Something clicked inside Leigh's brain.

"Good heavens!" she blurted out, wondering why she hadn't considered the possibility before. It wasn't as though his last name was a common one. "Are you talking about *Gulliver's Travels?*"

John nodded, his posture relaxing a few degrees. "That's right."

"I can't believe this! I met two of your clients a few months ago. Marcy-Anne and Maxwell Gregg. They were staying at a local inn as part of a fiftieth anniversary trip your agency organized for them and they came into my shop—I own a bookstore near the village green—several times. They were so warm and friendly. And they had nothing but raves for Gulliver's Travels. If Marcy-Anne mentioned your agency once, she mentioned it a dozen times."

"Mrs. Gregg had some very complimentary things to say about you, too."

This pulled Leigh up short. "You...talked to her about me?"

"Not exclusively. The Greggs sent some photographs from their trip to the agency's office manager and she passed them along to me. I followed up with a phone call. The Greggs have used Gulliver's Travels a number of times in the past and I wanted them to know I value their business."

Leigh nodded slowly. What he'd just said had sounded perfectly plausible. But it had also sounded rather...canned. As though he'd thought the answer out in advance and practiced it.

"In the course of our conversation," John continued, "Mrs. Gregg mentioned you and your shop." One corner of his mouth quirked up. "As well as a number of other things."

The wryly understated addendum prompted Leigh's own lips to curve into a reluctant half-smile. Although she'd liked the fluttery and flirtatious Marcy-Anne immensely, there was no denying that she'd found her garrulousness a bit overwhelming.

There was also no denying that she'd been unnerved when the older woman had begun interrogating her about her personal

life and background. Over the years, her relocation inspector
had given her a great deal of cogent advice on how to answer—or, more accurately, how to avert or evade—potentially
compromising inquiries. The most effective tactic seemed to be
to reverse the conversational flow and get the questioner talking about him- or herself. Still, it was a stressful proposition.
Always being on guard was difficult. Leigh missed the luxury
of casual chitchat, the pleasure of saying whatever happened to
pop into her head.

Marcy-Anne Gregg's version of the third degree might have
proved more than she could handle but for one fortunate cir-
cumstance. Although the older woman had asked dozens of
intimate questions, she'd almost never paused to hear the answer to them!

"I can imagine," Leigh said with a hint of humor. "Marcy-
Anne seemed to have a lot to say on a lot of subjects."

"Did that Gregg lady say how to get to our house, John?"
Andy suddenly queried.

Leigh's heart skipped a beat as she registered the implications of her son's innocent question. Her stomach knotted.
God! she thought, appalled by her carelessness. Why hadn't it
occurred to her to wonder how John Gulliver had discovered
their address?

"I don't think Mrs. Gregg has any idea where you live,
Andy," John said.

"Then—then h-how did you find us?" The inchoate anxiety that had nagged at her from the first moment she'd laid eyes
on the man now sitting next to her son coalesced into a genuine sense of alarm. She struggled to keep what she was feeling
off her face and out of her voice. If their visitor had a satisfac-
tory explanation for how he'd happened to turn up at her front
door one day after his dramatic entrance into her life, she didn't
want him thinking she was paranoid or had something to hide.
But if he didn't . . .

John looked at her, his gaze very direct. His expression told
her that her efforts to disguise her unruly emotions had been
only marginally successful.

I know you, it said. *I know all your secrets.*

"I knew your last name, Leigh," John stated quietly. "Remember? The staffer at the clinic who came into the examin-

ing room called you Ms. McKay. So I looked up McKay in the phonebook, but I didn't find anything. Then I called the operator. She said your number was unlisted.''

"I know it!" Andy volunteered. "It's five-five-fi—"

"Shush," Leigh said, cutting him off.

"But—"

John turned toward the little boy. "I'll bet you have an 'absolute rule' about not giving your phone number to strangers, don't you?"

"Well . . . yeah." Andy blinked rapidly, glancing from John to his mother, obviously trying to figure out what was going on. "And one about not takin' candy from strangers or gettin' into cars with 'em, either. And there's a special rule that I don't have to let *anybody* give me bad touches. Ever. Not even if I know them really good and they say it's okay. But . . . you're not a stranger, John. I mean, you *helped* me." He looked at Leigh again. "He did, Mommy. I heard you tell Nonna P. he was like a hero! So how come I can't tell him our phone number?"

"You can, honey," she replied, striving for a soothing tone. "Just not right now. Right now, you have to let him finish telling us how he found out where we live. It's . . . important." She waited a beat or two then asked, "Okay?"

Pulling a face, Andy fingered the feathers of his tomahawk. Finally he sank back against the sofa cushions and muttered, "Okay."

Leigh returned her attention to John. He leaned forward, his gaze meeting hers without wavering. The force of his will—of his desire that she believe what he was about to say—was palpable.

"I wanted to get in touch with you," he told her. "To make sure Andy was all right. I didn't think the clinic would give me any information, so I drove over to the preschool and talked to Thalia Jenkins."

"And she just told you our address?"

"Only because of what happened yesterday." John was emphatic. "If she hadn't recognized me, I doubt I would have gotten a word out of her."

That wasn't good enough, the woman who'd once been Suzanne Whitney told herself. A chill of apprehension shivered through her. This lapse in security was her fault. She'd

assumed that the good, decent people at Andy's preschool
could be relied upon to protect his privacy. She should have
made it clear to everyone at the time of his enrollment that it
was vital—*absolutely vital*—that no information about him be
disclosed to anyone without her express permission.

"Leigh." John's voice was soft, yet threaded with steel. She
looked at him, her heart thudding heavily. "I'm sorry. If I'd
had any idea my showing up here would upset you like this, I
wouldn't have done it. I didn't...think. I should have had Miss
Jenkins phone ahead to ask if it would be all right. Or I could
have gone to your bookstore and left a message. I—I stopped
by there yesterday, as a matter of fact. Before Andy's accident. Before I, uh, knew you had a son. I was driving around
and I recognized the front window from one of the Greggs'
photographs. I had a conversation with your—ah—assistant,
I guess she must be? Deirdre Bleeker?"

Leigh nodded slowly. He had to be telling the truth, she
thought. The information he was providing was too detailed—
and too easily checkable—to be anything but accurate.

And yet...

And yet, *nothing!* she decided with a sudden surge of emotion. John Gulliver had done nothing wrong. Quite the contrary. He'd come to the aid of her son. He'd looked after him
like...like... Oh, Lord, there was only one way to describe it.
He'd looked after Andy like a father. And he'd asked no reward for what he'd done. He'd even turned aside her belated
efforts to thank him.

Still, he disturbed her. Deeply. There was no getting around
that fact. But it wasn't his fault. His behavior toward her had
been above reproach. Whereas hers toward him—

"Leigh?"

The invocation of her name was accompanied by a gentle
touch to the back of her right hand. The contact was brief, yet
it sang through her nervous system like an anthem. She quiv-
ered, impulses she believed permanently deadened stirring to
life.

"Mommy? Are you okay?"

Leigh inhaled on a tremulous breath and looked at her son.
"Yes, Andy," she said after a moment, her voice husky, her

body humming. She knew she was blushing. "Mommy's just fine."

"Are you *sure?*"

"Absolutely."

"You're not mad at John anymore?"

"No." Leigh shook her head, intensely aware of the teasing brush of her hair over the nape of her neck. She was similarly aware of the stiffening of her nipples against the fabric of her bra. Her eyes met their guest's yet again. She noticed for the first time that his dark brown irises held glints of gold. "I was never mad at John."

Andy turned to the man sitting on his right. "Are you mad at Mommy?"

"Not at all, buddy."

"Is anybody mad at me?"

"Oh, *honey*—"

John reached out and ruffled Andy's toffee-colored hair. "Of course not."

"So...everything's all right, right?"

Blue eyes met brown ones. Again, Leigh felt the surge of connection she'd experienced in the examining room. And she could see that John felt it, too. The hard lines around his mouth eased. His nostrils flared. The flecks of gold she'd spotted just a few moments before turned molten.

"Right," he said softly.

"Right," the former Suzanne Whitney echoed, uncertain whether she was telling the truth but unable to answer any other way.

"Good," Andy declared, smacking his tomahawk against the sofa cushion. He seemed much relieved. "Let's eat lunch."

The lawyer—a sleek, Ivy League rat with a cocaine habit— was nervous. Scared, even.

Taking this as a tribute to his power, Federal Prisoner No. 00394756 savored the signs of the other man's weakness.

The stink of sweat that no designer after-shave could fully mask.

The tremor that kept messing up the oh-so-classy diction.

The twitchy movements of carefully manicured hands and the flick-flick-flickering shift of hyperbright eyes.

Forget the "earning respect" crap some talked about, Federal Prisoner No. 00394756 thought with an inward sneer. Instilling fear was the way to go. It was much more effective. Much more . . . fun.

"Tell me," he ordered, nailing the lawyer with a look.

The other man swallowed, his Adam's apple bobbing above the collar of the shirt Anthony Stone was willing to bet had been custom-made for him. He was also willing to bet the garment was sodden beneath its wearer's armpits.

"There's been an . . . accident . . . involving your package."

Federal Prisoner No. 00394756 sat forward, his gut knotting, his hands gripping the edge of the table that separated him from his lawyer. He glanced up at the surveillance camera in the corner of the small room in which this tête-à-tête was taking place. Chill, he told himself.

"An accident?" he echoed after a moment, keeping his voice even. Although the confidentiality of this conversation supposedly was protected by attorney-client privilege, he didn't doubt the feds were listening in. Hence the need for a calm demeanor and cryptic language.

"Yes." The other man nodded. "No permanent damage, though. Still, your—uh—source thought you should know."

"When?"

"The day before yesterday. Monday."

"What happened?"

"Just . . . an accident."

Anthony Stone snorted contemptuously, his mind flashing back to a night five and a half years ago. He knew about accidents. And how to cause them.

"Look." The attorney made an uncharacteristically aggressive gesture. Maybe he'd suddenly gotten some guts. Then again, maybe he'd suddenly lost what few brains he had left after years of powdering his snotty-looking nose from the inside. "All I know is what your source told me. And if you don't trust—"

"I don't trust anybody," Federal Prisoner No. 00394756 snapped. "Not even my own flesh and blood." He paused, his mouth twisting. "*Especially* my own flesh and blood."

"But—"

"What about my other piece of property?"

It took the lawyer a moment to switch gears. "Uh . . . fine," he said, his flash of nerve fading. "As far as I know."

"Not involved in the accident?"

"No. Apparently not."

Federal Prisoner No. 00394756 eased back in his chair, anger beginning to bubble through his veins. *What's going on, Suzanne?* he demanded silently. *You know what I want of you. What I . . . expect. You're supposed to be taking care of my son. Now I find out he had some kind of "accident" and you weren't even around! So, where were you . . . ? Off someplace, in bed with another man?*

He didn't want to believe it. He knew what Suzanne Whitney was, of course. He hadn't been fooled by her protests the night he'd finally taken her. She'd been hot for it. And for him. She might look like an innocent angel, but she was really a slut.

Still, he'd been willing to give her the chance to change her ways. Having his son had purified her. All she'd had to do was keep herself clean until he came for her.

"Mr. Stone?" the attorney asked, properly deferential once again.

Federal Prisoner No. 00394756 made up his mind. He'd waited long enough.

"I want you to get in touch with our friend," he said, staring at the other man. He allowed himself the fleeting luxury of imagining the lawyer pinned to a board, like a bug. "I want to reach out—personally—and take care of my own."

"That . . . that may take some time."

"Then what the hell are you doing sitting here?"

Chapter 4

John Gulliver had done a lot of difficult things in his life. Only a few of them had tested his mettle more painfully than staying away from Leigh and Andy McKay on the day following his first visit to their home.

His head had counseled that it was necessary to pull back, to keep the level of contact casual for the time being. Leigh's skittishness was such that pursuing an acquaintanceship too obviously might alienate her completely. Even worse, it might send her running to the feds. Rebuilding their relationship—or was it more a matter of constructing a new one on the wreckage of the old?—had to be done carefully. Once he'd gained her trust, he would tell her the truth about himself and Nick Marchand.

Whether her trust would survive this truth-telling remained to be seen.

His heart—his gut, his groin—had advocated a more precipitous approach. *Claim what's yours*, they'd urged. *You've been cheated out of five and a half years with the woman you love and the son you never knew you had. Don't give up any more time!*

In the end, caution had carried the day. But it hadn't been an easy win. Indeed, there were moments when John wondered whether it might turn out to be a Pyrrhic victory.

Holing up in his hotel room, he kept himself occupied as best he could during his self-imposed period of separation. He was involved in a dozen enterprises besides Gulliver's Travels and they all demanded some degree of attention. Two hours at the computer keyboard and on the phone took care of the day's most urgent business. Another thirty minutes of electronic catalog shopping—with each purchase guaranteed for over-night delivery—augmented the very limited wardrobe he'd brought with him from Georgia.

From there he turned to the "discreet digging" he'd decided to do prior to Andy's accident. What he discovered about Deirdre Bleeker in the course of his illicit sleuthing in cyber-space unnerved him. Given his initial reaction to her, he couldn't say that he was wholly surprised by what he learned. But when he considered the implications of someone with her background being so close to Suz—

Leigh, he corrected himself for what seemed the millionth time, clicking the Save function on his PC. Adjusting to his former lover's new name was almost as trying for him as ad-justing to his new face. That he'd gotten through Tuesday's visit without making a slip struck him as a minor miracle. The name "Suzanne" had trembled on his tongue more times than he could count. He'd swallowed it repeatedly, coming close to the choking point on several occasions.

He'd had to swallow the urge to confess his previous iden-tity, too. In the end, Andy's presence had kept him silent. As eager as he was to acknowledge his son, there was no way he could drop an "I'm your daddy" bombshell on an innocent little boy.

But back to Deirdre Bleeker. According to the files he tapped into, she'd been born to an unwed teenage mother who'd abandoned her as toddler. She'd spent her formative years bouncing between foster homes and juvenile facilities, racking up a long record of disciplinary infractions and petty crimes. She'd been arrested twice for solicitation, but had had the charges knocked down to misdemeanors both times. A bust for possession of a controlled substance at age eighteen had gotten her a mandatory two-to-five.

She'd gone through drug rehabilitation and earned her GED while serving her sentence. Her postrelease record—which dated back a little less than three years—looked squeaky-clean. She was gainfully employed, attended weekly group-counseling sessions and paid her bills on time. She even did volunteer work with some church group.

Much as it might have soothed him to do so, experience—both personal and professional—prevented John from accepting this apparent redemption at face value. Yes, it was possible that Deirdre Bleeker had managed to straighten out her screwed-up life. It was also possible that her responsible new persona was some kind of con—that beneath the surface reformation lurked the same old rot.

And if it did . . .

And if that rot threatened Leigh or Andy. . .

No, he told himself, his muscles knotting on a primal surge of protectiveness. He was not going to let that happen. If Deirdre Bleeker was up to something, he would find out about it and stop her.

Ditto, Wes-the-Book-Orderer. A casual interrogation of the inn's proprietor had garnered the information that "Wes" was Wesley Warren, a local boy who'd enlisted in the army after graduating from high school. He'd gotten out of the service a little more than two years ago and returned home with enough cash to buy a half interest in an auto-repair shop.

John clicked to another of the background files he'd created. The military records he'd loaded into it indicated that Wesley Warren had been assigned to the motor pool after completing basic training and done just fine. His evaluations had been solid but not spectacular. If he'd ever bent a regulation or broken the law, he hadn't gotten caught at it.

The big question was where he'd obtained the money to put into the garage when he'd returned to civilian life. As far as John could determine, the six-figure sum involved hadn't been a loan or a legacy.

Could Wes have saved enough from his military salary? Oh, it was doable, John conceded, studying his PC screen with a critical eye. But it would have required squeezing nickels until the Thomas Jeffersons stamped on them squawked in protest. Legends of Yankee frugality notwithstanding, he found such a scenario hard to buy.

So where had the cash come from? he asked himself, frowning. *Was someone bankrolling the Norman Rockwell-esque Mr. Warren? If so, who? And why? Not to get rich quick, that was for certain.* While the financial records he'd tapped into showed that Wes's garage was doing all right, it hardly qualified as a gilt-edged investment.

Could somebody be using the place as a front for some kind of money-laundering operation? John wondered, remembering the syndicate Saint Nick had helped bring down. He clicked to another file, scanning the rows of numbers that appeared on the screen with a critical eye. *Mmm... Probably not.* The cash-flow patterns were wrong for that kind of scam.

A chop shop? he mused further. *Maybe. But if that was the case, wouldn't the volume of vehicles going in and out have tipped somebody off?* Using a busy urban garage to strip and ship stolen car parts was one thing. Setting up business in a garage in a town where traffic seemed to travel at a horse-and-buggy pace was something else entirely.

Okay, he decided. *Forget the chop-shop theory for now. What about a smuggling drop?* The Canadian border wasn't that far away. In fact, if he remembered the road map he'd picked up at the airport correctly, it was pretty much a straight shot on 91.

John turned the idea over in his mind several times, probing for weaknesses. Yeah, he finally told himself. Smuggling was definitely a possibility. Drugs. Booze. Cigarettes. He would definitely have to keep checking.

Closing the file he'd been studying, he let his thoughts drift from speculation about the true nature of Wes Warren's business to a review of the information he'd gathered about Leigh's bookshop. He'd done a cursory check of her bank statements and credit records the previous night. By his calculations, she was keeping her financial nose above water and that was about it.

Assailed by a sudden flash of anger, John expelled a harsh breath and slumped down in his chair. His parents had died in a plane crash when he was twenty-five, leaving him in sole possession of a small but solid fortune. He'd expanded that fortune considerably since that time. Leigh should have been sharing in his wealth during the past five and a half years, not scrimping to make ends meet! And as for Andy—

The truth hit him anew, resonating deep within his soul.

Andy.

He had a son named Andy.

John closed his eyes, replaying the moment when he'd looked down the McKays' front hall and spotted his little boy coming toward him. Temporarily bereft of speech, he'd found himself searching for some imprint of his paternity. He'd stared, trying to reconcile childish features with memories of an adult visage that no longer existed.

The shape of Andy's blue-gray eyes and the set of his mouth and chin had reminded him of Leigh. So, too, the seemingly poreless skin and silken hair. But if his son resembled him—him as he used to be—he hadn't been able to detect it.

Whatever disappointment he'd felt because of this had been swept away by his reaction to the beaming, baby-toothed smile Andy had offered him. He'd been pierced to the heart by the unguarded warmth in that dimple-bracketed grin. The rush of emotion he'd experienced had nearly knocked him to his knees.

And later, when Andy had hugged him . . .

Dear Lord.

There were no words to describe the effect that impulsive, thank-you embrace had had on him. Or if there were, the man who'd once been Nicholas Marchand wasn't familiar with them. He'd been stunned by the profundity of what he'd felt. Too stunned, frankly, to hug the little boy back.

Which probably had been for the best, all things considered. Because if he *had* managed to put his arms around his newly-discovered son, instinct told him that he would have had a lot of trouble letting go.

Heaven only knew how Leigh would have reacted to that!

Well, no, John amended, opening his eyes and straightening his spine. Not only heaven. He had a pretty accurate notion of what Leigh's response would have been, too.

She'd been disturbed by the way Andy had taken to him. He'd seen it in her fair, fine-boned face. He'd heard it in her cool, contralto voice. Although she'd become more skilled at disguising her emotion over the years, his attunement to the nuances of her expression and tone was still acute. If she'd gotten the impression that he was trying to stake some special claim on her son . . .

She would have fought him, he thought grimly. No matter the debt of gratitude she clearly believed she owed him for the aid he'd given Andy. No matter the attraction her blushes and body language made it clear she felt toward him. *She would have fought him, tooth and nail.*

There was a tempered strength in Leigh McKay that he'd never sensed in Suzanne Whitney, John reflected, his body beginning to stir. Which wasn't to say that Suzanne had been weak. She hadn't been. As Drake Nordling had pointed out on that fateful day in his hospital room, she'd been fending for herself since her late teens. That had taken spirit. And smarts.

Still, for all her intelligence and independence, the woman who'd given herself to Nicholas Marchand had been fundamentally ignorant about the ugliest realities of life. This naïveté had shielded her from those realities in some ways. It had made her shockingly vulnerable to them in others.

Leigh was vulnerable, too, of course. One look at her face in the examining room had told him that. But unlike Suzanne, she appeared to be intensely aware of how dangerous the world could be. What's more, she'd taken steps to protect herself. Many of those steps were small—the careful way she now chose her words, for example. A few of them, however—like her acquisition of a handgun—represented a huge change in attitude.

John Gulliver had never gone anywhere unarmed during the eighteen months he'd played the role of Nicholas Marchand. A lot of women had been turned on by this. More than a few had been perversely fascinated by his alter ego's carefully orchestrated reputation for violence, as well.

Suzanne, on the other hand, had been appalled to discover that he carried a weapon. And while she'd never flat-out said so, he'd come to believe that her decision to surrender her virginity had been fueled by a conviction that Saint Nick was not what he was said to be.

The stirring of John's body became a stiffening.

Memory beckoned.

The flavor of Suzanne's sweet, kiss-rouged lips as they'd opened to the coaxing courtship of his teeth and tongue...

The feel and fragrance of her passion-heated skin as he'd charted her nearly naked flesh with long, lavish strokes...

Yes, he thought, succumbing to the lure of erotic recollection. *Oh, yes.*

Suzanne had shivered like a leaf in a windstorm when he'd dipped his head to suckle at the taut nipples of her small but beautifully shaped breasts. He'd nipped delicately at the jewel-hard peaks, then licked the outlines of the lushly pink areolae from which they rose. Her hands had come up at some point during those tactile ministrations, her slender fingers spasming in the dark hair that curled over the nape of his neck. A wild little sound—part plea, part protest—had broken from her throat.

"Don't be afraid, sweetheart," the man known as Saint Nick had whispered, levering himself up a few inches and staring down into his about-to-be-lover's emotion-clouded eyes.

"I'm not." Suzanne had shifted her body in a seemingly irrepressible movement. "Not...with you."

She'd tried to hurry him then, her caresses awkward but ardent. Although his libido had vehemently argued otherwise, he'd responded by slowing the pace. He'd done so for the same reason he'd stopped her earlier in the evening when she'd started to refill her wineglass for the third time. He'd wanted her wholly aware—and utterly sure—of what she was doing.

Well, no. Not wholly aware. Not utterly sure. Because that would have required his revealing the truth about who he really was. And that had been something he hadn't been able to do.

"Easy, love," he'd said huskily, gripping Suzanne's hips and holding her still. He'd shoved the goad of conscience aside, telling himself that his lies were this woman's greatest form of protection. All impulses toward honesty had to be deferred until his assignment was over and her safety could be assured. "We have all night."

She'd said his name in a hushed, half-suffocated voice, her gaze imploring. "Please," she'd entreated, the color in her cheeks fluctuating wildly.

"Not yet." He'd brushed his mouth over hers. Her tongue had stolen out for a heady moment to meet and mate with his. "There's no rush. I want to make sure you're . . . ready."

She'd been beyond readiness—all wet heat and wanton innocence—by the time he'd finally taken what she was offering. Fiercely aroused, he'd still been afraid of hurting her.

He'd eased into her slowly. Very slowly. So slowly that he'd shuddered with the stress of trying to control urges that were nearly uncontrollable. Constraint had caused his heart to hammer violently. He'd felt the force of each pounding beat from the tips of his toes to the top of his skull.

Despite his desperately careful precautions, there'd been an instant of pain. The sudden stiffening of Suzanne's previously pliant body and an involuntary whimper had made that brutally obvious. Appalled by what he'd done, ashamed by the duplicity that had brought him to this consummation, he'd started to withdraw. His no-longer virginal bed partner had clutched at his shoulders, her nails digging sharply into his tautly muscled flesh.

"N-no," she'd disputed on a shattered cry. "Oh...Nicholas. No."

"Suzanne—"

He'd felt her hands move down his back, pausing a scant inch or so above the crescent-shaped birthmark near the base of his spine. The pressure of her smooth palms had been a wordless but eloquent expression of her need. She'd raised her hips, taking him deeper inside herself. His bones had begun to liquefy.

"Please," she'd begged, arching again. "Please. D-don't . . . stop."

He hadn't. Whether he would have been capable of doing so, had she asked it of him, John Gulliver genuinely hadn't known. But somewhere in the back of his desire-hazed brain he'd been deeply grateful that she hadn't. He'd waited a long time to make love with Suzanne Whitney. The clamor for completion had been almost overwhelming.

He'd slid forward gently, increasing the extent of his possession by a small but critical increment. He'd been rewarded with a breathless gasp that held no hint of hurt. He'd moved again, still exercising great care. Reluctant tissue had relaxed, gloving his flagrantly hard flesh with a compellingly sensuous warmth. A luscious wave of sensation had rolled through him, sweeping him closer to ecstatic release.

"Yes," Suzanne had whispered heatedly, her fingers tightening. She'd kissed the side of his throat, licking at his sweat-dampened skin with feline delicacy. "Oh . . . *yes.*"

"Suzanne," he'd groaned, sinking a little deeper into her slick, feminine tightness. Nothing in his life had ever felt so right. So good. So meant to be. "Sweet . . . Suzanne."

"N-Nick—"

The sudden shrill of a telephone shattered John's reverie. He returned to the present with a start. His lungs were laboring as though he'd just completed a marathon. His body pulsed with carnal vitality, primed for a sexual explosion.

He glanced around, momentarily disoriented. Then he remembered where he was. And why.

The telephone rang again.

Getting to his feet, he walked an unsteady path over to the rucked-up four-poster bed in which he'd spent a very restless night. The phone sat on a small wooden table positioned next to it, along with a lamp and clock radio.

He picked up the receiver with his left hand, forking the none-too-steady fingers of his scarred right one through his hair. "Yes," he snapped into the mouthpiece. "What is it?"

There was an audible gulp from the other end of the line. Then, very tentatively, "Mr. . . . Gulliver?"

John experienced another flash of disorientation. A part of his psyche was still tangled in the potent web of memories spun from the life-altering period he'd spent as Nicholas Marchand and he wasn't sure how to tear it loose. Turning slightly, he caught a glimpse of himself in the mirror that hung above a chest of drawers set against the wall across from the foot of the bed. The image he saw did nothing to clarify his sense of identity.

God, he thought with a hint of desperation. How was he going to persuade Suz—*Leigh,* dammit!—about the truth of who he was if he could barely keep track of it himself?

"Gulliver," he finally repeated, hanging on to the name like a mental lifeline. He cleared his throat. "Yes. That's right. This is John Gulliver."

"Oh, good. This is Edith from housekeeping, Mr. Gulliver. I know you have your Do Not Disturb sign up, so I apologize for calling. But it's getting late in the day and I wanted to see whether you'd like your room cleaned."

John eyes flicked toward the bedside clock. The numbers on its digital readout gave him a shock. Late in the day, indeed. It was nearly 7:00 p.m.

"Uh—no, Edith," he responded after a few seconds. "But thank you for checking."

"You need fresh towels? Soap? A change of linen? Anything at all?"

"I'm fine."

"Well, if you're *sure*." A sigh came through the line. "My cousin made me promise I'd take special care of you."

John sank down on the edge of the unmade bed, the insistent throbbing in his body moderating a few degrees. "Your...cousin?"

"Thalia Jenkins. From the preschool. She's my second cousin, actually. On my mother's side."

"I see." He should have anticipated something like this, he thought with a grimace. Small-town rule of thumb: Everybody was related to everybody else by blood or business and they all knew each other's secrets.

"She told me what you did the day before yesterday. Went on and on about it."

It occurred to John that Thalia Jenkins could use a few lessons in discretion. While her garrulousness had proven useful to him—providing him with cover, should Leigh decide to pursue the touchy issue of how he'd discovered her home address—he had an innate aversion to people with loose lips. Careless talk could kill.

"I did what needed doing," he said flatly, wanting to discourage the woman's interest. "Anyone else would have done the same."

"That's not what Thalia says," Edith countered. "And I'll just bet it's not what that little McKay boy's mother says, either."

"Don't you understand? It doesn't matter that he lied about who he is and why he's here! He's the only man I've ever—"

"He's back."

Leigh started guiltily, her gaze slewing from the over-wrought action on the screen of the small television she kept in her office to the thin, frowning face of her assistant.

"D-Dee," she stammered, reaching for the set's volume control and turning it down. She couldn't quite bring herself to switch off the program entirely. It was a hospital-based soap opera she'd begun watching years ago, with her mother. Melodramatic though it might be—among the current story lines were a custody fight over a pair of switched-at-birth babies and the angst of an amnesiac bride-to-be—she was hooked. She'd even scheduled her bookshop's weekly story hour not to conflict with it. "I'm sorry. What did you say?"

"That guy's back."

"What ... guy?"

The redhead fiddled with the cuff of the baggy beige blouse she was wearing. The color was extremely unbecoming, emphasizing the sallow undertones of her milk-pale skin. Leigh knew that the unflattering attire had been deliberately chosen. While it pained her to see her assistant reject her natural prettiness, she understood the demons that drove her to do so too well to criticize.

"I didn't mention it because you had enough on your mind with Andy. This guy came into the shop Monday, while you were in Brattleboro. Tall. Dark. Definitely not your ordinary tourist-type. I would have remembered him even without the scars—"

"John Gulliver?" Leigh interrupted, her heart skipping a beat. She stood, smoothing the front of the raspberry-pink sweater she wore.

"You *know* him?"

The question triggered a strange tremor in Leigh's nervous system. Did she "know" John Gulliver?

No. She didn't.

Not really.

And yet ...

She remembered again the visceral sense of affinity she'd experienced when their gazes had connected in the clinic's examining room. She remembered, too, the rush of physical response he'd evoked when he'd stroked the back of her hand with his fingertips during his visit to her home on Tuesday.

She'd never been a believer in reincarnation or the transmigration of souls. But if she had—

"Leigh?" Dee prompted.

She blinked, swatting away a stray lock of hair and telling herself to stop being foolish. "John Gulliver is the man who drove Andy to the clinic after he had his accident, Dee."

"*Him?*"

"Yes, him. Why do you find that so difficult to believe?"

Dee hesitated, shifting her weight. "I don't know, exactly," she finally admitted, her voice constricted. The line of her jaw fretted. "Something about him . . . bothers me."

Leigh stiffened. Something about John Gulliver bothered her, too. Intensely. She didn't want to think it was the same thing that was bothering her assistant. Disciplining her voice into neutrality, she commented, "He certainly makes a very strong impression."

"You want to know the truth?" the redhead demanded with a hint of defiance. "If I were still on the street, I'd make him for a cop."

"A *cop?*"

"Yeah." A jerky nod underscored the affirmation. "Absolutely."

Leigh didn't know what to say. She was aware of her assistant's checkered history, of course. Dee had been painfully frank on her employment application. Given what the other woman had gone through, she supposed she should give some credence to her assessment. But it just didn't . . . jibe.

She had more than a passing familiarity with law-enforcement types, herself. It wasn't the kind of familiarity she'd gone looking for. Quite the contrary. But circumstances beyond her control had given her a crash course in cops. How they walked. How they talked. How they viewed the world. And if she had to "make" John Gulliver for anything other than what he claimed to be, it certainly wouldn't be a police officer!

She wouldn't have made Nicholas Marchand for a criminal, either, she suddenly reflected. Even after he'd confirmed with his own lips that the stories she'd heard whispered about him were more or less accurate, a part of her had still refused to believe—

Leigh inhaled sharply, clenching her fingers until their nails jabbed into the tender flesh of her palms. Nick was dead, she told herself. What they'd shared was gone. Thinking about him, about what he had and hadn't been, was dangerous. Not just to her, but to her son. *She had to stop it.*

"Wes doesn't like him either."

"Wh-what?"

"Wes," Dee repeated, flushing from the prim neckline of her blouse to her furrowed brow. "He doesn't like your Mr. Gullible either."

"Gulliver." The correction was automatic. So was what came next. "And he's certainly not *mine*."

"Well, Wes thinks—"

"How does Wes know him well enough to have an opinion, anyway?"

"He, uh, met him. Sort of. He dropped by the bookshop Monday, too."

Leigh studied her assistant for several seconds. "When did you and Wes Warren start comparing notes on people?"

"We don't!" The color in Dee's face intensified, clashing violently with her coppery-red hair. "Wes and I aren't— He doesn't even— I mean, we're not— God! I just *knew* . . . you know?"

"You just knew that Wes had taken one look at a total stranger and decided he didn't like him?"

"Yeah." The other woman made an awkward gesture. "Sort of. Oh, look, Leigh. I got this feeling from him, all right? From Wes. He didn't *say* anything. He hardly ever says anything to me. But . . . still. I could tell how he felt."

"I see." Leigh let a moment or two tick by. Out of the corner of her eye, she saw the end-of-show credits beginning to roll on her soap. "Where is he?"

"Wes?"

"John."

"Oh. I guess he's still out front."

"Do you have any idea what he wants?" Leigh reached over and switched off the TV. Her hand wasn't entirely steady. Neither was her pulse.

Dee grimaced. "He *said* he's here for story hour."

The wisdom of returning to Leigh's bookstore was something John Gulliver refused to debate with himself. He'd *had* to come. It was that simple.

Or that complicated, depending on one's point of view.

Still, he couldn't help wondering whether he mightn't have picked a more propitious moment to drop by. Preferably one when Deirdre Bleeker was off duty and the place wasn't crawling with kids.

Well, no. Not *crawling*. None of the dozen-or-so youngsters gathered in the cozy shop was crawling. Running, jumping, whirling around, kick boxing and playing patty-cake, yes. But crawling . . . no. Not that he could see.

John glanced toward the back of the store. The redheaded salesclerk had disappeared in that direction a few moments after he'd arrived, presumably to fetch her boss. He wondered what was taking so long.

What if Leigh didn't want to see him? he asked himself. While they'd parted on friendly terms at the end of Tuesday's visit, he'd sensed a great deal of tension lurking beneath the surface of his former lover's cordiality.

Maybe he'd been wrong to hold back the truth about who he was and what he'd been to Suzanne Whitney, he thought. Perhaps waiting was going to make an incredibly difficult situation even worse.

Then again . . . maybe he should abandon the idea of spilling the beans altogether. The past was the past. Suzanne had obviously moved beyond it. She had a new name. A new life. Perhaps he, too, should—

"John! John!"

John bobbled the hardcover book he had hadn't even realized he'd picked up, narrowly avoiding dropping it. He turned, his heart thudding.

"Hey, there, buddy," he greeted the bundled-up little boy who'd just skidded to a stop about a foot away from him. He hunkered down to kid's-eye level, controlling the urge to reach out and hug the youngster. He settled for a guy-to-guy wink. "How are you doing?"

"Pretty okay." Andy pulled off his mittens and stuffed them into the pockets of his bright blue snow jacket. His eyes were clear, his dimpled cheeks pink and glowing. The only visual reminder of his recent ordeal was a rectangular gauze bandage affixed to the side of his head. "'Cept my owwie keeps itchin' and itchin' and itchin'. Only I'm not s'posed to scratch it cuz the germ things might get in it and then I'd be in big trouble."

John nodded sympathetically, inwardly savoring a surge of paternal pride at this last sentence. Impartial judge or not, Leigh had been right. Their son *was* exceptional. How many other four-going-on-five-year-olds knew enough to articulate a concern about germs?

"You have to watch out for those germ things," he agreed.

"No kidding." After a few seconds of fumbling for the proper tab, Andy unzipped his bulky jacket and started to squirm out of it. "My friend Bryan—"

"The boy with the exploded appendix?"

Andy paused in mid-wriggle, the jacket half-on, half-off. He blinked several times. "You know Bryan?"

"Not personally. You told me about him when we were at the clinic."

"Oh. Yeah. Right."

The struggle to shed the snow jacket resumed. John considered offering some help but decided it would be better to keep hands off unless his assistance was specifically requested. The sigh of satisfaction Andy heaved once he'd fought his way free told him that this had been the correct course of action.

"Anyways," the little boy continued determinedly. "About why I know you have to be careful of germs. My friend Bryan fell down when he was trick-or-treatin' at Halloween and got a really wicked cut on his leg. It was all bloody and everything. But after a while—I don't know how long—a scab growed on it. Only Bryan didn't leave it alone. The scab, I mean. He picked at it. And itched it, too. And then his cut got in-fex-ted. It swelled up with that, uh, whaddya-call-it—uh— Oh, yeah. *Pus.* It swelled up with pus. And Bryan had to go to the doctor's and get a giant needle stuck in him to suck out all the yucky stuff. Because if he didn't, maybe his whole *leg* would've gotten in-fex-ted. And then he prob'ly would've had to get it chopped off. Cuz they do that, you know. Chop pieces off people when they get in-fex-ted. So just 'magine what would happen if I scratched at my owwie and my *head* got in-fex-ted!''

"Uh—"

The arrival of a stocky, middle-aged woman spared John the necessity of contemplating the grotesque scenario his "exceptional" son had just suggested.

"You shouldn't bother your mother's customers, Andy," she chided in a firm but gentle voice as John rose from his squatting position.

"He's not a *customer*, Nonna P.," Andy protested, turning to face the newcomer. "This is *John*. John Gul'ver. The man who saved me when I almost got that con-cushing. 'Member? Mommy told you 'bout him. And I showed you the cool tommy-hawk he gave me." He shifted his gaze back toward John, gesturing expansively. "John, this is Nonna P. She's takin' care of me today. She bringed 'freshments for story hour, too."

"Glad to meet you." John extended his right hand, studying the older woman with interest. He liked what he saw. Appearance-wise, Nonna P. was rather plain—her eyes were a bit too small, her nose was a bit too large and her shape bordered on the rotund. But she exuded an aura of rock-solid competence. The expression on her face when she looked at her young charge was deeply affectionate.

"Mr. Gulliver." Nonna P. clasped his hand and shook it, scrutinizing him as thoroughly as he was scrutinizing her. Although her gaze lingered on his scars, she did not seem put off by them. After a moment, she inclined her silver-haired head, apparently granting him her provisional stamp of approval. "It was a very good thing you did for Andy."

"I'm just glad I was there."

There was a pause. John looked toward the rear of the shop again, then glanced around. The story-hour crowd appeared to have doubled during the past few minutes. Deirdre Bleeker had returned and was trying—none too successfully—to get everyone to sit down and be quiet.

"John likes your cookies, Nonna P.," Andy piped up, compelling John's attention once again.

"He's had my pastries?" The older woman seemed surprised.

"Uh-huh." Andy nodded vigorously, not giving John a chance to respond. His eagerness to promote a friendship between his longtime sitter and his new, grown-up pal was endearing. "When he comed and visited me. It was on the same day you did, only after. Mommy said I should give him 'freshments from your goody basket cuz he was our guest, so I did." Wide blue-gray eyes peered up at John. "Today Nonna P. maked chocolate brownies. And cookies with raisins and sinnymin. I helped her put in the—" He broke off suddenly, his mouth curving into a smile.

John turned. His breath quickened as his gaze locked with Leigh's across the distance of several yards and the heads of about a half-dozen little children. A host of images—intimate, erotic, irresistible—flickered through his mind's eye. His pulse accelerated into overdrive.

"Come on, John," he heard Andy say. The words were partially muffled by the thunder of his blood. A moment later, he felt his son's small left hand slip trustingly into his disfigured right one. "You can sit by me."

How she accomplished it, he never knew. Perhaps she drew on some special sort of maternal magic. But with a quick clap of her palms and a cheerful cry—"Story Hour!"—Leigh McKay brought order out of chaos.

How she held a group of more than two dozen itchy-twitchy youngsters mesmerized for sixty minutes was easier to puzzle out. Her mellifluous voice was pure enchantment, full of lively humor one moment, dropping into a thrilling whisper the next. She didn't simply read from a printed page. She brought it to life.

John ached as he watched and listened. She was so beautiful, he thought. So vibrant. And he wanted her so badly he hurt with it.

Five and a half years, a voice inside him kept saying. *You've lost five and a half years you should have had with this woman. Don't lose any more!*

Several times during the session, Leigh's eyes strayed in his direction. Once her gaze flicked back and forth between him and Andy, who was sitting to his right. She seemed to falter for an instant, but regained control so quickly he couldn't be certain whether the break had really occurred. A quick glance around did nothing to clarify the matter. If others had noticed the fractional pause, they gave no sign of it.

Story hour concluded with laughter, applause and the presentation of Nonna P.'s brownies and cinnamon-raisin cookies. The throng thinned out slowly. John noticed that nearly all of the adults who had attended purchased a book or two before leaving the shop.

He took his time in approaching Leigh. He picked a moment when she was kneeling down, apparently engrossed in a conversation with a pixie-pretty little brunette who was clutching a gingham-clad rag doll. The tiny girl scampered away to the refreshment setup as he drew near. Leigh started to get to her feet.

She overbalanced as she rose. He reached out reflexively, catching her arm and steadying her. He felt a tremor of reaction run through her at the contact. The muscles of his belly tightened.

"John!" she exclaimed, pivoting to face him. A tinge of color entered her cheeks. She edged back a half step as she'd done in her foyer two days ago, but remained within touching distance. "Hello."

"Hello, Leigh." The fresh scent of her skin, more provocative than any perfume, tantalized his nostrils.

"I... I didn't expect to see you here today."

"What can I say?" he responded with what he hoped looked like a casual shrug. "I'm a sucker for a good story."

An emotion he couldn't put a name to shimmered through the depths of his former lover's sky-colored eyes. "I see."

"You don't mind, do you?"

"Your coming to story hour, you mean?"

"Mmm."

"Of course not." She shook her head, her pale hair feathering around her fine-boned face. The tips of his fingers tingled with a desire to feel the silken strands. "Andy was obviously thrilled you dropped by."

John glanced toward the refreshment table. Andy was standing next to it, a brownie in one hand and a "sinny-min" cookie in the other. He was chatting animatedly with another young boy. "He looks even better than he did Tuesday."

"Oh, he is." Leigh's voice was rich with relief. She smiled at John as he returned his gaze to her. "I was ready to let him stay home another day, but he insisted on going back to preschool this morning."

"Got tired of lolling around on the sofa, hmm?"

"That probably had something to do with it. Plus the fact that Thursday is show-and-tell day."

"Andy brought in the tomahawk?"

"Of course, he brought in the tomahawk. I don't think he's let it out of his sight since you gave it to him."

John was assailed by a complex combination of emotions. "Look, uh, Leigh," he began. "I know that probably wasn't the kind of get-well present you would have wanted—"

"No, it wasn't. But then, I'm not the one you picked it out for, was I?"

"Well . . . no." Leigh's candor startled him. For all Suzanne Whitney's transparent-as-glass honesty, she'd had a tendency to sugarcoat unpalatable truths. "Still, I hope you didn't find it—uh—"

"Tacky?"

John had to laugh. He also had to concede that the tomahawk was something of an eyesore. "I was thinking more along the lines of politically incorrect, actually."

Leigh fluffed her hair, her gaze shifting toward Andy, then back to John's face. While the look she gave him wasn't flirtatious, it held a provocative hint of complicity. Whether or not this was intentional was impossible to say. John sensed a curious disconnection between her instinctive actions and her conscious behavior.

This disconnection was different from the shyness that had inhibited so many of Suzanne Whitney's responses when she'd been with Nicholas Marchand. He wondered what could have caused it. The burden of single motherhood, perhaps? For all that she obviously adored her son, was Leigh ashamed of having borne a child out of wedlock?

"I'm afraid I have trouble keeping up in that area," she confessed with a wry laugh. "Every time I think I have the rules figured out, somebody changes them."

"I know the feeling."

There was a pause. Then, "Leigh—"

"John—"

They spoke simultaneously. They stopped the same way.

"Ladies before gentlemen," John quickly said. He caught a glimpse of Deirdre Bleeker. She was watching them. She didn't seem happy. He'd noticed her looking at him twice during story hour. The first time, she'd averted her gaze the moment he'd glanced her way. The second time, her pale face had hardened and she'd done her damnedest to stare him down. Although she'd lost the battle of wills, her attitude had exacerbated his determination to find out exactly what she was up to.

Leigh hesitated, nibbling on her lower lip. It was a mannerism he remembered from the past. "I've been thinking about the way I acted Tuesday when you came to visit," she admitted after a few moments, seeming to measure out each syllable before speaking it. "I hope I didn't— I mean, if I seemed, uh, *defensive*—"

"You were totally within your rights to be upset, Leigh," he interrupted, meaning it. "You and Andy, living alone—it's not just a matter of protecting your privacy. Unpleasant as it is to contemplate, we live in an uncertain world populated with some very scary people. Anyone with a grain of common sense is concerned about their personal security. I was wrong to ask Thalia Jenkins for your address. And she was wrong to give it to me, even though I'm sure she intended no harm. I meant it when I apologized to you Tuesday. I shouldn't have just shown up on your doorstep."

Again Leigh hesitated, her eyes searching his. John held his breath, hoping that whatever she saw there would reassure her. He wanted—*needed*—her to trust him. To feel safe with him.

"I just didn't want you to get the impression that I'm paranoid or anything like that," she finally said.

"I didn't."

"Good." She nodded, her posture relaxing. "I'm glad. Now... what were you going to say?"

"Not say. Ask." He paused, warning himself to keep his tone casual. "Will you have dinner with me?"

"Dinner?"

"Yes. You and Andy. Say, Saturday night?"

"Well—"

"I owe you two a meal."

"*You* owe *us?* After what you did—"

"You gave me lunch on Tuesday, remember?"

"Frozen pizza!"

"With pepperoni," John emphasized, smiling. "A veritable gourmet feast."

For a moment, Leigh seemed thoroughly nonplused. Then her eyes sparked sapphire. "You sound like Andy," she said with a musical laugh. "Although I'm not sure how he'd pronounce 'veritable.'"

Something inside him went very still at the first part of her comment. His son. She thought he sounded like his son!

Tell her, his heart urged. *Tell her... now.*

You have to wait, his head countered. *She needs to get to know John Gulliver. And John Gulliver needs to get to know Leigh McKay.*

"Dinner on Saturday?" he prompted. "You, me... and Andy?"

Her expression grew serious. She lifted her chin slightly, her cheeks pinkening. Then, softly, she gave him the answer he'd hoped to hear.

Chapter 5

She'd been right to say yes, Leigh told herself a little more than forty-eight hours later. She took a final bite of the braised duckling she'd ordered as her entrée, savoring the subtle richness of its fruited sauce. It was good for her to start getting out. And good for her son, too. He needed to see her having a normal social life.

"You can do your work anyplace you want, right?" Andy was asking, studying the man sitting to his right with great interest. "Like, you could be sittin' on the beach. Or stayin' at home in your jammies."

The notion of John Gulliver wearing "jammies" triggered a heated quivering in the pit of Leigh's stomach. She would be willing to bet that pajamas were not a part of his wardrobe. He'd probably been sleeping in briefs or less, since adolescence.

She could envision him wrapped in a dressing gown, though. Dark, heavyweight silk, a potent complement to his harsh masculine appeal. He would probably wear the garment casually, its belt knotted loosely around his narrow waist. And when he moved his arms, the upper half of the robe would gape apart, revealing a triangle of hair-whorled, sleekly muscled—

She wondered whether she'd made a sound. A sigh, perhaps. Or a moan. Because something caused John to glance at her. She saw his eyes narrow. His nostrils flared on a sharply expelled breath.

Setting down her fork, Leigh reached for the glass of mineral water sitting to her right and took a quick sip. She was trembling. That she would succumb to sexual fantasizing was disturbing enough. That the object of the fantasy would *realize* . . .

"Pretty much," John replied with enviable aplomb, shifting his gaze back to his preschool interrogator. "As long as I have access to a phone and a place to plug in my computer, I can work."

"And your job is makin' people go places, huh." Andy plucked a shoestring potato from his almost-emptied plate and munched it down. He'd never eaten in what he called a "grown-up" restaurant before and Leigh knew that he'd been a little wary about the food served by this establishment. Discovering that one of the specials of the day was venison—"It's from a deer?" he'd demanded of their waiter, his eyes round with horror. "You mean, like . . . Bambi?"— had done nothing to allay his anxieties. He'd been relieved when John had pointed out that the regular menu included "normal stuff" like chopped beefsteak—sans the proffered wild mushroom sauce, of course—and french fries.

"Not exactly."

"But you said your company in 'Lanta is a travel company. Doesn't that mean tellin' people how they should take trips and stuff?"

"Ah—"

"John owns a travel agency, honey," Leigh interpolated, surprised by the steadiness of her voice. "A travel agency doesn't *tell* people what to do. Customers come to one, explain where they want to go and how much they want to spend, and the agents who work there help them make their plans."

Andy considered this information for a few moments before transferring his attention back to John. "So, like, if I came to Gul'ver's Travels and said I wanted to have a really cool vacation in Disneyland for almost free, you could fix it up for me, right?"

"I'd certainly try," John answered. "But to tell you the truth, Andy, I don't do the kinds of things your mother was just talking about. Even though Gulliver's Travels belongs to me, I'm not a travel agent."

"Then what are you?"

"It's a little hard to explain. I own a lot of businesses, but I don't run them day-to-day. I hire other people to do that. A woman named Lucy Falco manages Gulliver's Travels for me. I'm basically an investor."

Leigh fingered the stem of her water goblet, conscious of the sudden jab of a singularly nasty emotion. Marcy-Anne Gregg had mentioned Lucy Falco several times. She'd described her as a "darlin'" girl. Ditto, an unmarried one. What if John Gulliver and his "darlingly" eligible employee—

"But what does a 'vestor *do?*" Andy pressed, disrupting her troubled speculations.

John smiled wryly. "Smart question, buddy. If I had to boil it down . . . well, I guess I'd say that what I do is go around looking for good businesses that need a little extra boost. And when I find one, I put my money in it. If things work out right, the good business gets better and I make a profit."

"Oh." Andy picked up the glass of milk he'd ordered to go with his meat-and-potato meal and drank deeply. He emerged with a damp, dairy mustache on his upper lip. Plunking down the glass he announced, "I put *my* money in a jar at home. I have maybe a million pennies. And some nickels and dimes and quarters. Dollars, too. Mommy puts her money in a bank. Only sometimes it's not very much."

"Andy!" Leigh gasped, genuinely shocked. She'd had no idea that her son was aware how tight their finances were. And even if she had, she never would have dreamed that he would discuss the situation in public!

Andy looked at her with innocent eyes. "What?"

John was watching her closely. She could feel it. She could also feel herself starting to blush. Maybe this night out hadn't been such a good idea, after all.

"We don't talk about our money in front of other people," she said after a moment, striving for an even, reasonable tone. What she achieved bordered on prissiness.

"John talked about his in front of us."

"That's—" oh, Lord, was she really going to take refuge behind what had to be one of the lamest responses in her parental repertoire? "—different."

"Why?"

"Uh—uh—" Great. Just great! Flummoxed by a three-letter question from a not-yet-five-year-old!

"Because it is, Andy."

Andy turned toward John, clearly taken aback. Leigh was a bit startled, too. And oddly bemused. The "Because" ploy was even lamer than her "That's different" gambit!

"Grown-ups *always* say that," Andy groused, making a face. His hitherto-perfect hero apparently had fallen a few points in his esteem. He shifted back toward Leigh again. She saw a hint of mulishness enter his expression and she braced herself.

"I don't see what's wrong with talkin' about money, Mommy," he declared. "Maybe John could 'vest some of his in your bookstore. It's a really good business. Everybody says. And if he gave us that little extra-boost thing, I bet we could get rich enough to buy a baby for Christmas. Or maybe just some of those seeds the daddy's s'posed to—"

"Andrew McKay, that's quite enough!" Leigh knew she should have cut him off several sentences earlier. Unfortunately, she'd been too stunned by what she'd been hearing to speak.

"I don't—"

"I said, that's *enough.* Take your napkin and wipe your mouth. It's got milk all over it."

"But, *Mommy*—"

She fixed her son with her most uncompromising I-mean-it-young-man glare. Eventually, he did as he'd been bidden. His obedience was grumblingly reluctant, to be sure, but at least he acquiesced to her authority.

She then forced herself to look at John. His expression was difficult to read. But there was a hint of something in his dark, deep-set eyes. Could it be...regret? she wondered. Yes. Perhaps. Although what he would have to regret in this situation she could not begin to imagine.

There was tenderness in his eyes, too. At least, she thought it was tenderness. Whatever it was, it triggered a soft, stirring warmth deep within her.

"I—" she slipped her hands beneath the table to wipe her suddenly damp palms on her napkin "—I'm sorry."

"For what, Leigh?"

It *was* tenderness she was seeing, she thought, licking her lips. And desire. And much, much more. *Where were these emotions coming from?*

"My son can be a little too... candid... at times," she replied after a moment, her voice throaty.

"You *told* me to always tell the truth," Andy muttered in a mutinous undertone.

An odd look passed over John's angular face. His eyes turned opaque. Leigh watched as he glanced at the pouty-mouthed little boy seated to his left.

"And you always should, Andy," he said quietly. "But you have to be careful how you tell it... and to whom."

You telged *me to always tell the truth.*
But you have to be careful how you tell it... and to whom.
Those two sentiments stayed with Leigh throughout the rest of their meal and during the half-hour ride back from the restaurant. She was still turning them over in her mind when John came downstairs after a good-night chat with Andy.

You telged *me to always tell the truth.*
How could she advocate honesty when so much about her life was a sham? she asked herself poignantly, leaning her forehead against the chilly glass of the living room's main window. She couldn't remember the last time she'd offered someone the truth, the whole truth, and nothing but the truth!

But you have to be careful how you tell it... and to whom.
Careful? Lord. Scared speechless part of the time—and preoccupied with keeping track of her lies the rest of it—was closer to the mark.

Worrying her lower lip with the edge of her front teeth, Leigh stared out into the wintry darkness. It had started to snow several hours earlier. Gentle flurries at first. Now, great fat flakes. She knew the roads were treacherous. John's concentration during the drive home had been a palpable thing. Even Andy had seemed to sense—

She didn't hear John come back into the living room. She *felt* him. Awareness of his presence rippled through her like a

heated tide, making her body tingle. Even before he spoke, she
was turning away from the window to face him.

"I think Andy's down for the count," he commented,
crossing to her. He moved like a jungle cat. No discernible
footsteps. Scarcely a squeak out of the room's normally noisy
hardwood floor.

"Good," she responded, brushing at the fabric of her skirt
with a slightly shaky hand. She caught a brief whiff of his after-shave. The subtly spicy fragrance was unfamiliar to her. But
beneath it was a scent that teased at her olfactory nerves and
sent a shiver skittering along the surface of her suddenly sensitized skin.

There was an element of anticipation in the shiver. Of expectation. As though she knew what the scent portended.

There was flash of anxiety, too, for precisely the same reason.

"You didn't mind, did you?" John asked quietly. Although
he was within touching distance, he wasn't crowding her. The
distance between them was nicely judged. Too well-calibrated
to be accidental.

"Mind what?"

"Andy insisting I stay upstairs and talk after you tucked him
in."

Leigh stiffened. Of course, she'd minded! Although her son
and she had shared their usual night-night kiss and cuddle,
Andy had punctuated this loving ritual by dismissing her from
his room so he could have a private conversation with his new
best buddy. The jealousy she'd experienced during John's initial visit to their home had returned full force. So, too, her in-
security about her ability to provide the kind of guidance a boy
needed on his journey into manhood.

"It was good of you to spend the time with him," she said
after a moment or two, picking her words with great care.

John cocked an eyebrow, the scarring on his temple furrow-
ing. "You weren't so diplomatic the day before yesterday when
you were talking about my tacky tomahawk."

Leigh lifted her chin, responding to the challenge in his observation. The angle felt . . . familiar. A split second later she
realized why. She'd tilted her head to precisely the same degree

to look up into Nicholas Marchand's eyes many, many times in the past.

Her breath caught.

Her pulse scrambled, then accelerated into a nervy, hip-hop rhythm.

Stop it, she ordered herself, a prickle of panic running up her spine in response to the unbidden encroachment of memory. *Just stop it!* So what if John Gulliver is the same height as Nick was? Millions of men are—

"Leigh?"

She started, blinking rapidly. Her heart was thumping. "Wh-what?"

"Are you all right?" John had closed most of the distance between them. He'd also taken hold of her, his palms curving to fit the shape of her shoulders. She could feel the virile heat of his body, sense his aggressively masculine power.

And yet . . . she wasn't afraid of him. Urgently aware of his proximity, yes. Acutely conscious of his physical superiority, too. But afraid, no. Not at all. Because something—his quiet, controlled tone? the disciplined gentleness of his touch?—persuaded her that John Gulliver would never hurt her.

This was not to say that she thought him harmless. Quite the contrary. The woman who'd once been Suzanne Whitney didn't doubt for a second that the man standing before her was capable of doing harm to another human being. Yet every instinct she had also assured her that he represented no threat to her.

Unless . . .

Unless she lowered her guard and allowed him to become one. And in that case, the fault would be hers—not his.

"Yes, John," Leigh managed, astonished by the steadiness of her voice. "I'm just . . . fine."

His gold-flecked brown eyes shifted back and forth several times as though he were trying to gauge the real meaning of her words. She sustained his searching gaze, even as she felt herself start to flush.

Finally, John's grip moderated. He slid his hands off her shoulders and halfway down her arms, then let go of her. "You looked a little rocky," he commented, stepping back a pace as though to underscore her release.

"Sorry."

"No need to apologize. You're *sure* you're all right?"

"Positive." Several seconds ticked by. Leigh finally broke eye contact and gestured in the direction of the sofa. She knew the color in her cheeks was still higher than normal. "Would you like to sit down?"

John hesitated for a moment, seeming to want to press for further reassurance. Then something changed his mind. He nodded, saying, "Okay. Thanks."

They moved to the sofa and seated themselves. There was an awkward pause. Just as the awkwardness was about to consolidate into something worse, Leigh asked, "So, what did you and Andy talk about?"

John shrugged. "This and that."

"Investment opportunities?"

"Not...exactly."

She grimaced inwardly, recognizing evasiveness when she heard it. She told herself that she and her son were going to have to have a serious discussion about the need for discretion in the very near future. She pretty much acquitted John of snooping. Why should the man pry? Andy had already demonstrated that he was ready to reveal all without any kind of prompting.

"Home arsenals?"

"Nope." This response was quicker and much more definite than the previous one.

Leigh crossed her right leg over her left, smoothing down the hem of her skirt as she did so. The fabric of her slip moved sleekly across her stocking-clad thighs, triggering a fluttering in her stomach. She caught another hint of the primal male scent beneath John's after-shave. The fluttering became more insistent.

"Baby...seeds?" she suggested.

John studied her for a few moments, as though trying to determine whether she was being deliberately provocative. She wished him luck in figuring it out. She wasn't certain herself. She only knew she couldn't let the issue alone.

"The subject did come up," he eventually allowed. His lips twisted as his eyes sparked with a sudden flash of humor. "Nothing I didn't know already, though."

Leigh caught her breath, knocked off-balance by the casual quip. A strange quiver ran through her. She could imagine Nicholas Marchand countering a question with exactly the same kind of—

No! she cried inwardly, cutting off the thought before she could complete it. *Don't imagine anything about Nick! He's dead!*

"Leigh?"

She steadied herself by sheer force of will.

"Sorry," she murmured, then wished she hadn't. A tremulous half-laugh worked its way up from her chest. This was— what? she wondered. The fourth time she'd been with John Gulliver? Yes. The fourth. And how many times during those four encounters had she felt compelled to apologize for her behavior? She couldn't exactly recall, but she knew the routine was beginning to wear a bit thin. "Have you noticed? I tend to say 'sorry' to you a lot."

"Some sort of vibe I'm giving off?"

"No!" She shook her head emphatically, but couldn't quite meet his eyes. "Of course not."

"But I do make you uncomfortable."

It was more assertion than inquiry and for a good ten seconds, Leigh had no idea how to respond to it. "That's *me,* John," she finally replied, fighting to keep her voice steady. "Not . . . you."

"Maybe it's both of us."

Her heart missed a beat. Shifting her position, she lifted a hand and began toying with her hair. Then she realized what she was doing and lowered the hand back to her side. She shifted again.

"We've known each other less than a week," she said at last.

"It feels longer."

"Yes, well, I can't rely on how a situation *feels,* John. I have to depend on how it really is."

There was a silence. Then, "Do you want me to go . . . Leigh?"

She shifted a third time, wondering tangentially about the peculiar way he'd just inflected her name. She'd heard him do it several times before. In a bizarre way, it reminded her of the terrible sense of disorientation she'd suffered during the first

months after she'd assumed her new identity. She'd been a beat
behind—a few degrees off—during that entire period. She'd
had to remind herself over and over that Suzanne Whitney was
no more. She was Leigh McKay. And she would be Leigh
McKay until the end of her days.

"Do you want to leave?"

"No."

His bluntness shook her. She'd assumed that John would try
to finesse her question as she'd finessed his. Equivocation she
could deal with. But this—

"Your turn," he prompted, holding her gaze with his.

"What?"

"Do you want me to go?"

She swallowed hard, a part of her wishing she could match
his frankness. "No," she admitted with a small shake of her
head. "I don't want you to go. Not . . . yet."

There was another break in their conversation. For reasons
she couldn't articulate, Leigh found this one was easier to endure than the ones that had come before. Unfortunately, John
chose to end it by broaching a very volatile topic.

"It must be tough for you," he observed reflectively.

"What?"

"Being a single mother."

Whether it was intended to do so or not, the remark hurt.
"I'm doing the best I can," Leigh retorted.

"I wasn't suggesting you weren't." John held up his hands
in a conciliatory gesture. "You've done an amazing job with
Andy. He's a terrific little boy."

"But he *is* a little boy." The words slipped out of their own
accord.

"Well . . . yes. Obviously."

"And little boys need more than their mommies if they're
going to grow up right."

John's gaze sharpened. He leaned toward her. "You're worried about there not being a . . . male influence . . . in Andy's
life?"

Leigh looked away, the bridge of her nose aching with the
sudden pressure of unshed tears. The stress of the last five days
had left her very thin-skinned. "I'm his mother. It's my job to
worry about everything."

"What about his father?"

Blue eyes collided with brown ones. Leigh's breath clogged alfway up her throat, compressing the hurt inherent in her ext words. "What about him?"

"I don't know. You tell me."

"He's not a part of our lives." It was the truth, but hardly e whole truth. She *didn't know* the whole truth. She'd spent ve and a half years clinging to the conviction that she didn't ally want to.

"You're divorced?"

"No." She bit the inside of her cheek. "We were never mared."

"He just . . . left you?"

"I don't want to talk about this anymore," Leigh abruptly eclared, getting up from the sofa. That she'd talked about it t all dismayed her. She'd declared the subject of Andy's parnity off-limits the day she'd learned she was pregnant, and e'd made the prohibition stick. Why had she abandoned her lence now? Why had *John Gulliver* been able to draw her out hen so many others—

"I'm sorry," he apologized, also rising to his feet. Reaching ut, he caught her left upper arm. "Leigh. Please. I'm sorry."

She pivoted toward him, pulling free of his grasp. He made o effort to hold on to her.

"I think you should leave, John," she said. "Now."

His instinct was to balk. She could see it in the hardening of is angular features and the tensing of his leanly powerful body. trangely enough, she felt no fear. The impression she'd formed arlier—that this man would do her no physical harm—reained intact.

"Are you sure?" John asked after a painful pause.

No, she wasn't.

"Yes," she lied.

He inclined his head. "All right, then. I'll go."

They walked to the front door in silence. John retrieved his an trench coat, donned it, then turned to face her. "I am sorry, eigh. Truly."

She lifted her chin, shutting her mind to the sense of déjà vu stirred. "So am I, John."

"Will you forgive me?"

"After everything you've done for Andy—"

"Is that what it comes down to?" he interrupted. "I get a pass because I helped your son?"

She inhaled sharply at the rasp of temper in his voice. The spicy scent of his after-shave—and the natural male musk it overlay—filled her nose. A melting warmth stole through her, muting her momentary flash of alarm. Her lashes fluttered down. She felt herself sway.

"Is it, Leigh?" The angry, injured edge was gone, superseded by an insinuating huskiness. As John spoke, his left hand came up to trace the curve of her right cheek. Gently. Oh, so gently.

"No," she admitted in a breathless whisper, wondering if he could tell how fast her pulse was pounding. She lifted her eyelids and gazed up at him. "This... I... It's not just because of Andy."

His fingers splayed. He eased his hand back, his hard palm cupping the side of her face with infinite care. "'This' being—?"

She lifted her own left hand and placed it against John's chest. She felt his muscles contract beneath the fine knit fabric of the dark turtleneck sweater he was wearing. The hammer stroke of his heartbeat was clearly discernible. She registered this evidence of the effect her touch had on him with an unsettling mixture of excitement and uncertainty.

"You *know* what this is," she said throatily, answering his question the only way she could.

"Yes," he concurred, buffing the pad of his thumb against the nerve-rich hollow just beneath her right ear. "I know."

And then he bent his head and touched his lips to hers.

The contact was featherlight at first. Cautious. Almost chaste. His mouth was teasing, hers tightly shut. She felt...next to nothing.

Or so Leigh told herself.

The coaxing glide of his tongue changed that. John traced the seam between her lips with a tantalizing stroke, murmuring her name in a velvety undertone. The caress of his hand against the side of her throat became more explicit in its eroticism. She shivered as a quicksilver thrill coursed through her veins.

Yes, she thought.

She opened to him on a melting sigh, tilting her head to the right as he tilted his to the left. There was no first-time awkwardness. No hesitation. Had every incremental alteration of position been choreographed, it could not have gone more smoothly. The uncertainty she'd experienced a few minutes before disintegrated in the face of an inexplicable sense of familiarity.

John insinuated his tongue slowly into her mouth, savoring her yielding sweetness with languorous strokes. After a few ready moments, she reciprocated.

He tasted of the espresso he'd drunk at the end of their meal. He tasted of the voluptuously rich chocolate mousse he'd consumed for dessert, too. And there was something else. An underlying flavor that had nothing to do with food and everything to do with hunger. Leigh knew the flavor as though it had been imprinted on her DNA.

Yes, she thought again, a spark streaking downward to ignite a wildfire flame deep inside her. She closed her eyes. *Oh...yes. Please.*

The intensity of the kiss escalated as though by mutual agreement. Leigh moved her hand up his chest to clasp his shoulder. John's right arm slid around her waist, his hand settling possessively at the base of her spine.

She did not dispute the claim implicit in his embrace. It felt too good. Too right. Rather, she exerted one of her own, stroking her hand from his shoulder to the nape of his neck.

Her partner urged her closer, his fingers insistent against the small of her back. She let herself be gathered in. It seemed preordained that she should do so. She moved her hips restlessly, conscious of the adamant press of John's masculine arousal against her lower body. He groaned something deep in his throat. She moved her hips again, her soft, secret places throbbing with need.

She'd been here before, she realized, ravished by sense memories she'd thought had been obliterated. She'd surrendered herself to this same delirious, don't-care-about-the-consequences swirl of desire in the past.

But how could that be?

How could she be feeling now what she'd felt back then?

She opened her eyes, staring wonderingly up into the compellingly male face she was just beginning to know. She saw a complex array of emotions, including signs of an inner tumult that was as great as her own.

A single-syllable name fought its way to the tip of her tongue, battling rationality every millimeter of the way. The name wasn't John.

She scraped together a breath, intending to speak. Exactly what she would have said, she never knew. She was forestalled by a summons from the top of the stairs.

"Mommy?" her son called down in a decidedly unhappy voice. "You have to come up right now. I didn't mean to, but I wetted in my bed."

John Gulliver left Leigh McKay's home with the taste of his former lover's kisses lingering on his lips and the memory of her uncharacteristically mercurial behavior weighing on his mind.

He returned to her front door twenty minutes later cursing a blue streak and chilled to the bone, but still torqued up by what had happened prior to his departure.

In the interim, he'd discovered that his rental car had given up the ghost and that nothing—but *nothing*—he tried could bring it back to life. In point of fact, he hadn't even been able to determine what was wrong with the damned thing.

"J-John," Leigh stammered when she opened the door to him. She was holding the neck of a bulging, brightly patterned pillowcase with her left hand. John assumed it contained the "wetted" sheets from Andy's bed. Poor little kid. He'd been so humiliated by his accident. His embarrassment had added impetus to John's exit. Someday he would have to assure his son there was no need to feel ashamed about what had happened. "What—?"

"I'm sorry," he apologized, keeping his voice down. "My car won't start."

Leigh's sky-colored eyes flicked away from his, darting in the direction of her driveway.

"I know, I know," he said quickly, flexing and unflexing his cold-numbed fingers inside the pockets of his raincoat. "It sounds like a con. But it isn't. I swear."

There was a sudden gust of wind. He hunched his shoulders against the arctic blast. Leigh stepped back, her clothing spackled with glistening flakes of snow. Shivering visibly, she gestured him inside with her free hand. He accepted the invitation with alacrity.

"Thanks." He shut the door.

"You're w-w-welcome." The response was delivered through chattering teeth. Dropping the pillowcase, Leigh wrapped her arms around herself. "So, what's wrong?"

John grimaced, resisting the urge to stomp his feet against the hardwood floor. He could hardly feel his toes. "Beats me."

"Mmm." Again, her gaze darted away from his.

"Leigh—"

She silenced him with a look. A rather amused look, in point of fact.

"I believe you, John," she said, an unexpected hint of humor playing around the corners of her soft lips. "If this *were* a con, I'm sure you would have come up with something more persuasive than the old my-car-won't-start ploy."

John stared, taken aback by this comment in much the same way he'd been taken aback by her post-story-hour remarks about the tomahawk he'd given Andy. Suzanne Whitney would never have said something so... so deliberately flippant. In all the time she'd been with Saint Nick Marchand, he'd never heard her use her wit to score a point over another person.

"Thanks," he responded dryly after a second or two. "I think."

Leigh inclined her head, her fair hair gleaming in the illumination from the foyer's overhead lighting fixture. John swallowed hard, his body starting to warm. He waited for his former lover to say something. She didn't.

"Do you have a set of jumper cables?" he finally asked.

"Jumper cables?" Leigh furrowed her brow. "Uh...no. I don't. Sorry."

"Well, then, can I use your phone?"

"To call—?"

"A tow truck."

"Oh, dear. There's only one garage in the area. It closes at six."

Somehow, that didn't surprise him. "Taxi service?"

"Not really. And in this kind of weather..."

"Great." John raked a hand through his snow-sodden hair, considering his options. He couldn't very well ask to borrow Leigh's car. That would leave her and Andy stranded. And he didn't want to suggest that she drive him back to the inn. Wait! The inn! What if he phoned and asked the proprietor—

"You could stay here."

He stiffened, genuinely surprised. It wasn't that Leigh's proposal was so untoward. He'd thought of it himself. But he'd refused to broach it for a variety of reasons. And he'd certainly never expected—

"Would you be all right with that?" he questioned bluntly.

Although he believed he'd made some real progress in gaining Leigh's trust this evening, he recognized that it had been a two-steps-forward-one-step-back kind of thing. What would have happened had Andy not put a, uh, *damper* on the flame rekindled by their kiss was a major question mark.

"If you'd be all right with sleeping downstairs on the sofa."

"Are you sure?" Instinct told him it probably seemed suspicious to push, but he couldn't help himself. He'd seen how skittish Leigh was. He couldn't help but wonder how she would handle having him stay in her home overnight. He had a fleeting vision of her sitting on the edge of her bed, her face pale and strained, her fingers clutching a loaded gun....

"Positive." Leigh smiled mischievously, suddenly looking a great deal like her young son. John's heart contracted. "You can thank me in the morning by digging out the driveway."

He let a moment or two slip by, watching her very carefully. Then he matched her smile with one of his own and said, "Deal."

She settled him quickly. So quickly that John found himself wondering about it. Maybe Leigh McKay wasn't as unaccustomed to sleep-over guests as he'd assumed.

The possibility disturbed him. A lot. It also brought back the memory of the masculine territoriality he'd detected in Wesley Warren's eyes when they'd encountered each other in the bookstore. God, he thought, his gut knotting. Maybe it wasn't Wes's *professional* affairs he should be checking into!

He had no right to be jealous, he reminded himself. He had let Suzanne Whitney go. He'd acquiesced in the conspiracy that had allowed her to believe that he—or rather, Saint Nick Marchand—was dead.

So, if she'd moved on . . .

If she'd taken another lover or lovers . . .

No. Not *her*. Leigh McKay. Because Leigh McKay was the person Suzanne Whitney had become.

Although exactly who Leigh McKay was—

"Anything else you need, John?"

Time, his head said firmly.

You, his heart insisted. *Right now.*

"No," he answered, gazing at the delicately featured face of the woman he loved but was still getting to know. "Thanks."

"You're welcome. I'll see you in the morning." She turned toward the stairs.

"Leigh?"

She pivoted back, her movement graceful, her expression slightly wary. "Yes?"

"About the, uh, baby . . . seeds."

She blushed, her hand lifting to the base of her throat. "John—"

"What I said about nothing I didn't know already," he went on in a rush. "I wasn't talking about the facts of life."

"Well—" she swallowed quickly "—I should *hope* not!"

"Andy told me about wanting a baby brother while we were waiting for you at the clinic on Monday. He also told me he didn't think it was going to work out because he didn't have a, uh, daddy around."

"Oh, God." The rosy color in Leigh's cheeks intensified. "Is there *anything* you two didn't talk about?"

"You."

She went still as a statue. "M-me?"

"And how lucky any little boy would be to have you as his mother."

Chapter 6

The image of John Gulliver bedding down on her living-room sofa caused Leigh's pulse to throb at a faster-than-normal rate as she carried out her nightly check of her home's second floor. Still, she stuck to her self-appointed rounds, disciplining herself against the distraction of her physical responses, trying not to think about the man who had caused them.

She tested each window to make certain that it was locked and secure. She opened every closet to reassure herself that there were no bogeymen lurking within. She even pulled back the shower curtain in the bathroom . . . just in case.

All was as it should be.

Or so it seemed.

She lingered a few minutes when she reached her son's toy-strewn, nightlight-illuminated room. Andy was sprawled crosswise on his twin-size mattress, the Batman pajama top he'd donned after his accident rucked up around his armpits, the freshly changed bedclothes wound tightly around his legs. He was clutching his precious plastic tomahawk in his left hand, the brightly colored feathers tickling beneath his nose. The garish fluff stirred slightly each time he exhaled. He appeared to be fast asleep.

She knew he'd been terribly embarrassed by his loss of bladder control. Bad enough that he'd regressed after many, many months of accident-free nights. But that his hero had been present to witness his disgrace as well! Andy had been horribly humiliated. There'd been a few dicey moments when Leigh had feared that his painfully obvious sense of shame would lead to a tearful scene.

John had handled the situation with remarkable sensitivity, all things considered. While he'd stuck around long enough to make it clear to his young buddy that he didn't think any less of him because of the bed-wetting, he'd seemed to understand that the little boy required privacy to recover from his upset. He'd tactfully taken his leave about twenty minutes after Andy's initial announcement.

To say that Leigh had had mixed feelings about his departure was to understate the case. Still, given the incendiary implications of what had happened in the minutes before her son had called down from upstairs, she'd told herself that his exit was for the best. The kiss she and John Gulliver had shared had rocked her in more ways than she could count. She'd needed time to sort through her reactions, to decide what she was going to do about them.

Sighing, Leigh gently extricated the tomahawk from Andy's stubby-fingered grasp and set it aside. He made a whiny sound of distress as she did so, his brow corrugating like cardboard and his mouth twisting. For a second, he seemed on the verge of waking up.

"Shh," she soothed, stroking his furrowed forehead with the tips of her fingers. "I'm putting your tomahawk right here by your bed, Andy. You can play with it first thing in the morning."

Her words must have penetrated at some level of consciousness because Andy calmed as soon as she spoke them. His inarticulate protestation softened into a breathy murmur of contentment. His features relaxed, his lips easing into a mysterious little smile.

Leigh studied him for several seconds, debating whether to disturb him further. He couldn't be comfortable with the bedclothes twisted around him the way they were, she finally told herself. And he would probably catch cold if he wasn't properly covered up.

Straightening his sleepwear was a relatively easy task.

Rearranging the bed linen was a tad more complicated. She'd just gotten Andy free of the sheets when he'd decided to flop over onto his stomach. In addition to retangling his legs, he almost tumbled off the side of the bed. She caught him just in time, narrowly avoiding getting smacked in the face by his flailing right hand as she did so.

"Numm . . . *kummeez,*" he said loudly, then giggled.

"Numm-kummeez yourself, slugger," she retorted with a wry half-laugh, easing him into a less precarious position and drawing the covers up and over him. Rolling onto his left side, Andy brought his knees up toward his chest and curled into a ball. He smacked his lips together two or three times, then settled back into a deep slumber.

Leigh watched over him for another minute or so, her heart very full. When all was said and done, she had to rate herself an extraordinarily fortunate woman. While the circumstances of Andy's birth were an ugly far cry from the fairy-tale dreams of marriage and maternity she'd once entertained, her son himself was a blessing.

Even if he *did* have a big mouth.

She nibbled on her lower lip, flashing back to the remarkable exchange she and John Gulliver had had earlier in the evening.

"Andy told me about wanting a baby brother while we were waiting for you at the clinic on Monday," he'd admitted to her. "He also told me he didn't think it was going to work out because he didn't have a, uh, daddy around."

"Oh, God," she'd groaned, knowing her cheeks must be as red as radishes with mortification. "Is there *anything* you two didn't talk about?"

"You."

She'd gone very still. Whatever she'd expected John to say in response to her essentially rhetorical question, it hadn't been this. After a moment she'd managed to stutter, "M-me?"

"And how lucky any little boy would be to have you as his mother."

Leigh leaned down and brushed her mouth against her son's cheek. "I do the best I can, sweetie," she murmured, breathing in the faintly soapy scent of his skin. "If I make mistakes, I'm sorry. Just remember—you're my extra-special boy and I love you very, very much."

"Mmm..." Andy sighed blissfully, burrowing his cheek into his pillow.

Straightening, Leigh picked a careful path away from the bed. "Night-night," she whispered over her shoulder as she stepped out into the hallway. She pulled the bedroom door almost—but not totally—shut.

A gust of wind rattled her home's outside walls and howled up under the eaves like a wild animal seeking refuge. She heard the roof groan. A floorboard creaked beneath its covering of foot-worn carpeting as she headed down the hall.

Although such sounds had disturbed her peace of mind when she'd first moved in, she'd become accustomed to them over the years. It had been a long time since she'd paid them much heed.

She heeded them now.

Now...when her body thrummed with desires she'd thought tainted beyond cleansing by an act of violation and an enduring sense of shame.

Now...when a man she'd known for less than a week was sleeping on her downstairs sofa at her invitation.

"It feels longer," that man had observed scarcely two hours ago when she'd reminded him of the brevity of their acquaintanceship.

She'd understood what he meant, of course, although she'd had no intention of admitting so. She'd shied from the intimacy he seemed to be asserting. She wasn't ready for it. She didn't know whether she would ever be ready for it!

"Yes, well, I can't rely on how a situation *feels*, John," she'd answered. "I have to depend on how it really is."

One big problem. She had yet to determine what this "reality" on which she'd maintained she needed to depend actually was. It seemed to be one thing when she was apart from John Gulliver, a whole host of others when she was with him.

Reality wasn't supposed to change—was it?

Leigh paused on the threshold of her bedroom, listening to the wind and the discordant sounds it elicited from her home.

After a moment or two she felt for the light switch on the wall and flipped it on, narrowing her eyes against the sudden flare of illumination from a pair of bedside lamps. Then she stepped inside and firmly shut the door behind her.

Where Andy's bedroom was a celebration of primary colors and joyful kid-style junk, hers was a study in impeccably matched pales and monastic neatness. The last adult male to enter it had been a furniture deliveryman, nearly four years ago. He'd brought the old, oak-framed cheval glass that stood in the far corner of the room.

Nothing in the room had belonged to her for longer than five and a half years. Save for a small suitcase filled with a hodge-podge of clothing and toiletries, she'd been allowed to take nothing with her the morning the federal authorities who had informed her of Nicholas Marchand's death had escorted her to what they'd described as a "neutral" site. What had happened to the items she'd left behind—among them, silver-framed photographs of her late parents, scores of books she'd purchased from secondhand shops and the ruins of a highly personal gift she'd received from her first and only lover—she didn't know. She hadn't asked. The men who'd taken her away from her "old" life had indicated that it would better for all concerned if she didn't.

Crossing to her quilt-covered bed, Leigh slipped off her shoes and began to undress. The process was methodical. Unthinking. She was down to her ecru-colored brassiere and matching panties when she caught a glimpse of her seminude body in the mirror in the corner.

Her first impulse was to turn away. Although she disguised it more cleverly than Deirdre Bleeker, she was as wary about the implications of her appearance as her assistant was about the messages sent by hers. But something inside her overrode this wariness. After a few moments of mental struggle, she succumbed to the lure of her mirrored image and moved slowly toward the cheval glass. She came to a stop about a foot in front of it.

The pattern of her breathing ruffled as a strange quiver of awareness shimmered through her nervous system. She watched as a flush of color stole up her throat and into her face. Outside, the wintry night wind continued to blow with haunting force.

Slowly, Leigh lifted her hands to the small clasp that nestled at the base of the cleft between her creamy-skinned breasts. She undid the fastener with trembling fingers, then brushed the flesh-toned bra cups aside. A second or two later she slipped the garment off and let it drop to the floor.

Bared to the waist, she contemplated her reflection. Her heart had begun to thud with hammer-to-anvil deliberation. There was an aching tightness between her thighs.

Suzanne Whitney had been slow to achieve physical maturity. Her breasts had seemed little more than bee-sting bumps until she was nearly seventeen, and she'd been targeted for a great many mocking gibes because of it. As a result, she'd been terribly self-conscious about her shape when she'd finally started to develop a figure.

Not only had she bloomed late, she'd bloomed a lot less than most of the girls she knew. In fact, to say she'd "bloomed" was probably an exaggeration. The only child of Nancy and George Whitney had graduated from high school feeling as though she'd barely budded. The indifference she'd seemed to inspire in members of the opposite sex—she hadn't even had a date to the senior prom, for heaven's sake!—had underscored her bruised sense of feminine inadequacy.

Unfortunately, there had been no one for her to talk to about her self-doubts. Her mother had been a straitlaced, duty-conscious woman who had handed her a pamphlet about menstruation rather than sit down for a face-to-face conversation about the facts of life. And her father—Lord! While he'd been a dependable and decent man, he'd been even more distant than his wife. Suzanne could no more have initiated a discussion about her sexual insecurities with him than she could have sprouted wings and flown away to Florida.

As for friends . . . well, she hadn't really had any. Acquaintances, yes. But she'd been too shy to venture beyond casual chitchat with them. As often happened in such situations, those around her had interpreted her innate reticence as snobbery. Rather than realizing that she held back because of very shaky self-esteem, her classmates had categorized her as stuck-up and far too sure of herself.

Her mother had died of ovarian cancer two months after she'd turned eighteen. Her father had been felled by a massive coronary seven weeks later. Their sudden deaths had shattered Suzanne Whitney's insular world, leaving her bereft of economic as well as emotional support. Her concerns about her physical endowments—or lack of them—had ceased to matter. So, too, her worries about her nonexistent social life.

Digging deep inside the numbness that had descended upon her in the wake of her devastating loss, Suzanne had discovered a strength she'd never known she had. She hadn't questioned its source. She hadn't wasted time regretting that she hadn't found it sooner, either. She'd simply grabbed on to it with both hands and prayed that it would be enough to see her through.

It had been. Somehow, some way, she'd survived. Not thrived, exactly, but endured.

And after a little more than four years of enduring, she'd met Nicholas "Saint Nick" Marchand.

She'd known who he was the Friday morning they'd shared an elevator in the office building where she'd been working as a secretary for nearly three years. She'd also known what he was supposed to be. She should have been afraid or appalled or both. Instead, she'd been instantaneously attracted.

He'd been enamored, too. Or so it had seemed. Although he'd spoken not a word to her in the elevator, he'd had a dozen pale pink, tightly furled roses delivered to her desk within an hour of their encounter. The flowers had been accompanied by a handwritten card that had boldly asserted, "These made me think of you."

He'd also turned up outside the building when she'd left work at the end of the day. She'd spotted him lounging indolently against a low-slung, imported sports car that had undoubtedly cost several times her annual salary. If he'd had any qualms about the fact that his vehicle was angled into a clearly marked No Parking zone, she hadn't been unable to detect them.

"Have dinner with me, Suzanne," he'd said in a velvet-soft voice, opening the passenger-side door of the shiny black car.

She'd hesitated, a long list of reasons for refusing his invitation—or was it closer to being an order?—unspooling in her brain. The reasons had been individually sound, collectively convincing. She would have bowed to them but for one ineluctable fact.

She'd wanted to say yes. No matter that she'd understood with absolute certainty she should do anything but. She'd wanted to say yes to Nicholas Marchand.

"Thank you," she'd finally replied, then gotten into the car.

They'd dined at a quietly expensive restaurant where no one had seemed aware of Nick's identity. While the taste of the beluga caviar he'd coaxed her into sampling had been a bit much for her unsophisticated palate, she'd feasted on the freshly broiled lobster he'd ordered for her with such greedy relish that he'd laughed aloud.

Having picked and sucked every delectable shred of meat from her entrée, she'd asserted that she was too full for dessert. Brushing aside her protests, Nick had insisted that she try a single bite of the hot chocolate soufflé he'd claimed was a famous specialty of the house. One luscious spoonful and she'd been hooked. She'd ended up eating an entire serving of the voluptuously delicious concoction. The temptation to lift the soufflé dish and lick it clean had been strong, but she'd managed to resist.

After dinner they'd gone dancing at a noisily extravagant club where her suavely dictatorial companion was obviously well-known. Her presence on his arm had generated a great deal of attention, not all of it flattering. The man nicknamed "Saint Nick" had fended off his acquaintances' curiosity with a ruthless politesse that she might have found unnerving under other circumstances. As it was, she'd been thankful for his coolly efficient method of parrying people's questions.

He'd driven her home shortly before one. He hadn't bothered to inquire about the address, he'd simply taken her to it.

He'd kissed her good-night at the door to her apartment, wooing her lips with carefully controlled ardor. Braced for a sexual aggressiveness that seemed in keeping with his reputation and imperious manner, Suzanne had been stunned by the eroticism of his restraint. Nicholas Marchand had not sought to "take" from her. Rather, he'd aroused in her a searingly sweet urge to yield up all she'd had to give.

Whether the nearly-twenty-three-year-old virgin she'd been that night would have gone to bed with the man she'd known for less than nine hours was a question Leigh McKay had never pressed herself to answer. Suffice it to say that the man involved hadn't asked and Suzanne Whitney, for all her nascent sensuality, had lacked the confidence to offer.

Suzanne had tormented herself with questions about what else she may have lacked during the three weeks that had followed that first mind-blowing kiss. She'd done so because Nicholas Marchand had dropped out of her life as suddenly as he'd dropped into it.

He hadn't come by.

He hadn't called.

He'd made no effort whatsoever to contact her.

Bitterly hurt and desperately confused, she'd ripped up the provocatively worded card and thrown out the roses. She'd also spent several miserable nights sobbing into her pillow. Finally she'd reviewed all the things she'd heard whispered about her escort-for-a-single-evening and tried to persuade herself that she'd actually had a lucky escape.

Twenty-one days after he'd deserted her on her doorstep, Nick had shown up at her apartment unannounced. "I couldn't stay away," he'd told her, his voice low and strained, his posture tense.

"I'm glad," she'd said with helpless honesty, then stepped back a pace and gestured him inside.

She'd wondered later whether Nick had come hoping that she would turn him away. If so, he'd badly miscalculated. This was not to say that she hadn't experienced a fleeting urge to slam her door in his face in the first few seconds after she'd opened it. The pain he'd inflicted by his unexplained withdrawal from her had been acute. But the impulse to reject had dissolved in a rush of compassion when she'd looked up into his deep-set brown eyes and realized that he'd been hurting, too. Steering clear of her had cost him in ways that she, in her inexperience, could only vaguely imagine.

They'd become lovers six weeks later. Two months after that, Nicholas Marchand had been killed in a fiery car crash. And in a very real sense, the woman he'd been en route to visiting had perished that same night.

Leigh closed her eyes for a moment, allowing herself the dangerous indulgence of summoning up the devilishly handsome image of the man upon whom Suzanne Whitney had willingly bestowed both her physical innocence and her heart.

The dark, rakishly styled hair.

The classically chiseled cheekbones and cleft chin.

The sensual, crook-cornered mouth.

"Nick," she murmured. "Oh . . . God. *Nick.*"

She opened her eyes, focusing once again on the reflection in the mirror. For the first time in five and a half years, she assessed herself as a woman. Not as a mother. Not as a . . . victim.

Although her breasts had gotten a little fuller with maternity, they were hardly the stuff of centerfold fantasy. The nipples were more prominent than they had been, though. They'd darkened from a fragile petal pink—the exact shade of the bouquet Nick had sent her, to be precise—to a rich, dusky rose sometime during her pregnancy.

Leigh lifted her hands, cupping her softly curving flesh with her palms. A moment or two later she feathered the pads of her thumbs over the stiffening peaks and the pebbling areolae that encircled them. Her breath snagged in her throat as a thrill of response arrowed downward toward her womb.

The muscles of her legs started to tremble. The ache between her thighs became a melting, pulsating warmth. The crotch of her demure cotton panties dampened.

She wanted to be able to want again, she thought with a fierce surge of conviction. To want freely. Without fear or shame. And she wanted to be wanted in return by a man to whom it would be safe to entrust herself and her son.

Could John Gulliver be that man?

Her long, pale lashes fluttered down to rest against the upper rise of her flushed cheeks. The masculine visage that filled her mind was very different from the one she'd conjured up with such foolish vividness a few moments ago.

The hair was no longer glossily dark and fashionably long. It was now heavily brindled with gray and neatly barbered around the ears and at the nape.

Matinee-idol handsomeness had given way to features that were harshly hewn and angularly irregular, yet compelling in their masculine integrity. They were also irreparably scarred.

One of the hands that had caressed her earlier in the evening had been disfigured, too, she remembered with a pang. But the sensations that hand had evoked had been so poignantly beautiful, it had seemed unblemished and whole.

Leigh opened her eyes once again, her breathing shallow and unsteady. Gazing at her reflection, she stroked her right hand downward from her breasts. Pregnancy had softened her once-taut figure in a way that no amount of exercise or dieting could fully undo. It had also marred the skin of her hips and stomach with silvery striations.

Her fingertips brushed the elasticized waistband of her panties. She traced the top edge of the garment with her nails for a few tremulous seconds, then slipped her hand beneath it. Her palm felt very warm.

A moment later she touched herself through the fine golden fleece that clustered at the juncture of her pale thighs. A voluptuous heat suffused her, rushing through her veins, inundating her already primed senses.

She touched herself again. Something deep within her clenched as she stroked the slick, folded flesh that marked the portal of the passage to her feminine core. Her body spasmed in shockingly potent response.

So long, she thought, arching into the sensation. It had been so...long.

A single-syllable name teetered on the tip of her tongue, then broke from her lips. The name wasn't *Nick*.

Outside, the wind continued to howl—a cruel reminder of how unwise it could be to consider oneself safe in a fundamentally insecure world.

Downstairs, the man Leigh McKay had recognized at some inexplicable level the first time her eyes had met his, slept. And as he did so, he dreamed of the woman reflected in the cheval glass.

Hundreds of miles away, Anthony Stone lay in a cell fantasizing about his possession of Suzanne Whitney and the murder of Nicholas Marchand.

Chapter 7

The feeling of being stared at summoned John Gulliver out of an intensely sensual paradise early the next morning. Although the transition from blissful oblivion to full awareness was an instantaneous one, he opted to pretend he was still asleep. The decision to do so was instinctive. Until he knew for certain who was scrutinizing him and why—

"John?"

It was Andy. His little boy, Andy.

"John?" The repetition of his name was hushed but penetrating and accompanied by a kittenish puff of breath. A second or two later something—a finger? the handle of a tacky plastic tomahawk?—nudged his right shoulder. "Are you still asleep?"

John opened his eyes with melodramatic suddenness. His son, who was practically nose-to-nose with him, gave a yelp of surprise and jerked back. The feather-decorated war club he'd had clutched in his left hand slipped from his grasp and hit the floor.

"Yes," he replied in a grave monotone, closing his mind to the heaviness in his groin. "I'm still asleep."

Andy stared at him for a moment, his eyes round with shock. Then he started to giggle. The sound was a tad shaky at first, but quickly steadied into genuine merriment.

"No, you're not," he contradicted, his tender features acquiring a smug, you-can't-fool-me cast. "You're *awake!*"

"How can you be so sure?" John challenged, willing himself not to shift his position. He wasn't certain how his sexually charged body would react to movement.

"Because—" there was more fizzy laughter "—you're *talking!*"

"Haven't you ever heard of people talking in their sleep?"

The giggling stopped. Andy blinked several times, obviously thrown by this inquiry. Finally he conceded, "Yeah. I guess."

"Maybe that's what I'm doing."

Andy chewed on his lower lip, considering. Whether the mannerism was inherited or acquired through unconscious imitation, it reminded John very strongly of Leigh. Where was she? he wondered. He didn't sense her presence in the room. Perhaps she was still upstairs—

"Nuh-uh," the little boy interrupted his speculation. The tone of the assertion was very definite. "You can't be. Cuz people who talk in their sleep don't have conber—um—conber-*say*-shins."

John was amused by the mispronunciation but proud that Andy had attempted such a sophisticated word in the proper context. "Is that what I'm doing?" he countered. "Having a conversation?"

"Yep." Andy gave an emphatic nod. "With me."

"You're sure about that?"

"Totally sure!"

"Well . . ." He paused, manufacturing a sigh of resignation. "I guess that must mean I'm not talking in my sleep."

"It means you're *awake!*" Andy bent to pick up his tomahawk, then fixed John with a pointed look. "Just like I told you already."

"Pretty smart, aren't you?"

"Yeah." The acknowledgment was endearingly matter-of-fact. Andy punctuated it by scratching the tip of his faintly freckled nose with the edge of the tomahawk's plastic head.

"Mommy says I'm 'ceptional. I heard her. Did she ask you to sleep over?"

"Sort . . . of."

"Huh?"

Deciding he was going to have to risk embarrassing himself, John tossed back the eiderdown coverlet Leigh had given him the previous evening and sat up. He shivered, his nearly-naked body protesting the sudden exposure to the room's cool air. He didn't dare glance down to check his below-the-belt reaction to the chill. "My car wouldn't start and I couldn't go back to my hotel."

"Oh." Andy seemed perfectly content with this explanation. "Well, she's still sleepin'. Mommy, I mean. I opened her door a little before I came downstairs and tippy-toed over to her bed, really quiet. I think she was havin' a nice dream. Her face looked all soft and she was smilin'."

A vision of a smiling-in-her-sleep Leigh McKay blossomed in John's highly suggestible mind. He did his damnedest to root it out. Surging to his feet, he reached for the pair of trousers he'd draped over the back of the sofa before he'd bedded down for the night. He donned the garment swiftly, turning away from Andy in the interests of modesty as he did so. He then pivoted back to face his son. He was startled to find himself the target of an unblinking, blue-gray stare.

The scars, he thought instantly, mentally cursing the carelessness bred by years of living alone. He'd forgotten about the scars on his shoulders and right arm.

"Andy—" he began, his voice thickening with concern. What if his son was repulsed by what he was seeing?

"Do your hairs itch you, John?" the little boy asked, cocking his head to one side and wrinkling his nose.

It took John a moment to realize what the boy was referring to. He glanced down at his chest. "Uh, no," he replied with a hint of awkwardness. "Not particularly."

"I think Bryan's daddy's hairs itch *him*. He scratches a lot. He has more than you on his chest, though. And whole bunches on his back and arms. Last summer he taked off his shirt when he was mowin' their lawn and it was like he had on a *sweater* underneath."

"Different men have different amounts of hair, Andy."

The little boy nodded knowingly. "Like on their heads. Bryan's daddy doesn't have many hairs on his. It's kind of bald. He scratches it, too, sometimes. The bald part, I mean."

"I ... see."

Andy got to his bunny-slippered feet, tomahawk still in hand. He frowned down at himself and sighed. "My chest is bald."

John controlled a smile. "It won't always be, buddy."

"It *won't?*"

The uncertain tone of the question made John hesitate. Adults he could handle, he reflected. Manipulate. Control. But an innocent little kid? Man, oh, man. He was working without a net here, psychologically speaking. What if he inadvertently said something that screwed up his son for life?

"Probably not, buddy," he responded after a moment, retrieving his shirt and putting it on. "Little boys get hair on their chests as they grow up."

"Really?" Andy lifted his eyes, his expression intrigued. And trusting. Oh, God. So trusting. As though he believed that anything John Gulliver told him had to be true.

"Yes, really." John debated whether he should detail any of the other physiological changes that went with maturity. He decided that discretion might be the better part of valor in this instance. While he didn't want to be accused of holding anything back, he also felt that there were some facts of life a preschooler might not be prepared to hear.

"Hairs like you have?" his young companion pressed.

"More or less."

"When?"

"When you're fourteen. Or fifteen. Sixteen, maybe. It depends."

Andy took a few seconds to mull this over, then asked in a tentative voice, "Will it hurt?"

"Growing hairs?"

"Yeah."

"Not at all. It's a very natural thing. It happens to all us guys."

Andy's eyes brightened. He puffed up a bit, clearly thrilled to be considered a *guy*. "But not to girls."

"Definitely not to girls," John concurred, releasing the smile he'd previously suppressed. He felt pretty smug. Invoking male solidarity had been a smart thing to do, he told himself.

"How come?"

The smile faded. So did the inclination toward self-congratulation. John swallowed. "How come...girls don't get hairs on their, uh, chests?"

"Yeah."

"Well—"

"Is it cuz they get other stuff there?"

"That's—ahem—part of the reason, Andy." John felt himself start to flush like a hormonally-challenged schoolboy. He braced himself for a request for a description of the "other stuff" in question. Or worse, the offer of one.

"It's *private* stuff," Andy asserted confidently. "What girls get on their chests, I mean."

"Very private." John shifted his stance uneasily, suddenly remembering the ploy Leigh had used to divert their son from the subject of her handgun ownership. The food feint had worked once. Maybe it would work again. It was certainly worth a try.

"Mommy says girls have—"

"Are you hungry, buddy?"

Andy blinked, plainly startled by the interruption but not visibly offended by it. After a moment he asked, "You mean, like, for breakfast?"

"Exactly." The boy could have declared himself starving for pickled pigs feet or a hot fudge sundae, for all John cared at this moment. He just wanted to put an end to this discussion of gender differences. "Are you?"

"Well . . . yeah. Sure."

"Me, too."

"You're hungry for breakfast?"

"Very."

Andy cocked his head and twiddled with the beads on his tomahawk, a mischievous gleam of calculation entering his blue-gray eyes. An uh-oh prickle of apprehension skittered up John's spine. He quickly assured himself that whatever was on his son's clever mind, it had to be less unnerving than a discussion of the physiological differences between male and female.

"*I* know," the little boy announced triumphantly, flashing his dimples. "Let's make pancakes!"

Leigh surfaced from slumber with a drowsy yawn and a long, luxurious stretch. She felt strangely at peace with herself. As though she'd made some sort of critically important decision as she'd slept.

The storm must have blown itself out, she decided, noting the lambent sunshine filtering through the cracks in the window shades. At the very least, the wind had died away.

She rolled over, focusing dreamily on the face of her bed-side clock. A quarter past nine, it told her. What a nice time of—

A quarter past nine!

Leigh stiffened, staring at the digital readout in disbelief. It had to be wrong. She never slept this late! Even if she'd been inclined to laze around, Andy was always up and—

Oh, no.

Andy.

She sat up, swiping a handful of hair back from her face. Her gaze slewed toward her bedroom door. It had been closed when she'd gone to sleep. She was positive of that. Now it was par-tially open. Which could only mean that someone must have— Oh. Oh, God.

The floodgates of memory gave way. The events of the pre-vious evening sluiced through Leigh's brain and stimulated her body into action.

She flung aside the bedclothes and practically hurtled off the mattress. The room's hardwood floor was freezing against the soles of her bare feet but she didn't care.

Grabbing her robe from the foot of the bed, Leigh dashed out into the hall. A quick glance told her that the door to her son's room was wide open. Heart pounding, she hurried to the stairs.

"Andy?" she called urgently as she descended. "Sweetie, are you down here?"

A crash of cutlery from the kitchen arrested her headlong flight. She froze midway down the staircase, one hand spasm-ing on the banister, the other rising to the base of her throat. *What in the name of—*

And then she smelled it. The slightly acrid scent teased her nostrils for a second or two before her emotion-roiled brain recognized what it signified.

Someone was cooking—or perhaps that should be *over-cooking*—one of her son's "most favoritest" foods in the world.

The door to the kitchen swung open. A moment later Andy materialized at the foot of the stairs. He was clutching a spatula as though it were his treasured tomahawk. There was a purple smear on his chin. His pajama top was dusted with flour and dotted with— Lord! Were those shreds of potato? A piece of eggshell ornamented the toe of his right bunny slipper. What the brown gunky stuff dribbled on the ears of the left one was, Leigh didn't dare speculate.

"Hi, Mommy," her son said, beaming up at her. "Guess what me and John are makin'?"

"We got a little carried away," John conceded with an awkward gesture when he finally found his voice.

The unwitting intimacy of Leigh's appearance—the tousled hair, the sleep-flushed cheeks, the bare feet—had knocked him for a loop. And the *robe* she was wearing! Never mind that its fuzzy, powder-blue bulk covered her primly from ankle to throat. The garment made her look so sexily cuddlesome that it was all he could do not to cross to where she was standing and gather her into his arms.

"So I noticed." The response was as dry as unbuttered toast.

He'd never seen Suzanne Whitney in a morning-after situation, John realized with a jolt, trying not to stare. She'd been too shy to spend an entire night in Saint Nick's apartment. And he— Well, he'd felt too guilty about too many aspects of their illicit affair to sleep over at hers.

He'd seen her in a nightgown only once. It had been an exquisite piece of lingerie, a shimmering sluice of ivory silk that had clung to the curves of her beautiful breasts and teased against the provocative cleft between her thighs. He'd given it to her three nights before Nicholas Marchand had been killed. While she'd been enchanted by the garment's fragile beauty from the moment she opened the tissue-lined box in which it had been packed, he'd had to pressure her into accepting it.

Getting her to try it on once that had been accomplished had required a more delicately seductive form of persuasion. Likewise, the process of getting her to take it off.

Which wasn't to suggest that he'd regretted the effort. Quite the contrary. And if truth be told, part of the pleasure he'd experienced had stemmed from his belief that Suzanne had very much enjoyed his method of coaxing her into acquiesence.

Although trauma had blunted his ability to recall many specifics, John had the vague impression that on the evening of his supposed death, Saint Nick had been heading to his lover's apartment expecting to find her wearing nothing but his blatantly sensual gift and a spritz of the delicately floral perfume she favored. He harbored an equally nebulous notion that this expectation had been based on something Suzanne had said in a telephone call.

"We been 'sperry-menting, Mommy," Andy volunteered in a cheery tone.

"Experimenting?" Leigh repeated, arching an eyebrow. John winced as he watched her glance around. Her cream-and-yellow kitchen had been tidy enough for a photo shoot when he and Andy had set out to make themselves breakfast. It was now... Well, the phrase "disaster area" suggested itself rather strongly. He hadn't really noticed how messy he'd allowed things to get. He'd been too busy enjoying himself.

"We had to," his partner in culinary misadventure blithely explained. "You forgetted to buy maple syrup the last time you goed grocery shoppin'."

"This is *my* fault?" Although the query was ostensibly directed at her son, Leigh's eyes were focused on John.

"We, uh, needed something to put on our pancakes," he offered after a fractional pause, trying not to let his gaze drift downward. He also tried not to speculate about what—if anything—Leigh had on beneath her robe. The thought of that fuzzy blue fabric rubbing against bare skin had a decidedly unsettling effect on his pulse rate. "So we... improvised."

"We did tests." Andy waved the greasy spatula he was holding, indicating the motley collection of jars, boxes, bags, bowls and plates that was spread out on the kitchen counters. "To see what tasted the goodest."

"You put grape jelly, canned corn and *pickle relish* on pancakes?"

"Not all together, Mommy." A giggle dismissed the suggestion as silly. "The pickle relish was yucky, but that was like a joke. Nonna P.'s s'ghetti sauce, too. 'Specially since it was cold. And the corn we put *in,* not on. We dumped some in the batter stuff *before* we cooked it. That was John's idea."

"I . . . see."

"So was the crispy pancake with shredded-up potato. John's idea, I mean. I didn't want to eat it at first, but he said I should hold my nose and take a bite and I did. It was pretty good. Then I let go of my nose and taked another bite and it was *very* good. Sort of like smooshed-up Tater Tots. I ate it all." Andy waved the spatula again. "We can cook you one if you want."

"Well—"

"Oh! Oh! Wait!" Andy did an excited little jig, evidently recalling something he had to share right then or burst. "Did you know there's a kind of pancake you can set on *fire?*"

John groaned inwardly. He'd forgotten that he'd made a passing reference to crêpes Suzette early on in the proceedings. He'd been so damned eager to hold his son's interest—so desperate to impress him—that he'd yammered on like Marcy-Anne Gregg. He wanted to kick himself. What kind of idiot talked about flambéed desserts in front of not-yet-five-year-old?

Accusing blue eyes slammed into defensive brown ones.

"You *didn't—*"

"No, I didn't."

"Didn't what?"

"Nothing!" Leigh and John blurted out simultaneously.

Andy's artless gaze ping-ponged back and forth between the two adults for several seconds. "Oh," he eventually said, shrugging his small shoulders. "Okay. What about pancakes with teeny chocolate chips, extra-crunchy peanut butter and melted marshmallows, Mommy? I 'vented them all by myself."

John watched Leigh turn back to his—*their*—son, her mouth curving into a slightly strained but still-lovely smile. "Pancakes with teeny chocolate chips, extra-crunchy peanut butter and melted marshmallows?'' she repeated. "Why, honey, that sounds . . . delicious.''

The hours that followed were full of light and laughter and, it seemed to John, the promise of a loving future.

To the casual observer, nothing much happened. To John, everything that occurred was freighted with tender significance.

The kitchen was eventually cleaned up. Andy got around to trading his food-stained pajamas for a spanking-fresh sweatshirt and a pair of jeans. Leigh shed her absurdly alluring bathrobe for a loose-fitting sweater and trim corduroy slacks.

Although his hostess protested that it really wasn't necessary, John kept his pledge and dug out her driveway. That he ruined a very good pair of leather shoes doing so bothered him very little. That the task took twice as long as it needed to because Andy insisted on helping troubled him even less.

He and his son were just heading in for a late lunch when Wesley Warren pulled up behind his moribund rental car in a tow truck.

"Why don't you go along without me, buddy," John said quietly, thrusting his hands into his pockets.

"Naw," Andy replied, waving enthusiastically at the man in the truck. "That's okay."

"Your mom's got the food ready."

"She won't mind. She likes Mr. Warren. Me, too. Last time we were at his garage, he let me hold a wrench for him. *And* squirt some oil on this squeaky thing. Mommy said he fixed our station wagon good as new, even though it's sort of old."

"That's terrific," John declared evenly, lying through his teeth. "I still think you should go inside."

"But, John—"

"Go."

Although clearly disgruntled, Andy did.

John walked toward Wesley Warren slowly, taking his measure, preparing himself for . . . whatever.

"Busy day?" he asked, his breath condensing in the chilly air.

"Don't usually work Sundays," the other man replied, easing back the hood of his parka. "Folks started callin' me at home 'bout six this morning, though, 'cause of the storm. Couldn't very well say no. Told Ms. McKay when she phoned it'd be a while 'fore I got out here. First come, first served.''

John nodded, wondering about the formality of the reference to Leigh. He remembered that Warren had called Deirdre Bleeker "Dee.''

"Had car trouble last night, did you?'' The mechanic looked from John to John's rental vehicle and back again.

"Yeah.''

"Convenient.''

You son of a—

"No,'' he said. "Not very.''

"See you stayed over.''

John stiffened, torn between a desire to stake a public claim on Leigh and the recognition that doing so would likely damage her reputation. Small-town gossip could be a very nasty thing. "Downstairs. On the sofa,'' he finally clarified, holding the other man's gaze, biting off the words. "Not that it's any of your business.''

An emotion he couldn't put a name to flickered through the depths of Wesley Warren's hazel eyes. It might have been jealousy. "Lot of people 'round here are fond of Ms. McKay,'' the former military man observed after a moment. "Her little boy, too. Wouldn't like 'em to get . . . hurt.''

Nicholas Marchand's instincts—predatory, possessive— stirred within the man who'd lived by them for eighteen pressure-filled months. "Neither would I, friend,'' he responded, his voice carrying a mix of razor and rasp. *"Neither . . . would . . . I.''*

Chapter 8

Monday turned out to be an unusually slow day in Leigh's bookstore. Although the lack of business boded ill for her bottom line, she was grateful for the respite. She knew that she was too preoccupied with thoughts of John Gulliver and the time they'd spent together to deal effectively with customers.

What she didn't realize until late in the afternoon was that her distracted mental state had kept her from noticing that her assistant was very upset about something. She experienced a rush of guilt. Although Dee could be prickly to the point of unpleasantness at times, Leigh genuinely cared about her.

Her admiration for Deirdre Bleeker's fight to break with a sordid past and begin a clean new life ran deeper than she could ever fully express. She saw a number of parallels in their situations. She also recognized that while her fresh start had been organized and underwritten by the government, her assistant had been forced to scrabble for a second chance unaided.

Which wasn't to imply that Deirdre Bleeker would have found it easy to operate on any other than solitary and suspicious terms. Based on everything she'd gleaned about Dee, Leigh suspected that she would have rejected any and all offers of help.

"Why did you give me this job?" the redhead had stormed into Leigh's office and demanded about a month after she'd begun working at the bookstore.

"I didn't 'give' you anything," Leigh had replied quietly. She'd had a feeling this kind of confrontation was brewing and she'd tried to prepare herself for it. "You earned it. You were the best applicant."

"Oh, right." A sneer. "A junkie-whore convict."

"Ex."

"What?"

"*Ex*-junkie. *Ex*-whore. *Ex*-convict."

Dee's eyes had widened as though she'd been shocked that Leigh was able to utter the word "whore" without choking on it. Leigh had let the reaction pass unremarked. The explanation for her equanimity—that she'd heard herself labeled much worse the night the man to whom she'd given her heart had been taken from her—was something she hadn't been able to share.

"This is some kind of pity thing, right?" the redhead had accused, taking another tack. "You feel sorry for me and my 'dysfunctional' background."

"I don't think I'd dare."

"Then why the hell did you hire me?"

Leigh had lifted her chin, accepting the challenge by offering one of her own. "Why not, Dee? Did you answer my Help Wanted ad because you thought you were unqualified?"

"No!"

"Did you accept my offer intending to screw up at the first opportunity?"

"Of course not!" Dee had flushed violently, her eyes turning glassy with anguish and outrage. "I wanted this job so much I could taste it! And not just because my only other choice was slinging hash at some stupid roadhouse, either. I like books. I didn't much when I was in school, but I do now. Books take you places. They teach you stuff. They make you believe you can change the world if you try hard enough. And as for screwing up— *God!* I've been working my butt off for you, lady! I come in early. I stay late. I bring home the inventory lists to memorize so I can know everything you have in stock. I even read reviews so I can tell people what's good and what's garbage. You couldn't have somebody better than me working for you, and you damned well know it!''

"You're right," Leigh had concurred, unruffled. She'd understood that the outburst was proof of the intensity of Dee's feelings. "I *do* know it. I knew it when I hired you."

The redhead had stared at her mutely for several seconds, shivering visibly as the residue of her anger drained away. Finally, her face milky pale, her voice fragile as a blown-glass bubble, she'd asked, "R-Really?"

"Really."

"You're not bull—uh—fooling me?"

"Absolutely not."

"I was the b-best applicant you had?"

"Mmm-hmm."

"Let me guess." Dee's mouth had twisted. "The other ones were so dumb they couldn't spell AT & T without a dictionary."

Although the hurt she'd heard lurking behind the humor had made it difficult, Leigh had smiled. She'd realized it was expected. Then she'd replied, "The competition was pretty tough, actually. I think the deciding factor was your listing the Bible, *To Kill a Mockingbird* and *Green Eggs and Ham* as your three favorite books."

"I . . . almost crossed the last one out."

"I'm glad you didn't. It made me certain everything else you wrote down was true."

"Oh, it was." Dee's expression had turned pleading. Almost desperate. "It *is*. Every single word on my application is God's own truth, Ms. McKay. I swear it."

"Leigh, please. Call me Leigh."

"Are you . . . sure?"

"Very."

"All right. L-Leigh, then."

Things had improved considerably after that episode. But now . . .

"Dee?" Leigh began softly, chiding herself for not picking up on her assistant's agitation earlier. "Is there something you'd like to talk about?"

"No," the redhead said flatly, shuffling a rack of paper-backs into alphabetical order. She was obsessive about keeping the store's merchandise properly organized.

"I can see you're upset—"

"Can you?" The question was accompanied by a short, sharp glance.

Leigh recoiled from the accusation in her assistant's eyes. Dee had looked at her as though she felt she'd been betrayed at some fundamental and unforgivable level.

But why?

"Dee," she tried again, doing her best to keep her voice steady. Whatever was going on, it clearly was a lot more serious than one of her assistant's periodic attacks of self-doubt and ultradefensiveness. "I'm sorry. I realize I've been... distracted...today. I didn't mean to be insensitive toward you. If you've got a problem, please, let me try to help you." She made a gesture of supplication. "I think we know each other well enough—"

"I don't."

"Don't...what?"

"Know you well enough. I thought I did, but I was wrong."

The look of accusation was back in Dee's eyes. And there was something else, as well. It was disillusionment, Leigh realized with a shock. Bleak, bitter disillusionment.

"I don't understand," she said after a few moments, deeply shaken. If truth be told, she hadn't believed her assistant capable of being disillusioned. Of being hurt, yes. Dee was vulnerable in a great many ways. But she didn't seem to trust anyone or anything. And if a person didn't trust, he or she couldn't be let down or disillusioned.

Or so Leigh McKay had assumed.

Dee's thin face contorted. She looked terribly young, yet horribly used up. For a moment she appeared to be on the verge of tears. Then she swallowed convulsively and said in a half-strangled tone, "I never thought you were like me, Leigh."

"Like...you?"

"Y-yes." Dee jerked her head up and down. "You know."

"No, I don't."

"With men!"

Men?

"You had him at your house Saturday night, didn't you?" Dee blurted out. "That John Gulliver. You had him. And *Andy* was there!"

Leigh felt the blood drain out of her cheeks. She swayed slightly, her vision blurring as though she might black out. As she fought against the swirling dizziness, a complex combination of emotions buffeted her. Anger was part of the equation. So was shame. Not so much because of what she'd done; more because of what she'd contemplated doing.

"No," she managed to choke out.

"Yes!" the other woman disputed, growing more distraught. "I thought you were good! In all the time I've worked for you, you n-never once—I never saw or heard—*never*, Leigh! Never any men. And I wanted— You were my model, don't you see? When I went through rehab, the counselors said we should find p-people to look up to. So I found you. From the first day I came into the bookstore, I wanted to be like y-you. Just like you. *Only now I find out you're just like m-m-me!*"

There was a disastrous silence.

"Oh...Dee," Leigh finally said, her throat tight and aching. The impulse toward swooning had passed. She now felt as though she'd been dropped into an earthquake zone equipped with nothing more than a dented teaspoon and an order to restore the landscape. "Oh, honey. I...I had no idea. No idea at all."

The redhead had begun to cry. Huge tears rolled down her cheeks. "You weren't—" a sodden hiccup was punctuated by a long sniffle "—s-s-supposed to."

Another silence.

"Okay," Leigh said at last, slipping a supportive arm around her sobbing assistant. "Shh. Shh." She patted and stroked the younger woman in much the same way she'd patted and stroked Andy when he'd broken down in the clinic examining room after his playground accident. Had that been just one week ago? she questioned fleetingly. Lord! It seemed like a lifetime. "It's okay, Dee."

"N-n-no...it's not."

"Yes, it is." Leigh glanced toward the front door, coming to a snap decision. Some things were more important than business. "Look, honey. I want you to go into my office, all right? I'm going to lock up the shop. Then I'll come back to you and we can talk."

"There's nuh-huh—" another hiccup "—nothing to t-t-talk about."

"There most certainly is." Leigh patted the other woman again, instinctively slipping into her mom-in-charge mode. "Now, go. There's a box of tissues in my bottom right-hand drawer. Use all you need."

While Dee had pretty much stopped crying by the time Leigh joined her in the back office, her emotions were still obviously raw. Leigh sighed inwardly, bracing herself for the possibility of another outburst. She also prayed for the wisdom to undo the harm she feared she'd unwittingly caused through her failure to comprehend what had been going on inside her assistant's head.

Deirdre Bleeker had chosen *her* as a role model? she thought, still stunned by the notion. Lord! What a mess!

"I'm . . . s-sorry," Dee apologized, blotting her nose with a damp wad of tissue. She was hunched over in Leigh's desk chair, trembling like a whipped puppy. Her eyes were red and puffy. Her skin was blotchy. She looked as bad as she'd ever looked, and that was saying something.

"Sorry for what?" Leigh countered gently, gesturing the shaky redhead back into the chair when she started to get up. She'd tried to formulate some kind of agenda while she'd been locking the shop. She'd decided that her first task was to make an effort to explain why John Gulliver had spent Saturday night—and a good chunk of Sunday—at her home. Second on her list was finding a way to deal with Dee's distorted image of her. Telling the truth would help her in terms of the former. But when it came to the latter . . .

"Sorry for everything."

"I think that's a bit much, honey."

Dee snuffled moistly into the tissues and glanced toward the television on the corner of Leigh's desk. "You're missing your show," she remarked irrelevantly.

Leigh glanced toward the set, startled to see it was on. The amnesiac bride-to-be was on the screen, apparently suffering some kind of flashback. Her prospective groom—or was it the prospective groom's evil twin?—was arguing with her.

"Oh. That." She reached over and turned off the TV, genuinely indifferent to the melodramatic proceedings. "Who needs soap operas?" she asked rhetorically, leaning against the edge of the desk.

Dee blew her nose. "People with lousy lives?" she suggested, balling up the tissues she'd been using and tossing them into the wastebasket to the left of the desk.

Leigh stiffened slightly, but decided after a second or two that the response had been prompted by misery, not malice. "Could be," she agreed in a neutral voice, then drew a steadying breath. "Let's start with John Gulliver, all right? Where did you hear about his spending Saturday night at my house?"

"It doesn't matter."

"Yes, it does." Although Leigh made the assertion firmly, she was inclined to think Dee might be right. Still. She wanted to know. She figured she might as well start with the most obvious suspect. "Was it from Wes Warren?"

The redhead's eyes filled again. She grabbed another handful of tissues and swiped at them with clumsy strokes. "Not...exactly."

"What does that mean, Dee?"

"Well—" she gave a sniff "—I went to church yesterday morning, just like I always do. There weren't as many people as usual because of the snow." Another sniff. "And things got started a little late because Father Purcell had to find a replacement altar boy. While I was waiting for the service to begin, I heard these two women behind me talking. I'm not sure who they were. I...I didn't want to turn around and look."

"These woman were talking about me?"

"Yeah. One of them said she'd seen you and Andy having dinner Saturday night with a man who had scars on his temple and neck."

Leigh didn't bother trying to puzzle out the identities of the churchgoing gossipers. She'd spotted about a half-dozen women she knew—or at least vaguely recognized—at the restaurant.

"How did you make the leap from my having dinner with John Gulliver to his staying overnight at my house and doing...whatever?" she pressed.

"You don't really want to hear."

"Yes, I do."

"Okay." Dee heaved a weary-sounding sigh and dabbed at her nostrils. "I went back to church for my fellowship meeting about seven. We've been collecting old toys and fixing them up to give away at Christmas. Last night we were supposed to finish wrapping them. Thalia Jenkins from the preschool was there. So was her cousin, Edith. She's a housekeeper at that inn on the outskirts of town."

Leigh grimaced, beginning to sense where this meandering monologue was heading. The local grapevine. Her relocation inspector had warned her about the dangers of getting ensnared in it. Small-town gossips should not be underestimated, he'd said, then suggested that more than a few of them could give the FBI lessons in effective interrogation techniques and intelligence gathering.

He'd smiled slightly when he'd made this observation, but Leigh hadn't gotten the impression that he'd been joking.

"Anyway," the redhead continued, "Thalia started talking about Andy's accident, going on and on about how this dynamic stranger—John Gulliver—had shown up out of nowhere and saved the day. Then Edith chimed in to say that he's been a guest at the inn for about a week. He only got a room because somebody canceled out at the last minute. He *said* he's intending to stay through Christmas, only he arrived with nothing but an overnight bag and a very fancy laptop computer. I guess that seemed sort of suspicious. Then he flashed one of those platinum credit cards *and* ID proving he owns this travel agency down south somewhere, so it was all okay. A day or so later he got about a dozen overnight deliveries from a bunch of catalog places. Clothes, mostly, according to Edith. And not cheap stuff, either."

"I see," Leigh responded slowly. She gnawed on her lower lip, temporarily diverted from her exploration of the question of how Dee—and, she suspected, most of the people in town—had discovered that she'd had an overnight guest to a consideration of the information she'd just been given.

While her assistant's recitation hadn't contradicted the sketchy explanation John had offered for his presence in the area in any substantive way, there was something...odd about it, she reflected with a trace of uneasiness. Then again, maybe John Gulliver's investments were lucrative enough to underwrite the kind of impulsively eccentric behavior she'd just heard described.

Nicholas Marchand had had an extravagant streak, she suddenly recalled. Accustomed to living on a budget that had been calculated down to the penny, Suzanne Whitney had found his free-spending ways more than a little shocking. Although being on the receiving end of the generosity that had earned him the sobriquet "Saint" Nick had been exciting—

Stop it! Stop it right now!

"Wh-what?" Dee asked uncertainly, the wad of tissue she'd been wielding falling from her fingers and into her lap.

Leigh clenched the edge of the desk with white-knuckled force, hoping she hadn't spoken her panicked self-command aloud.

"Nothing," she said after a moment. "Go on."

"Are you—"

"*Please,* Dee. Just finish your story."

"All right." The redhead retrieved the tissues she'd dropped and began shredding them. "There's not that much more, anyway. Edith doesn't usually work Sundays but she got called in for a few hours because the inn was short-staffed. She said she didn't mind because she could use the overtime, what with Christmas coming and all that. When she let herself into John Gulliver's room—Thalia had asked her to make a special point of looking after him, you see, because of Andy—she realized it was exactly the way it'd been when she'd turned down the bed the evening before. She got worried and phoned the front desk. The manager said Mr. Gulliver had called earlier to explain that he'd had car trouble and got stuck spending the night someplace else."

"And you assumed that it was my house, with me and my son."

Dee averted her face, her pasty cheeks flooding with color. "I saw W-Wes this morning. I stopped in at the café to get a muffin and he was there. He...he mentioned something about having to come out to your place with a tow truck."

"John really did have car trouble, Dee."

"Yeah." The flush got darker. "Wes . . . said."

"And he spent the night downstairs, on my sofa."

"Wes said that, t-too."

"*Wes* said?"

Dee looked at her again. "That . . . h-he said."

"'He' being John?" Leigh frowned, thinking back. Andy had tromped into the house right after Wes had arrived. He'd been grumbling about something, but she hadn't really paid much attention. John had come in a few minutes later and announced that he was going to ride back to town with Wes. He'd seemed edgy. Very different from the man who'd taught her son how to make crispy pancakes with shredded potatoes. And when he'd kissed her goodbye...

She brought her right hand to her lips, a tremor running through her. John's kiss had been brief but unexpectedly potent. It had also been imbued with a possessiveness that had provoked a very confused response from her. She hadn't known whether she'd wanted to succumb to the embrace or struggle against it.

John had lifted his mouth from hers before she'd arrived at the point where she would have had to make a choice. Gazing up into his dark eyes, she'd experienced that same disorienting rush of connection she'd first experienced in the clinic's examining room less than a week before. *Who are you?* she'd almost asked. *And why do I feel as though I know you?*

"Thank you . . . Leigh," he'd told her, his raspy voice a note or two lower than it had been, his inflection of her name exquisitely careful. "For everything."

And then he'd left.

"'He' being . . . J-John," Dee confirmed, beginning to tear the shredded tissues into even tinier pieces.

"Wes didn't believe him?"

"I . . . uh . . ."

"*You* didn't believe him."

Dee's fingers froze. She dipped her head, her throat working. "I s-saw how he looked at you," she muttered. "That day at story hour. And I saw how y-you looked at him."

"Which means you don't believe *me*."

The redhead looked up, her face pale again, her eyes huge and haunted. "I want to, Leigh."

"But if I've been with a man I can't be trusted?"

"I'm s-s-sorry."

"There's nothing to be sorry for," Leigh said, a rush of compassion welling up within her. She'd realized that her assistant had been damaged by what she'd done and had been done to her, of course. But she hadn't until now understood how bad the damage was.

"You hate me, don't you?"

"No, I don't hate you. I could never hate you. I just— Oh, look. What you said earlier. When we were out front. About your thinking that I was, uh, 'good' because I didn't have any... men in my life."

"Y-yeah?"

Leigh hesitated, knowing what needed to be said but uncertain how to say it. Finally, she opted to be as direct as she could.

"I'm a single woman with a son, Dee. I'm an unwed mother. I'm not—" she took a deep breath, asking forgiveness for what was probably going to come out sounding like blasphemy "—the Virgin Mary."

"Having Andy doesn't make you bad."

"But being with a man would?"

Dee flinched as though she'd been struck. "It made me bad."

The assertion seared Leigh like acid, reminding her of the dark desperation that had nearly overwhelmed Suzanne Whitney during the months following her lover's death. She understood what it was like to feel physically soiled and emotionally stained. The birth of an innocent baby—*her* baby—had helped purge her soul of the poisons it had taken on.

But Deirdre Bleeker had no child to hold and hug. No little boy to snuggle up against her and whisper words of unconditional affection. She had... only herself.

No, Leigh thought on a powerful surge of emotion. *She has me, too. For whatever it's worth, she has me, too.*

Pushing herself away from the desk, she took hold of her assistant's narrow shoulders. "Look at me," she ordered sharply.

After a moment, the other woman did.

"You are *not* bad, Dee," she said fiercely. "You can disbelieve everything else I say, but don't disbelieve that. You are *not* bad!"

"You . . . you know what I d-did."

"*Did.* Past tense. Not *are.* Yes, you made some terrible mistakes. Yes, you broke the law. And you paid a price for it. You went to prison. *But you are not bad!* You kicked your drug habit. You earned your GED. You started a brand-new life. A bad person wouldn't do that, Dee! A bad person would just keep on . . . being bad."

"You don't understand!" It was a cry from the heart. "You've never—you *aren't* like m-me, Leigh. I know I s-said you were. But I was wrong. I—I see that n-now. You—you—"

"You don't think I've made mistakes?" Leigh gave the other woman a little shake, desperate to get through to her. "You don't think I've done things I'll regret until the day I die?"

The redhead went very still, her eyes shifting back and forth, back and forth. "Y-you?" she finally whispered, her skepticism a palpable thing.

Leigh bit the inside of her cheek so hard she tasted blood. The coppery tang triggered a sense memory so vile she almost vomited. Choking down the bile that had risen in her throat, she decided what she had to do.

"Yes, me," she quietly affirmed, releasing Dee's shoulders and straightening. She took a step back. "About six years ago, I got involved with a man. He was a criminal."

"You . . . didn't know?" Dee's tone suggested that she was painfully familiar with tales of good girls duped by bad men.

"Oh, I knew, all right. From the very beginning, I knew exactly what he was." Leigh paused, remembering several off-kilter moments when Suzanne Whitney had glanced at Nicholas Marchand and caught a glimpse of a man she hadn't recognized at all yet to whom she'd been powerfully drawn. She'd wondered once or twice whether it hadn't been this man she'd surrendered to, rather than Saint Nick. "I knew what people said he was," she resumed, correcting herself. "But it didn't matter."

"Because you l-loved him?"

"Yes. And because I wanted him. This wasn't some chaste romance. I wanted this man, Dee. This . . . criminal. I wanted the taste of him. The smell of him. The *feel* of him. I knew it was wrong. It went against every rule I'd been taught when I was growing up. Against every standard I'd set for myself. *But it just didn't matter.*"

"Did he love you?"

Leigh closed her eyes. "He . . . never said."

"But he w-wanted you."

"Yes." Oh, God, yes. Saint Nick had wanted her. Or, rather, the woman she'd once been.

"What happened?"

Leigh opened her eyes, meeting the redhead's searching gaze once again. "He died. In a car crash. He was on his way to visit me."

There was a long pause. Then, very quietly, Dee asked, "Was this man Andy's father?"

Leigh wanted to look away but found she couldn't. Tangible as the tilting of a child's teeter-totter, the emotional balance in the room had shifted. Where she'd been strong, she now felt weak. Where Deirdre Blecker had been shattered and unsure, she now appeared calm and capable of offering succor.

"I'm not sure," answered the woman who'd spent seven nights dreaming of a man whose outer scars seemed strangely matched to her own inner wounds. "I'm not . . . sure."

More than that, Leigh McKay couldn't—wouldn't—say. She'd never told anyone what had happened between the end of Suzanne Whitney's final phone conversation with Nicholas Marchand and the arrival at her apartment of the law-enforcement officials who'd informed her of his death. She wasn't sure she ever would.

Dee's expression changed. Leigh saw in her face the same flooding compassion she'd felt earlier.

She knew.

Somehow, some way, Deirdre Blecker knew what had happened to her.

The redhead got to her feet, bits of tissues fluttering to the floor like confetti. She took a step toward Leigh. Then, very awkwardly, as though she were unfamiliar with the mechanics of the gesture, she put her arms around her and gave her a hug.

"It's okay, Leigh," she said in a gentle voice. "It's . . . okay."

Chapter 9

John frowned at the Closed sign hanging inside the front door of Leigh's bookshop, then checked his wristwatch for the second time.

It said 4:45 p.m.

According to the neatly lettered schedule in the window, the store was supposed to be open from 9:00 a.m. to 6:00 p.m., Monday through Saturday.

The lights were off, he observed with a trace of uneasiness. But Leigh's station wagon—the "sort of old" one that Wesley Warren supposedly had fixed as good as new—was parked by the curb.

He glanced at the bouquet of flowers he'd purchased from the florist down the street. He'd gone into the place on impulse, thinking that Leigh might enjoy a bit of spring in the middle of winter. The first thing that had caught his eye was a bunch of blush-pink roses. The sight had jolted him, triggering a host of memories.

"Pretty, aren't they?" the florist had asked, sizing him up in a politely mercantile way.

"Yes, they are," he'd agreed, stroking the velvety outer petals of one of the tightly furled blossoms with the tip of his right index finger.

"Twenty-five a dozen, including a couple of nice sprays of baby's breath and some fresh greenery."

He'd been tempted, but only for a moment. Because, lovely though they'd been, blush-pink rosebuds had seemed inappropriate for the woman Suzanne Whitney had become. Lush cream ones with well-guarded hearts and a few hidden thorns would have been closer to the mark, if they'd been available.

He'd ended up picking out an assortment of flowers. Exactly what he'd bought, he had no idea. He'd simply pointed at items he thought would appeal to Leigh. A couple of those whatever-they-were with the ruffled petals. Three—no, four— of the big blue ones with the purple centers. A couple of bunches of those golden orchidy-looking things. And two of those. And two of these. And a half-dozen sprays of the good-smelling white ones.

The florist had seemed mildly amused about the haphazard selection process but more than a little pleased by the final tab.

John checked his watch again. Something was wrong, he decided. Leigh wouldn't hang up a Closed sign during business hours unless there were. What if she'd taken ill? What if there'd been an emergency involving Andy? What if Deirdre Bleeker—

He froze, his attention riveted on the shop's unlit interior.

Movement! Dammit, yes, there was movement in the back of the store. Someone was inside.

Fisting his left hand, John banged it against the door. "Hello?" he called through the glass. "Hello?"

Nothing.

He banged again, harder. "*Hello?* Anybody in there?"

A moment later several of the shop's overhead lights flickered on. A moment after that, the redhead emerged from the shadows.

She'd been crying. John made that out long before she reached the door. Even viewed through a finger-smudged piece of glass at a distance of eight or nine feet, she looked as though she'd been bawling her eyes out.

She also looked . . . well, not happy exactly. He had a feeling that "happy" hadn't been in Deirdre Bleeker's emotional repertoire for a long time. But there was a hint of softness in her face that he'd never seen before.

Trick of the lighting, he thought as he watched her begin to unlock the door. Or maybe just a trick.

The door opened with a silvery jingle.

"Mr. Gulliver," she greeted him, blotting her nose with a mangled piece of tissue. "H-hi."

Thrown by the comparative cordiality of her tone, John stepped inside and glanced around. Dee shut the door but did not relock it. She also flipped the Closed sign over. The move seemed automatic.

"Are you...all right, Dee?" he asked, following her over to the checkout counter. He was careful not to crowd her.

"Oh, yeah," she said, starting to straighten a stack of bookmarks. Like the move with the Closed sign, the action appeared automatic. "I'm sorry about the door. Leigh and I—"

"Is she here?"

"She's in the back. She'll be out in a minute. She, uh, decided to lock up early because it was a really slow day. But then we, uh, got hooked on this old movie—Leigh has a little TV in her office—and we sort of, uh, lost track of time. It was one of those, uh, ten-hankie deals." She gestured with the bunch of tissues she'd been using. "Or ten hunks of tissue, as the case may be."

Two realizations struck John almost simultaneously. The first was that Deirdre Bleeker had just made a joke. A very weak joke, to be sure. But still a joke. The second realization was that Leigh's assistant was a lousy liar. A *really* lousy liar.

"I . . . see," he said.

"Are those for Leigh?" she asked, indicating the flowers.

"That's right."

"They're beautiful."

"You think?"

"Especially the freesia."

"Excuse me?"

"The little white ones. They smell terrific, you know."

"Yeah." He nodded. "I noticed. Freesia, hmm? The florist said the name when I picked them out. I—uh—thought she'd sneezed."

Dee laughed, just a bit. Then she sniffed and began dabbing at her nose.

"Here." Before he really considered the implications of what he was doing, John plucked a spray of freesia from the bouquet and extended it.

The redhead stiffened, a hint of panic entering her expression. "N-no. I couldn't."

"Please."

"John?"

He had it bad, he thought. The sound of Leigh McKay saying his name made his breath catch and his heart stand still. And he'd only kissed her twice!

He turned.

She'd been crying, too. A lot. Yet there was something in her expression that suggested the tears had been a much-needed catharsis. It suddenly occurred to John that he—or rather, Nicholas Marchand—had never seen Suzanne Whitney weep. Not that he'd wanted to. God, no! But it was another example of the emotional reticence he'd sometimes found so frustrating.

Which had been damnably unfair of him, considering how much he'd held back from her. Like who he really was. What he really did. How he actually felt about her.

"Leigh!" Dee exclaimed, retreating a step. "I was just explaining to Mr., uh, G-Gulliver about the, uh, old movie we were, uh, watching. On your TV. In the back. It was a, uh, real sobfest, huh?"

"A total tearjerker," Leigh smoothly agreed, hooking a lock of pale blond hair back behind her right ear as she came forward. She offered John a gentle smile. Like the one in the photograph Lucy Falco had sent him the day before Thanksgiving, it didn't quite touch her eyes.

Evidently the catharsis hadn't been as cathartic for the employer as it had been for the employee, he reflected with an inward frown. On the other hand, Leigh McKay appeared to be a lot more at ease with prevarication than Deirdre Bleeker was.

At least in this particular instance.

"He brought you flowers."

Another smile. And this one *did* brighten Andy's mother's beautiful sky-blue eyes.

"Thank you," Leigh said, accepting the bouquet. Her fingertips brushed John's as she did so. A hint of color stole up into her cheeks. She lifted the flowers to her nose and inhaled. "Mmm. Freesia."

"I was trying to get Dee to take some," John said after a moment, conscious of a stirring in his groin. He made an awkward gesture with the stem he was still holding.

"I told him I couldn't," Dee said quickly.

"Why not?" Leigh asked.

"You wouldn't...mind?"

"Of course not."

The redhead turned toward John, her expression uncertain. He simply held out the spray. In the same instant she took it, the front door opened with a bright ring-ting-a-ling and a brief burst of wintry air.

"Dee?"

Deirdre flushed, clutching the freesia to the front of her dun-colored sweater. "W-Wes!" she exclaimed, pivoting around.

The mechanic walked forward, his eyes shifting from Dee to John to Leigh and back to Dee again. "Came by about a half hour ago, sign said you were closed," he reported. "Thought maybe there was some kind of problem."

"The ladies were having a private sobfest," John said, noticing the way the other man's gaze kept drifting toward the freesia nestled against Dee's flat chest, then jerking back up to her blotchy face.

"Huh?" Wes demanded, a frown creasing his face.

"Dee and I were watching an old movie, Wes," Leigh elaborated easily. "A classic weepie."

"Which movie was that?"

For a moment John thought Wes was trying to trap the women in their obvious lie. Then he realized that the guy had accepted Leigh's spiel as gospel. The mechanic was interested in the movie's title. Sincerely interested.

Something very weird was going on.

"*Doctor Zhivago*," Dee blurted out.

"*Anna Karenina*," Leigh responded in the same breath.

Wes seemed flummoxed.

"It was a double feature," John interpolated, beginning to wonder whether he might have misread the other man. "Tragic Russian romances."

"Huh." Wes took a moment to absorb this bit of information then looked straight at Dee. "From books?"

"Y-yes," the redhead stammered. "Boris Pasternak and Leo T-Tolstoy."

"In stock?"

"I . . . uh . . . think. We c-c-could . . . look."

"Sounds good."

The two moved off. An obviously odd couple, but strangely in sync.

"You want to tell me the real reason for the waterworks?" John asked in an undertone after a beat or two.

"A . . . misunderstanding."

"About?" He shifted, edging nearer to Leigh. The sweet fragrance of the flowers she was holding tantalized his nostrils. The ear she'd revealed when she'd brushed her hair back looked incredibly tempting to him. He wanted to trace its delicate outer curve with his tongue. To nibble on its dainty lobe with the edge of this teeth.

She raised her eyes to his. Something sparked in their sapphire depths. Racheting up her chin another notch she said, "Dee was upset because you spent Saturday night at my house."

Arousal gave way to anger. *"Wes told her—"*

"No." Leigh laid a restraining hand on his forearm. John shut up. He didn't have much choice. The feel of her fingers— even experienced through several layers of clothing—caused his throat to close up. "Not really. Yesterday morning at church, she overheard some woman talking about having seen Andy and me having dinner with you. And later, Thalia Jenkins's cousin—"

"Edith from housekeeping," John managed as Leigh removed her hand. "And she's Thalia's second cousin. On her mother's side, if I recall correctly."

"You know her?"

"We've spoken on the phone."

"Ah. Well, Edith and Thalia belong to the same fellowship group as Dee and during last night's meeting your name came up in connection with Andy's accident. One thing led to another and Edith apparently mentioned that your room at the inn hadn't been slept in Saturday night."

"And Dee assumed—"

"Exactly. She also ran into Wes this morning at the café."

"Small-town gossips," John muttered acidly, shaking his head. "Man. They could teach the FBI a thing or two about surveillance."

Leigh's face lost much of its color. She took a step back, gathering the bouquet against her as though it were a shield.

What the—? John wondered, recognizing shock when he saw it.

"Leigh?" he asked. "What's wrong?"

"N-nothing." The denial was quick and palpably false. "It's just that— I mean—uh— What an . . . odd thing to say. About the FBI."

"You'd never heard it before?"

"Not exactly." Andy's mother took a deep breath, obviously willing herself to calm down. After a moment she summoned up a slightly crooked smile and said, "Although—now that I consider, it makes a lot of sense. The idea that the residents of small towns would have a certain, uh, expertise in keeping track of people, that is. I mean, they *do* tend to know their neighbors . . . and their neighbors' business."

"Which you'd just as soon they didn't in your case?"

She fingered the bouquet, not meeting his gaze, not bothering to reply.

"Leigh, I'm sorry if my staying over has caused a problem for you."

Her hand stilled. Then she lifted her eyes to meet his once again. The strength he saw in her face reminded him again of how much she'd changed in the five and a half years of their enforced separation. She was so much . . . more . . . than Suzanne Whitney had been.

"It's nothing I can't handle, John," she said steadily. "Besides. You and I know the truth."

The truth . . .

Tell her, his heart commanded.

Not yet, his head countered. *But soon.*

"Yes," he agreed huskily. "I guess we do. Still, if I've stirred up something between you and Dee—"

"It's settled."

John glanced toward the rear of the store. Dee was handing Wes a book.

"I thought I had things settled with Wes," he commented edgily. "About what happened at your house, I mean. Or... didn't happen."

"You did."

"But you said Dee talked to him this morning—"

"He told her you'd told him you'd spent the night on my sofa." Leigh tilted her head, a curious expression coming over her face. "Although why you felt compelled to say anything in the first place..."

"I didn't want him to get the wrong idea."

"Ah."

John expelled a breath on a frustrated hiss, feeling strangely off-balance. "Something about the guy rubs me the wrong way."

"Really?"

What was *that* supposed to mean? he wondered. If he didn't know better, he would think Leigh was enjoying a joke at his expense.

Whoa. Wait a second. Maybe he didn't know better. That Suzanne Whitney would never have dreamed of teasing Nicholas Marchand, he was absolutely certain. But what liberties Leigh McKay might consider taking with John Gulliver...

"Let's forget about Wes, okay?" he suggested abruptly. "Unless you think he didn't believe what he told Dee I told him. Because if that's the case—"

"He wouldn't have repeated it if he'd thought it was a lie."

John raked a hand through his hair, considering the implications of this assertion. "Then Dee's the one who doesn't believe."

"Didn't. Does now. As I said, we pretty much sorted things out."

"Oh."

There was a pause.

"So, John," Leigh finally said, lifting the bouquet to her nose and taking another sniff. "Did you have a reason for stopping by? Aside from bringing me these gorgeous flowers, that is."

Actually, he had.

"I have to fly down to New York tonight," he replied. "A business problem."

"Not something you can take care of via computer while lounging around in your jammies, hmm?"

He chuckled, understanding the reference. "Unfortunately, no. I expect to be back early tomorrow evening, though, and I was wondering if I could talk you and Andy into having dinner with me again."

"Dutch treat?" The suggestion came after a brief hesitation.

"Fine with me," he immediately acquiesced, sensing the pride that underlay the offer. Then he winked. "Or we could stick Andy with the bill. Get him to shell out some of those millions of pennies he has in his savings jar."

Leigh laughed. "Speaking of my son—"

"I know. I know." He'd already anticipated the caveat. "He wouldn't want to go back to a restaurant that serves Bambi au poivre."

"Something like that."

"Is there a pancake house in the vicinity?"

His companion's soft lips twisted. "I don't think so."

"How about the local pizza joint?"

"Been there. Done that."

"No craving for pepperoni, huh?"

"I happen to prefer anchovies and black olives, thank you very much."

John feigned a shudder of disgust. "Now *that* sounds awful."

"How about hamburgers?"

"How about it?"

"There's a place nearby that specializes in overcooked burgers, greasy fries and shakes with less milk in them than artificial coffee creamers."

"It's a date."

* * *

"I'm sorry. I told you the arrangements would take time."

"Time's up," Federal Prisoner No. 00394756 replied, trying to bore a hole in his lawyer's skull with his eyes. "Someone's been messing with what's mine."

"H-how—?"

"My source."

"You . . . spoke directly to your source?"

"You have a problem with that?"

"No. No, of course not, Mr. Stone. It's perfectly understandable. Given that your source is—" the lawyer glanced nervously toward the omnipresent surveillance camera "—I mean—"

"I don't give a damn what you mean. I don't *pay* you to mean. I pay you to do what I tell you."

"I . . . y-yes. Yes. Absolutely."

"When?"

"Another week."

"Too long."

"Maybe . . . maybe six days."

Six days, thought Federal Prisoner No. 00394756 with a slow smile of expectation.

Six days.

In six days he would be on his way to disposing of Suzanne Whitney—that faithless witch!—and reclaiming his only son. Maybe en route he could find Saint Nick Marchand's grave and spit on it.

"Mr. S-Stone?" the Ivy League shyster asked.

"Six days. No more."

Chapter 10

"Is not."

"Is, too!"

"Is *not!*"

"*Is, too!*"

"Hey, chill out, you guys," John commanded, stepping between a glaring, red-faced Andy McKay and an equally bellicose little boy with a roly-poly build and curly black hair. Although he would have preferred to spend the interlude watching Leigh, he'd felt compelled to keep an eye on these two youngsters during the story hour just past. Instinct had told him that they were spoiling for some kind of square-off. When they'd moved away from the refreshment table and headed toward the back of the bookstore, he'd decided to follow—just in case. "What's going on?"

Andy turned, his blue-gray eyes incandescent with indignation. "Bryan says his 'pendix scar is gooder than my head owwie and it's not!"

"Is so!" the aforementioned Bryan insisted, also turning toward John. There was a smear of chocolate on his plump upper lip, a souvenir of the frosted snack cake that John had seen him wolf down in three huge bites. The boy had also packed away four or five peanut-butter cookies and at least two raisin-studded fruit bars. "Wanna see?"

John frowned, not immediately understanding the implications of this artless query. Then he realized that the curly-haired kid had hooked his thumbs into the drawstring waistband of his sweatpants and was preparing to yank them down. A split second later he recalled what Andy had told him about his friend's penchant for showing off the scar on his stomach.

"No!"

"Huh?" Bryan froze in mid-tug. He seemed mildly puzzled by the vehemence with which his offer had been rejected.

"I don't, uh, need to see your appendix scar, uh, Bryan," John said, making a conscious effort to moderate his tone. He glanced toward the front of the store. Leigh was standing by the door, bidding farewell to a pregnant woman and a pair of identically dressed twin girls. Each of the little girls was clutching her very own copy of the book of poems from which Leigh had read at the close of story hour. "I'm sure it's . . . terrific."

"More terrificker than my head owwie?" Andy asked, a whiny edge entering his voice.

John brought his gaze back to the two boys, trying to focus his thoughts. "Not necessarily."

"What's that mean?" Bryan demanded. "Not 'cess-a-sarily?"

Good question, John acknowledged with an inward grimace, struggling to formulate an adequate answer. "It means your scars are different," he elaborated after a moment. "You can't really compare them to each other."

"So—" Andy scrunched up his face "—they can both be terrific?"

"Uh . . . yes. They can both be terrific."

"Only not the *same* terrific, right?"

"Exactly."

Andy and Bryan exchanged looks. John held his breath, uncertain how his improvised reasoning would play with a pair of not-yet-five-year-olds. He released it in a relieved rush when the two little boys started to grin.

"Cool!" Bryan exclaimed, the enthusiasm of his tone making up for his less-than-eloquent choice of adjectives.

"Yeah," Andy concurred with a merry giggle, bobbing his head. The bandage that covered his wound was considerably smaller than the one he'd sported at the previous week's story hour. *"Cool."*

There was a pause. Eventually John bent down and extended his hand to Bryan. "I'm John Gulliver, Bryan," he said.

"I know," the curly-haired youngster replied, allowing his fat little fingers to be engulfed by John's long, lean ones.

"I get to call him John," Andy reported smugly. "Cuz he said I could. *You* have to call him Mr. Gul'ver."

John glanced at his son with a mixture of affection and exasperation. "He can call me John, too, if he'd like."

"Yeah!" Bryan cheered, sticking out his tongue at Andy. Andy promptly reciprocated.

"Guys," John reproved, feeling a bit like a referee. "Come on. I thought you two were supposed to be friends."

"Sometimes."

"Maybe."

"Well, *maybe* you could make this one of those 'sometimes'?"

The little boys traded another pair of glances, considering the proposition.

"'Kay," Andy finally acquiesced, shrugging.

"Yeah," Bryan concurred, twiddling with the drawstring on his sweatpants. "'Kay."

It wasn't quite peace in the Middle East, John reflected wryly, but it was better than a fistfight.

"John?" Bryan queried after a few seconds, cocking his head.

"Yes?"

"Did you get in an ax-ident? Is that why your face has that stuff on the side of it?"

John hesitated, trying to gauge whether the little boy was upset by his appearance. He didn't really seem to be. Still . . .

"Yes, Bryan," he replied after a moment. "I was in an accident. A car crash."

"Did somebody run into you?"

"No. I lost control and hit an embankment." Or so the official police report maintained. He had no memory of what had happened.

"He cried after," Andy contributed. "Even though he was a grown-up. Cuz what happened to him really hurt."

Bryan frowned. "My daddy says only sissies cry."

Again, John hesitated. There'd been a time when he, too, had subscribed to the notion that "real men" didn't weep. He hadn't realized until the episode with the clinic staffer who'd chided Andy for acting like a baby how far away from this attitude he'd moved. But just because he'd come to the conclusion that tears and masculinity weren't mutually exclusive didn't mean he had the right to impose his conviction on another man's son.

"John says it's okay to cry," Andy declared before he'd decided how to respond. "I cried kind of a lot when I got my head owwie, but he still told me I was brave."

"And you were, buddy," John said, finally finding his voice. He was deeply touched by his son's faith in his opinion. And humbled, too. He was accustomed to having people defer to his judgment in professional matters, of course. But this was different. This was from the heart. "You were very brave."

"Well . . . maybe," Bryan conceded.

Andy fixed his pudgy playmate with a inquisitive look. "Did you cry when the doctor sticked that giant needle in your leg to suck out all the pus and keep it from havin' to be chopped off?"

The curly-haired boy screwed up his mouth, the chocolate smear on his upper lip twisting like a caterpiller. "Some," he admitted with palpable reluctance. "But mostly I screamed. And after, my doodoo-head sister Allison said how it was all my fault cuz I didn't leave my cut alone like I was s'posed to. I wanted to sock her."

"Sisters are doodoo heads cuz they're girls," Andy asserted with a disdainful gesture. "That's how come I want a baby brother for Christmas."

"Yeah." Bryan nodded solemnly. "Brothers are much better. 'Cept if they do gucky stuff on you."

"Like poop."

"Or pee."

"Or—" Andy broke off, glancing beyond John. He lifted his hand and waggled his fingers. "Oh, hi, Mommy."

John had already started to turn. Something—a sound, a scent, *something*—had alerted him to Leigh's approach. He was conscious of an acceleration in his pulse. Likewise, of a twinge of uneasiness. How much of his conversation with Andy and Bryan had she overheard?

"Hi, guys," came the pleasant greeting.

"Wanna see my 'pendix scar, Ms. McKay?" Bryan questioned, his hands dropping to his waistband.

Leigh didn't miss a beat. Favoring her son's chubby chum with a serene smile she replied, "I've already seen it, thank you, Bryan."

"John was 'splainin' to us about owwies, Mommy," Andy informed her.

"Really?"

"Uh-huh. How, like, they're not all the same. And you can't com—uh—com-*pare* them. Did you know he cried when he got his?"

Blue eyes shifted toward brown ones, full of questions. John decided it was time to trot out the trusty distract-'em-with-food ploy. It had worked before; perhaps it would work again.

"You know, you two," he said, inclining his head toward the front of the store, "I think I see a couple of leftover chocolate snack cakes on the refreshment table. It'd be a shame to let them go to waste."

Bingo. The touchy issue of injuries suffered and tears shed in the wake of them was instantly abandoned.

Bryan's eyes widened in greedy anticipation. "Can we—?"

"Please, Mommy?" Andy wheedled, looking up at his mother.

Leigh's mouth quirked. "One apiece," she replied, shooing them off with a quick movement of her hands. "Go on."

The two preschoolers raced away.

There was a pause. Blue eyes met brown ones once again. Lord, she was lovely, John thought, his body tightening. Inside as well as out, Leigh McKay was absolutely beautiful. And he wanted her. In his arms. In his bed. *In his life.* He wanted her more than he'd ever wanted anyone.

Including Suzanne Whitney.

"You have quite a knack for dealing with little boys," she finally observed, her voice wry.

"Just borrowing a page from your book."

"Excuse me?"

"The first day I came to visit, when Andy got on the subject of your having a handgun in the house, you distracted him—"

"By suggesting he offer you some refreshments." Leigh colored delicately as she completed the sentence. Whether she was embarrassed by the reminder of her firearm—or by the revelation that her parental manipulations had not gone unnoticed—was impossible to say. Perhaps it was a combination of the two. "Yes. I remember."

"Well, I'm no expert on the younger set," John admitted frankly. Although he was determined to find out more about why his former lover had chosen to arm herself, he knew this wasn't the time to pursue the matter. "I figured I'd go with what I'd seen work. I hope you don't mind."

"Except for having to cope with the effects of a post-snack-cake sugar rush, not at all."

John glanced toward the front of the store, watching his—*their*—son. "Andy's a wonderful boy, Leigh."

"He likes you, too, John. Very much."

The tone of this statement brought his gaze back to her face. That his companion's softly spoken words were sincere, he didn't doubt. But there was a hint of...of...well, it sounded like regret lurking beneath the assertion, as well.

What about Andy's mother? John suddenly found himself wanting to demand. Did *she* like him very much?

He took a deep breath, forcing himself to push those questions aside. This was not the time or place to press. He summoned up what he hoped looked like a casual smile and said, "I had a great time at dinner last night."

Leigh responded to his smile with one of her own. He saw a look of relief shimmer through the depths of her sky-colored eyes. "Me, too."

"Of course, I probably consumed a hundred times the federal government's recommended daily allowance of grease in one sitting."

"I warned you about those fried onion rings."

"True. Although you neglected to mention that I'd still be tasting them twenty-four hours later."

They both laughed.

There was another pause. After a moment or two, Leigh looked away. She licked her lips. John clenched his hands at the sight of her pale pink tongue and the provocative sheen of moisture it left behind.

"Do you want to do it again?" he asked abruptly.

Leigh's gaze slewed back to his. She seemed genuinely startled. Had he harbored a suspicion that the lip-licking routine had been some kind of come-on, it would have died right then.

"Do what again, John?" she asked, flicking a lock of hair away from her face. "Go out for hamburgers?"

Cool down, he ordered himself. "Only if you insist."

"I don't—"

"Dinner," he quickly clarified. "You, me and Andy."

Confusion gave way to caution. And something more. John stiffened.

"What is it, Leigh?" he asked, taking a step closer. "What's wrong?"

"Nothing's wrong," she replied, fiddling with the cuff of the raspberry wool sweater she wore. The color flattered her fair complexion. "It's just that— Well, I know you're planning to stay here 'til Christmas—"

"You *know?*"

"I . . . heard."

Of course. He should have figured. "From Edith in housekeeping, no doubt."

"Indirectly."

Which meant she'd heard it from Dee Bleeker who'd heard it from Edith in housekeeping, he translated. "So?"

"So, you're not always going to be around."

"And?"

Leigh lifted her chin a notch, her beautiful blue eyes darkening with maternal determination. For all the fragility of her features, she looked quite fierce.

"Andy's become very attached to you, John," she said quietly. "I've realized what was happening since day one. But seeing you together last night and today— Well, I'm concerned about how he'll react when you leave."

Again, John wanted to ask about Andy's mother. How attached had *she* become, assuming she would confess to being attached at all? And how would *she* react when—if—he left?

Again, he choked back the queries as inappropriate and ill-timed.

"Maybe I won't," he replied after a few seconds.

"Won't . . . leave?"

He nodded, holding her gaze. "I was telling the truth when I told Andy I could pretty much run my businesses from anywhere there's a phone and an electrical outlet."

"But you *live* in Georgia."

"I have a house I own and occupy, Leigh. It's not the same thing." And it wasn't. He hadn't "lived" anywhere since the day he'd given up his claim on Suzanne Whitney. He'd simply been taking up space.

"Are you saying you might decide to . . . stay . . . around here?"

"How would you feel about that?"

Leigh blushed, raising her hand to the base of her throat. "It's not up to me."

"It could be."

"John—"

"I know. I know." He gestured. "It's been less than two weeks."

"But it feels longer."

She hadn't wanted to say it. He could see the resistance in her eyes. But he could also see that she hadn't been able to hold back the admission.

Tell her, dammit! his head commanded suddenly, switching sides in the battle he'd been waging within himself. *Tell her the truth before this goes any further!*

Don't! his heart contradicted, equally urgent, equally inconsistent. *This is about Leigh McKay and John Gulliver, not Suzanne Whitney and Nicholas Marchand. Leave the past alone . . . at least for now.*

"What about dinner?" he asked after several seconds, returning to the original issue. "The three of us. Tomorrow night. We'll try to find a middle ground between Hamburger Heaven and 'Chez Bambi.'"

Leigh lowered her hand. The hot color in her cheeks receded a little. "I—um—we can't. Andy's going on a sleepover tomorrow night."

John cleared his throat, riveted by the shift in pronouns. He'd been rejected in the collective. Did that mean that there was a chance for an individual acceptance of his invitation? Just he and Leigh together? No Andy?

"A sleepover?" he echoed carefully.

"It's a birthday party for one of his friends from pre-school." Her eyes strayed toward the front of the store. The elegantly sculpted line of her jaw fretted for an instant.

"First time away from home?" he guessed.

She looked at him, her expression holding a mix of vulnerability and ruefulness. "Is it that obvious?"

"Andy will be okay."

"Oh, I'm sure he will. The question is, will *I?*"

John smiled briefly, then succumbed to the temptation to lift his hand and touch her cheek. For one intoxicating instant, she seemed to turn her face into the curve of his palm.

"You'll be more than okay, sweetheart," he said huskily.

The endearment just slipped out. John's breath snagged as he saw Leigh's eyes widen in response to it. "Sweetheart" was what the man he'd pretended to be had called the innocent she'd actually been.

What if—?

He lowered his hand. His companion edged back a few inches. The look on her fine-boned face reminded him of the night Suzanne Whitney had made up her mind to surrender her virginity to Nicholas Marchand.

"Leigh?" he questioned softly, wanting to underscore the identity of the woman he was with.

"Why don't you come over to the house tomorrow night," she responded. "We can have dinner there."

"What do you know about this John Gulliver?" Donatella Pietra asked, stirring the pot of pasta sauce Leigh had left simmering on the back burner while she'd dashed upstairs to freshen her face and fluff her hair.

"Enough." Leigh consulted her watch. It was twenty past seven. John was scheduled to arrive in ten minutes. While she was grateful for the assistance Nonna P. had given her, she really wanted her to go. She was nervous enough without having the older woman hovering around, seeming to second-guess every move she made. Or was contemplating making. Or was contemplating contemplating. "He's been wonderful with Andy and a perfect gentleman with me."

"He stayed with you overnight."

"I've explained about that," Leigh replied, crossing to the refrigerator and opening it. She still needed to make a salad, she reminded herself. Plus some kind of dressing.

"He lives—where?"

Leigh paused in the act of sorting through the contents of the vegetable crisper, her memory skipping back to a fragment of the extraordinary exchange she and John had had in her bookstore less than twenty-four hours ago.

"But you *live* in Georgia," she'd protested, telling herself she must have misunderstood his previous words.

"I have a house I own and occupy, Leigh," he'd responded, the expression in his dark, deep-set eyes hinting at a loneliness she comprehended all too well. "It's not the same thing."

"Are you saying you might decide to...stay...around here?"

"How would you feel about that?"

She'd been shaken. Shocked. She'd felt her cheeks flame. "It's not up to me."

"It could be."

"John—"

"I know. I know." He'd held up his hand, obviously anticipating what she was going to say. "It's been less than two weeks."

"But it feels longer."

But it feels longer.

She hadn't intended to utter those words. Yet, having blurted them out, she'd found she couldn't deny them or the essential truth they contained. At some inexplicable level, her relationship with John Gulliver transcended time. A connection had been forged—*reaffirmed,* she would be tempted to say if she believed in such things—the instant their eyes had met.

"Leigh?" Nonna P. prompted.

Leigh grabbed a head of lettuce, a basket of cherry tomatoes and a cucumber, her hands only marginally more steady than her pulse. "John's staying at the inn on the outskirts of town at least until Christmas," she said, shutting the crisper. Straightening, she closed the refrigerator door and moved over to the sink. "He has a house in north Georgia."

"You'd like it better if he had a house around here."

Leigh set down the vegetables, acutely conscious of Nonna P.'s gaze on her back. Taking a steadying breath, she turned around and looked at her young son's beloved baby-sitter.

"Would it be wrong of me if I did?" she asked simply. It occurred to her that this was the kind of inquiry she would never have dared put to her mother.

The older woman's expression was difficult to decipher. Finally she observed, "You've been alone for a long time."

Leigh thought of the look she'd seen in John's eyes when he'd pointed out that there was a difference between occupying a house and living in it. She also recalled the rush of compassion she'd felt when she'd realized how terribly isolated Dee Bleeker had been as she'd struggled to begin her life anew. Finally, she remembered the sense of peace that had settled over her the first time she'd held her baby son.

"I've had Andy," she answered.

Nonna P. smiled briefly, the curving of her wide mouth illuminating her plain features with a curious kind of beauty. Then the smile faded away, taking the transitory loveliness with it. Donatella Pietra suddenly looked older than her fifty-plus years, and unbearably sad.

"Sometimes children aren't enough," she said.

The emotion in the other woman's voice and face caught Leigh off guard. While Nonna P. had spoken of having been married and widowed, she'd never mentioned having had a child.

"Nonna—" she began, genuinely concerned.

At that point, the front doorbell rang.

"You're a good woman, Leigh," Donatella Pietra said. "And everything I see and hear tells me this John Gulliver is a good man. Maybe more. So go answer the door. I'll put another pinch of oregano in the sauce and leave by the back way."

"One sip."

"Well . . ."

"Try it. You might like it."

Leigh smiled, uncertain whether she was continuing to refuse the Armagnac her dinner guest was offering because she

genuinely didn't want it or because she feared agreeing to drink
would put an end to a very enjoyable coaxing process.

John had handed her the brandy—plus two bottles of imported wine and a lush bouquet of cream-colored roses—when
he'd arrived. She'd experienced a queer flash of déjà vu when
she'd noticed the label on the liqueur. It had taken her a moment to realize that she'd seen the same label on a bottle in
Nicholas Marchand's apartment, nearly six years ago.

"Should I hold my nose?" she teased, remembering Andy's
story about his initial reluctance to taste John's crispy potato
pancake.

"Hold your—" her companion began, then stopped as he
obviously realized what had prompted the joking query. After
a moment he smiled and said, "No, sweetheart. You shouldn't
hold your nose. You'll miss the bouquet if you do."

The endearment sent a quiver streaking through a nervous
system that had been vibrating with a volatile mix of anxiety
and expectation all evening. Leigh shifted her position on the
sofa, her thigh brushing against John's. She exhaled on a shaky
breath, her body suffusing with a sudden rush of warmth.

"All right," she managed after a moment or two. "One sip."

The appearance of a faint flush along the angles of John's
cheekbones made it obvious that he, too, had been affected by
the accidental contact. "One sip," he repeated huskily, bringing the snifter to her mouth and easing it between her lips.

She took a small, cautious drink. Her taste buds tingled at
the Armagnac's potency. Her throat actually burned for an instant. But then a curious transmutation occurred and she found
herself savoring the headily complex flavor that lingered on her
tongue.

"Better than smooshed-up Tater Tots?" The query was
silken.

"Smooshed-up—?" She blinked, placing the absurd reference. "*Oh.* Oh, yes. Definitely better than smooshed-up Tater
Tots. It...mmm...*glows* in your mouth, doesn't it?"

John chuckled deep in his chest. Rotating the snifter, he took
a long, slow drink of the brandy. A split second later Leigh realized that by turning the glass as he had, he'd ended up placing his lips on exactly the same spot from which she'd imbibed

a few moments before. She also realized that John *knew* she'd
realized. . . .

"Glows in your mouth, hmm?" he echoed, the gold flecks
in his dark eyes turning molten with possibilities.

"I don't drink very much," she felt compelled to say.

"So I noticed." John set the snifter aside with great care.
"Only one glass of wine with dinner."

"It was very good, though."

"Thanks." Turning slightly, he reached forward and ran a
caressing fingertip down the curve of her cheek. "I picked it out
myself."

"D-did you?" A tremor ran through her. She struggled
against an urge to let her eyelids flutter closed. "I . . . I didn't
want you to think I didn't d-drink because I didn't . . . like it."

"I didn't."

Leigh swallowed, registering that her right hand had apparently lifted of its own volition and settled against the front of
the flannel shirt John was wearing. She could feel the heat of
his skin through the soft, subtle-plaid fabric. "I don't have
much, uh, tolerance for . . . alcohol."

"You wanted to keep a clear head this evening?"

Her fingers flexed involuntarily at the question. The ripple
and release of the tautly muscled chest beneath the shirt offered immediate testimony to the power her touch had over
him. A clear head? she thought dizzily. How could she keep a
clear head in the presence of a man whose scent affected her like
a narcotic?

"Something . . . like that," she eventually agreed.

John's hand drifted down to stroke the side of her throat,
then eased back through the curtain of her hair and cupped the
nape of her neck. His fingertips caressed the nerve-rich nob at
the top of her spine, sending a sweet flurry of sensation cas-
cading though her. "So you could be sure of what you're doing."

Another flash of déjà vu.

Another disorienting surge of the been-here-before familiarity that had tantalized and tormented her by turns for nearly
two weeks.

"Yes," she whispered, gazing deeply into a pair of eyes that seemed capable of penetrating to the center of her soul. "Y-yes..."

Did John kiss her then or did she kiss him? Leigh wondered about this much, much later. But in the breathlessly beguiling moment when their mouths met, the issue of who'd initiated and who'd acquiesced became irrelevant.

Lips mated.

Breaths merged.

Tongues intertwined, supple and sinuous as lovers.

"Yes," she murmured, tasting the primal flavor of male desire through the sophisticated tang of the Armagnac. An alluring warmth kindled deep within her, radiating outward with a promise of unalloyed bliss. "Oh . . . yes."

The kiss grew hotter. Hungrier. The fingers of the hand that had caressed the back of her neck splayed suddenly, then spasmed in the tumble of her hair. Leigh angled her face, offering a more intimate access to her mouth.

She wanted.

Oh, Lord, *she wanted*.

And she wasn't afraid. At least, not yet.

John lifted her. Shifted her. Settled her firmly on his lap. She moved once, conscious of the bold rise of his arousal. He groaned harshly, his free hand closing hard on her hip.

"Don't..." he implored, raising his mouth from hers for an anguished half-second.

Except for the frantic beating of her heart, she went still. His lips came down again, more insistent than before. She opened to him, welcoming the suggestive intrusion of his tongue once again. This time the flavor she tasted was partly her own.

The kiss went on. And on. Endlessly enticing. Erotically evocative. John ate at the acutely sensitized flesh of her lower lip, the nipping pressure of his teeth exquisitely calibrated. She shuddered, rocked by the most powerful sense of need she'd ever known.

And still, she felt no fear.

Yes, Leigh thought as John's tongue captured hers again and drew it into his mouth. She closed her eyes, yielding up her sweetness with a tremulous sigh of pleasure. Oh, yes. Oh, please . . .

Giving. Taking.

Offering. Receiving.

And wanting. Wanting so much she almost hurt with it.

Leigh's eyes flew open as she felt John surge to his feet, lifting her in his arms and cradling her to his hard chest as he rose.

"Wh-wha—?" she stammered, her sensation-jumbled brain spinning.

"Not here," he said, his voice thick with passion, his breath coming in short, shallow gasps. "Upstairs. In your bed."

John took the steps to the second floor two—maybe three—at a time. Leigh clung to him, her fingers kneading his strong shoulders through the fabric of his shirt. He moved down the hallway to her room at the same precipitous pace, shoving the partially closed door open with one foot and striding into the pale, pristine room that had been both sanctuary and prison to her.

He crossed to her quilt-covered bed and laid her down with infinite care. Then he reached over and flicked on the bedside lamp. She blinked, an instinctive protest rising to her lips. John silenced her before she could utter it by brushing a gentle fingertip against her quivering mouth.

"Just one light, sweetheart," he told her huskily, his dark gaze moving over her in a way that both soothed and stirred. "I need to see you."

She swallowed hard, staring up into his compellingly imperfect face. Slowly, she lifted her hand and traced the outline of the scar on his temple. She regretted its existence not because of how it looked, but because of the suffering it implied.

Andy had said he'd wept because of the pain.

"I need to see you, too," she said in a hushed voice, brushing back a lock of his thick, silver-threaded hair.

With kisses and caresses, John Gulliver divested Leigh McKay of every stitch of clothing she had on. There was nothing hurried about the procedure. Indeed, her lover-to-be seemed inclined to loiter over each newly revealed inch of skin.

"Beautiful," he whispered, brushing the cups of her bra away from her breasts. Her dusky rose nipples were already crinkled into aching peaks. John fondled them gently. Almost reverently. She closed her eyes for a moment, stunned by the potency of what he was making her feel. "So... beautiful.

"Beautiful," he whispered again as he slid down her panties, baring her completely. He stroked her belly, his palm warm
and firm against her skin. Then, slowly, he moved his hand
downward and slipped it between her thighs.

He seemed to know exactly where and how to touch. Leigh
arched up as his passion-slickened fingers slid over the petaled
secrets of her femininity. An inarticulate cry of response
erupted from her throat as pleasure detonated through her intensely primed senses. She'd never... *ever*... felt anything so
glorious.

John stood, undoing his flannel shirt with more speed than
finesse and casting it aside in a single, seamless movement. He
kicked off his shoes. Reaching into his left pants pocket, he
pulled out his wallet. Flipping it open, he extracted several foil-
wrapped packets. He placed them and the wallet on the nightstand. Then he unbuckled his belt and shucked off his trousers.

It was at this point that the woman who'd once been Suzanne Whitney experienced a flash of panic. She levered herself up into a sitting position as atavistic instincts coalesced with
memories she'd done her best to suppress for nearly five and a
half years. For a few shattered seconds, the identity of the man
who seemed to be looming over her didn't matter. All she saw
was the blatant, even brutal, thrust of his arousal. All she
sensed was the threat inherent in his superior size and strength.

And then, miraculously, something inside her began battling back against the fear. At the same time the man whose
identity actually made all the difference in the world spoke her
name on a note of urgent concern.

"Leigh?" John questioned, sitting down on the edge of the
bed. "Sweetheart? What is it?"

She inhaled on a shuddery breath, the darkness receding, its
power over her waning with each passing moment. "Nothing."

"You're trembling," he countered, encircling her with his
arms. Although he gathered her close, the contact was comforting rather than constraining. Leigh knew with absolute
certainty that if she tried to pull away, John Gulliver would
make no effort to hold her against her will.

"I'm all right," she said, breathing in the musk-male scent of his warm, naked flesh. The coarse silk of his chest hair teased against her skin. "Better than . . . all right."

There was a pause. John's embrace altered during the course of it, turning possessive although still not constraining. Leigh shifted languidly, her body starting to thrum. She heard his breathing pattern ruffle and re-form. Then, astonishingly, he asked, "Is it the scars?"

She drew back, her heart skipping a beat. "Wh-what?"

"The scars," he repeated. His eyes flicked back and forth, gauging her expression. "I know they aren't easy to look at. If you'd rather turn out the light—"

"No!" She shook her head, appalled at the idea. "I meant what I said, John. I need to see you tonight. I . . . *want* . . . to see you."

"You were afraid before." It wasn't a question. He *knew*.

"Not of the scars. Not of you." Leigh lifted her hands and cupped his rough-hewn face between her palms, willing him to believe what she was telling him. "Never of you, John."

And then she kissed him. And he kissed her back. First her mouth. Then the line of her throat and the curves of her shoulders. Then he eased her back and down against the mattress, charting the delicate upper swell of her breasts with his ardent, open mouth while his hands slid up to cup the rounded undersides.

"Leigh," he murmured, his breath hot against her skin. "Oh, Leigh."

She was half out of her mind by the time John finally shed his underwear and sheathed himself in one of the condoms he'd taken out of his wallet. He'd brought her to the brink of ecstasy and held her there with single-minded expertise until every fiber of her body seemed to be clamoring for release.

"Please," she moaned. "Oh . . . *please*."

A nudge of his knee parted her thighs. He moved up, positioning himself, then thrust into her yielding body, joining them with a strong, sure stroke. Leigh gasped, clutching at his upper arms.

Bracing himself, John withdrew partway, then thrust forward again. She arched up to meet him this time, the lift of her pelvis a perfect counterpoint to the downward movement of his hips. Her lover groaned deep in his chest, then covered her mouth with his, sealing in her soft cry of pleasure.

It felt right.

Utterly, absolutely right.

It also felt overwhelmingly familiar.

Except at the very end, when rationality gave way to untrammeled sensation. What Leigh experienced as she reached the peak and hurtled off it was beyond anything she'd ever known or imagined.

She might have feared this tumultuous journey into uncharted territory save for one thing.

She didn't make it alone.

She was partnered by the man she loved.

John stirred drowsily shortly after seven the following morning. He was coming awake far more gradually than he normally did. An intensely pleasurable kind of lassitude suffused him, seeming to penetrate to the marrow of his bones.

"Mmm . . ." he breathed.

Eyes still closed, he sought the warmly generous woman who'd granted him readmission to the paradise that he'd thought had been lost to him forever. Three times they'd joined together during the night. But instead of leaving him sated, each ecstatic coupling had whetted his appetite for the next. Even now, with his strength at low ebb, his body was beginning to stir in anticipation. Five and a half years was a lot of lost time to make up for.

"Suz—?" he said in a husky whisper, groping through the tangle of once-crisp sheets.

Recognition of the mistake he'd just made lasted less than a second before being swept away by the inundating realization that he was by himself in Leigh McKay's bed. The woman for whom he was reaching wasn't with him anymore.

Exhaustion fell away in the space of a single heartbeat. He sat bolt upright, his pulse pounding out an unsteady tattoo, his senses attuned for some indication of another person's presence. A moment later he kicked off the sheets and got up.

The clothing he'd discarded so carelessly the night before had been left in a tidy pile on the end of the bed. He yanked on his briefs and pants, then snatched up his flannel shirt, pulling it on as he headed for the door. Despite Leigh's passionate reassurances of the night before, he still felt a stab of uncertainty about exposing his scars to her in broad daylight.

The aroma of freshly brewed coffee reached him at the top of the stairs. He went a little weak in the knees.

His knees damned near buckled a few moments later when he eased open the kitchen door and saw Leigh. She had her back to him and she was clad in the same powder-blue robe she'd had on six mornings ago. The fuzzy cover-up had not lost one whit of its inexplicable allure. Quite the opposite.

She turned, her flaxen hair rippling around her shoulders, her expression warm and welcoming. "John!"

He crossed to her in three swift strides, catching her around the waist and drawing her against him. She melted into the embrace, tilting her head up for a kiss he was more than happy to bestow.

"You taste like heaven," he said when he finally lifted his mouth from hers.

"Heaven comes in peppermint?" she teased, stroking his hair-whorled chest with both hands. Her touch was like a benediction. "I thought it was brandy flavored."

"That depends—" he dipped his head and brushed his lips against the tip of her nose "—on the time of day."

She gave a breathless little laugh, her eyes sparking sapphire blue. "Oh, really?"

"Yes, really," he affirmed.

They kissed again. Slowly. Sweetly. As though they had all the time in the world.

"You wore this blue fuzzy thing to drive me crazy, didn't you?" John accused, nibbling on the lobe of her left ear.

"No." The reply was lush with a very feminine kind of amusement. "I wore it to keep warm."

"*I* would have done that if you'd stayed in bed with me," he countered, undoing the belt that held the robe closed. The garment parted, revealing an enticing flash of creamy pale skin. He slid a hand inside. Leigh trembled when he cupped her breast. The nipple budded against his palm.

"There's a difference between keeping someone warm," she managed after a moment, "and making them . . . hot."

It was undoubtedly the most overtly sexual thing she'd ever said to him. John's physical response was flagrant in its immediacy. His psychological one was more complex.

Suzanne Whitney had never been so bold, he thought, withdrawing his hand as he tried to ignore the pulsing heaviness between his thighs. Then again, Suzanne Whitney had never been afraid of him, either. For all her virginal inhibitions, she had never gazed at him with the fear he'd glimpsed in Leigh McKay's face for a few awful seconds the night before.

He still didn't understand the source of that fear, although he fully intended to ferret it out.

"John?" Leigh asked, the provocation of just moments before yielding to a poignant uncertainty. She'd crossed her hands in front of her, drawing the top of her robe closed once again. He noticed for the first time the blue-gray smudges of weariness beneath her eyes. The radiance of her complexion had disguised the effects of a nearly sleepless night.

It dawned on him then how fundamentally different their perspectives on this morning-after encounter must be. It was more than the usual male-female divergence that typified such situations. For him, last night had been an act of reunion. He was aware of the history they shared. He felt the bond and the burden of their mutual past. Whereas she . . .

"Is that what I do?" he asked, his voice several notes deeper than it had been the last time he'd spoken. "Make you...hot?"

Leigh flushed, her lips trembling, her eyes becoming very, very bright. "Oh, J-John," she said. "You make me...so many things. . . ."

He swept her into his arms again, claiming her mouth with his own. The kiss went on and on, growing deeper and more demanding with each passing heartbeat. His blood thundered in his ears.

Know me, Suzanne, he thought fiercely, trying to obliterate the loss of five and a half years by fusing past to present. *Recognize me.*

It wasn't until the woman he was trying so desperately to reach shoved him away and grabbed for a bread knife that he realized he'd made his supplication aloud.

Chapter 11

Leigh clutched the knife she'd snatched from the counter in a two-handed grip, aiming the point of the serrated blade at the man to whom she'd given herself so freely. So trustingly. She'd envisioned herself constructing a secure and loving future with him. But in the space of five short words, he'd transformed himself into a threat to everything she held dear.

He was standing perhaps a yard away, hands raised, palms facing forward. Although his stance clearly was meant to assure her that he intended no harm, she wasn't deceived. She could see the coiled-spring readiness in his posture. It was evident in the set of his strong back and broad shoulders. Clearer still, in the way he was balanced on the balls of his bare feet.

He was like a predator, poised for a strike. If she faltered for even an instant, he would be on her.

She would fight him if that happened, she vowed. She would battle him to the bitter end. The last time she'd been cornered by someone bigger and stronger, she'd given in. Given up. But never again.

Never, *ever* again.

"What did you call me?" she asked in a voice she didn't recognize as her own.

"Suzanne," the man who'd taken her to bliss and beyond answered evenly. His dark gaze shifted from her face to the knife blade and back to her face. He seemed to be trying to gauge whether she would have the nerve to stab or slash another human being. He apparently came to the conclusion that she would because he stayed where he was. "I called you Suzanne."

"No." She shook her head, denying everything and nothing at the same time.

"Yes."

"Why?"

"Because that's the name I originally knew you by."

"Knew—" her breath seemed to solidify somewhere between her lungs and her lips "—me b-by?"

"Yes."

"You c-couldn't."

"I did."

"I don't know you!" It was a cry of desperation. A last-ditch rejection of the implications of the inexplicable flashes of familiarity she'd been experiencing ever since they'd met.

"Yes, you do." The response was quiet but unequivocal, as though he was aware of what she'd been feeling. As though he'd been inside her brain and under her skin, sharing the sense of déjà vu. "And yes, you did."

Again she shook her head, her unbrushed hair shifting over the nape of her neck. A sudden stir of air against her naked breasts warned her that her robe had gaped open again. She wanted to pull it closed and cover herself but she was afraid to loosen her hold on the knife. Her palms were slick with perspiration. What if she dropped her weapon?

"Wh-who—?" she stammered, tightening her hold on the polished wooden handle.

"I'm John Gulliver, Leigh. I've been John Gulliver all my life. But seven years ago, I went undercover for the Justice Department. For eighteen months, I used the name Nicholas Marchand."

There were no words to describe what the woman who had been born Suzanne Whitney felt during the next few seconds. Indeed, she was never sure she felt anything at all. It was not that there was nothing for her to feel. Rather, there was so much that her capacity to respond to it completely shut down.

"N-n-no," she finally managed to choke out.

"Yes."

"You can't be."

Saint Nick was dead. They'd told her he was. The morning after the night that had taught her the meaning of degradation, grim-faced men flashing official badges had come to her door and told her. *Nicholas Marchand was dead.*

He had to be, she thought numbly. Because in a horrible way, Nick's violent demise had been the cornerstone of her new life. Losing her first lover had freed her to move on, to become Leigh McKay. While she'd never articulated it, she'd always felt a great deal of guilt about this turn of events. It seemed as though part of the price of her second chance had been paid in another person's blood.

"I am," John countered. "I was."

He lowered his hands at this point and took a step toward her. Leigh retreated involuntarily, a frightened gasp breaking from her throat when she realized that she'd backed up against the edge of a counter. She was trapped. She straightened her arms, thrusting forward with the knife, slicing through air. John froze in his tracks, what little color there was left in his scarred face draining away.

"No!" she cried rawly, her fingers spasming. She wondered dizzily if she was losing her mind. Maybe none of this was real. Maybe she was hallucinating. Hearing things. Insanity seemed to make more sense than the idea that the man to whom she'd surrendered her virginity had returned from the grave in the guise of a disfigured stranger who'd found a way to heal her wounded psyche and win her woman's heart. "No."

"Leigh. God. Please." John's expression was anguished. "I'm not going to hurt you."

A bubble of hysterical laughter worked its way up from the center of her chest. *Not going to hurt her?* she echoed mentally. Sweet God in heaven, what did he—whoever he was—think he'd already done?

"Nick's *dead!*" She spat out the words like a curse.

"Nick never existed."

"Never—?"

"It was me, sweetheart. Playing a part."

"You don't look anything like him!" she disputed wildly, flinching from the endearment.

"Plastic surgery. The car crash that supposedly killed Nicholas Marchand damned near killed me. It destroyed my face."

She couldn't contend with the horror this last statement conjured up. She shoved it away. "You don't know—"

"I know everything. Think back, Leigh. *Remember.* The first time you—Suzanne Whitney—saw Nicholas Marchand was in an elevator in the office building where she worked. Neither of them said a word. But Saint Nick sent her roses within the hour. Pale pink, barely opened roses. He sent Suzanne a handwritten note, too. It said the roses made him think of her."

Leigh started to tremble. Anyone could have found out about the bouquet, she reasoned desperately. The florist. The delivery boy. Her office colleagues. But the *note.* Oh, God. She'd never told anyone about the note!

Nick could have, though. He could have boasted about it. Or perhaps the oh-so-intimate line he'd used had been part of some standard seduction routine. She didn't know. She just didn't know!

"Nick was waiting for you—for Suzanne—that evening when she left work. He asked her to have dinner with him. Ordered her, really. She didn't say yes. She didn't say no. She simply said thank you and got into his car."

"Someone...someone could have seen...could have heard..."

"At the restaurant, he talked her into trying caviar as an appetizer. Suzanne didn't like it, but she was too polite to tell him. He ordered lobster for her entrée. That, she did like. Very much. But not as much as she liked the hot chocolate soufflé he persuaded her to have for dessert after she told him she was too full to take another bite."

Leigh recalled the flavor of the sinfully rich treat as though she'd eaten it six minutes—rather than nearly six years—ago. Her mouth flooded with saliva. She swallowed convulsively.

"It was a...public p-place...."

The man she'd taken into her bed and into her body the night before paid no attention to her feeble effort to explain away his knowledge of what had happened between Suzanne Whitney and Nicholas Marchand. He simply continued with his accurate-in-every-detail recitation.

"Nick took Suzanne dancing afterward. Bright lights. Loud music. Lots of people. His turf, not hers. Sometime around one in the morning he drove her home to her apartment. He didn't need to ask the address. He'd had someone pull her personnel file. He escorted her to her door and he kissed her. He knew she'd never been with a man. He could taste it. He could also taste that Suzanne would be willing to make love with him if he pushed her. And that's why he left."

Leigh made an inarticulate sound of protest. Although she tried frantically to keep her hands steady, the knife blade jerked and flashed.

Her throat started to close up. Her chest felt as though it had been lashed with straps of hammered steel. The straps began to tighten. She had to labor to fill her lungs.

"I stayed away as long as I could after that first night." The admission was strained. The expression that accompanied it, stark. "I should have stayed away, period. Getting involved with an innocent like Suzanne Whitney broke every rule in the book. I realized it was wrong. I realized— God help me, I realized it might be dangerous. *But I couldn't help myself.*"

John advanced on her as he spoke, catching her wrists and forcing the knife down between them. Despite her earlier vow to fight to the end, Leigh didn't struggle. His devastatingly sudden shift into the first person had under-cut her resistance in ways she couldn't begin to explain. By the time he'd finished his confession, there were only a few scant inches between them. She could feel the warmth of his body; smell the musky male scent of his skin; see the wild jump of his pulse at the base of his scarred, sinew-corded throat.

Tilting her head back, she stared up into the dark, deep-set eyes of a man she no longer recognized, but whom she nonetheless knew she knew.

Intimately. Absolutely.

In the same way that he knew her.

Nicholas "Saint Nick" Marchand.

John Gulliver.

They were one, she realized, but they were not the same.

Dots of light danced bizarrely across Leigh's field of vision. She felt her body go cold. Then hot. Then cold again. He'd been hurt, she thought suddenly, her blurring gaze fixing on the puckered skin that marred John's left temple. He'd been terribly hurt and in hideous pain, and she hadn't been there to comfort him.

She should have been. She would have been, had she been told the truth.

"Why?" she whispered.

"Because I fell in love with you six years ago." The husky-rough response seemed to reach her across a great and perilous distance. "And I never fell out."

Her heart cartwheeled. She swayed.

Love.

He said he'd fallen in love with her.

But who was *he?*

And who was the "her" with whom he claimed he was still enamored?

She wasn't Suzanne Whitney anymore, she told herself painfully. She was Leigh McKay. Survivor. Businesswoman. Single moth—

A name crashed into her consciousness like a comet, freighted with fear and a ferocious degree of maternal protectiveness.

Andy.

Oh, dear Lord.

Andy.

The dancing dots of light metastasized into great splotches of darkness.

Leigh's fingers went slack. The bread knife fell, clattering against the floor.

A moment later, she fainted.

John caught the only woman he'd ever loved as she sagged against him, then swung her up into his arms. Cursing the slip of the tongue that had unleashed such emotional havoc, he carried her out of the kitchen and into the living room. He laid her down on the sofa.

She was frighteningly pale. Worried about the possibility of shock, he sought for her pulse in the same way he'd sought for their son's on a wintry Monday afternoon less than two weeks ago. The beat-beat-beat he finally found and counted off was rapid but not irregular.

Breathing a prayer of thanks, he brushed Leigh's fair, tangled hair off her brow. Then he set about adjusting her fuzzy blue robe—drawing it closed, retying the belt. His responses throughout were rooted in compassion and concern, not carnality.

The instant she began to stir, he backed away. His deliberate crowding of her in the kitchen notwithstanding, he knew·that Leigh needed space. The encounter to come would be difficult enough without beginning it under the pressure of enforced proximity.

Tensely, he watched Leigh open her eyes. Her delicately veined lids fluttered up reluctantly, revealing eyes that were clouded with confusion. Her gaze wandered aimlessly around the room before finally meeting his.

He saw... nothing.

No hurt.

No hostility.

Certainly no happiness at the resurrection of her lover and the father of her only child.

For a few awful moments, she didn't seem to register his presence at all.

And then, in the space of a single pulsating second, everything changed. Leigh's expression went from unaware to overwhelmed. He could almost see the memories flooding back into her consciousness.

"I'm sorry," he said, forcing the words out of a tight, dry throat.

She blinked several times, levering herself up into a sitting position. Her movements were awkward. "For what?"

Where should he begin? he wondered wretchedly. The list of the mistakes he'd committed and the misjudgments he'd made was lengthy, indeed.

"For all the lies," he finally responded.

Leigh shuddered. She crossed her arms in front of her as though trying to stay warm. "They told me you were dead," she said in a small, shattered voice. "The police. The... men from the FBI. They *t-told* me."

"I know." He hadn't known when they'd told her, of course. But he'd found out later and assented to the conspiracy of silence, so that made him equally culpable.

"They never said anything about John G-Gulliver."

"I know that, too."

"You wanted me to believe—"

"No!" The word exploded out of him. John thrust his injured right hand through his hair, searching for an explanation. "I mean...God! I didn't *want* it, Leigh. But in the end—after the accident—I decided it would be better to let you go on thinking that I was Nicholas Marchand and that he'd been killed."

Her sky-colored eyes filled with tears. Her lips trembled. "Better for whom?"

The tone of the question stunned him. It wasn't accusatory. Rather, it was replete with self-directed guilt. It sounded as though Leigh somehow felt that she was to blame for what had happened.

John's control broke. He crossed to the sofa and sat down, encircling Leigh in his arms. She resisted the contact for a moment, then yielded to it with a gut-wrenching sob.

"Shh." He stroked her, trying to absorb her anguish. Seeing her hurting under any circumstances would have been difficult to bear. Knowing that he was the cause of her pain was unadulterated hell. "Shh, sweetheart."

"You didn't—t-trust me?" Leigh eventually asked, her voice partially muffled by his chest.

His hands stilled. His heart missed a beat. Again, he got the incredible impression that she was blaming herself, not him, for what had gone so terribly wrong five and a half years ago.

"In the beginning, when we—when Nick and Suzanne—met, I didn't trust anybody," he answered, his voice thick with emotion. "Including myself. It's like that, under cover." He paused, remembering the unrelenting pressure of the deception he had practiced for eighteen months. And then he saw a parallel that had never occurred to him before. It was not a pleasant notion to contemplate. He broached it carefully. "It's...probably like that, being in the Witness Security Program, too."

A choky sound and a violent shiver seemed to confirm his assumption. After a few moments Leigh eased back and lifted her face toward his. Her cheeks were wet, her lashes spangled with tears. "Y-yes," she replied with aching vulnerability. "Sometimes."

"Suzanne Whitney was so innocent," he murmured, blotting the fragile skin beneath her eyes with the pads of his thumbs. He knew the observation probably sounded like a non sequitur, but it really wasn't. "So...honest."

"You didn't think she'd—" Leigh inhaled on a hiccupy breath, then cut to the heart of the matter "—lie for Nick Marchand if you told her the truth?"

John hesitated, wondering if she was thinking about the fact that Suzanne Whitney *had* perjured herself on Saint Nick's behalf in the wake of his putative death. A fragment of the pitch Drake Nordling had made in his hospital room came rushing back to him.

She's obviously got feelings for you, the older man had told him. *Or maybe I should say, for Marchand. That comment I made about her being very cooperative doesn't apply to the subject of Saint Nick. About him, she's given us nothing. Nada. According to her, he was a perfect gentleman. A Boy Scout. If she found out...*

"I thought Suzanne might try," he admitted with difficulty, tracking the exquisitely symmetrical shape of her face with his fingertips before lowering his hands. "But I was afraid she wouldn't be able to pull it off. I didn't want to put her at more risk than she already was."

"And after the accident? After the risk was over?"

Again, John hesitated. Then, slowly, he began to relate the events that had prompted him to acquiesce in the fraud that had propelled her out of her old life and into a new one. He did not spare himself as he explained why he'd decided that the love he felt for Suzanne Whitney demanded he free her from the web of deception in which he'd entangled her. Nor did he shy from underscoring the ugly irony that the price of her liberation had been yet another lie.

It was only at the end that he sought to mitigate his actions. Taking a deep breath he concluded, "I had no idea you were pregnant, Leigh. I swear to heaven, I had no idea. Nordling never said a word.''

A queer spasm of emotion contorted Leigh's delicate features. John tightened his hold, fearing she was going to faint again.

But she didn't. Instead, she angled her chin up a notch and asserted with surprising steadiness, ''He didn't know.''

He gaped, feeling like a man who had assumed he was operating on solid ground only to look down and discover there was nothing beneath his feet but air. *''What?''*

''Drake Nordling didn't know I was carrying a baby.'' Leigh's eyes held his for a second or two, then slid away. Her lashes flicked down, veiling an expression he couldn't put a name to. ''I didn't know then, either. I was nearly three months along before I realized.''

John needed a few moments to begin adjusting to the implications of what he'd just heard. When he thought he could trust his voice he asked, ''You told him once you found out?''

''I told the marshal who was handling my relocation. I…had to.''

''Because there was no one else for you to turn to.''

Leigh's gaze came back to his. Once again, her eyes were bright with tears. His heart contracted as he forced himself to confront what it must have been like for her to confess to some hard-faced lawman that she was pregnant by a man she believed had been a criminal. He opened his mouth to beg for her forgiveness. She forestalled him with a question that stole his breath away.

''What about you, John?'' she demanded tremulously, the tears welling up over her lower lids and trickling down her cheeks. ''Who did *you* have to turn to? You nearly died! All those months in the hospital. All those operations. You were…you were *alone*. You were suffering. And I n-never knew. I would have— Oh, God. *If only you'd told me…*''

On the edge of weeping himself, John gathered Leigh against him once again. He caressed and cuddled her, nuzzling her silken hair with his lips and crooning sounds of comfort and caring.

''I love you,'' he said fervently, repeating the words over and over like a mantra. ''I love you so much.''

"J-John," came the sobbing response. "Oh...J-John."

Eventually, Leigh cried herself out. She lay quiescent in his embrace for nearly a minute afterward, her head tucked beneath his chin, her warm breath fanning his skin in unsteady little puffs. He continued to stroke her, trying to communicate the message that she was safe with him and always would be. He would have been happy to hold her next to his heart forever. But when he felt her stir and start to pull away, he made no attempt to restrain her.

"Why now?" she asked throatily, raising her gaze to his. "Why, after five and a half years of letting me think you were d-dead—if you honestly believed letting me go was the b-best thing to do—" She paused, biting her lower lip. Her eyes darted back and forth. "Was it— I mean, d-did you—did you find out about...Andy?"

John thought he understood the anxiety he heard threading through her disjointed inquiry. Leigh plainly feared that his profession of love for her was rooted in a desire to claim his son. Well, he couldn't deny that he yearned to acknowledge his flesh and blood. But he'd come to Vermont for *her* and only her, and he would do whatever it took to convince her of that.

"I 'found out' about Andy when you flung open the door of the examining room and snatched him away from me," he declared.

"Marcy-Anne Gregg hadn't said anything about him?"

"Not a word."

"Mr. Nordling—"

"We don't talk. We haven't talked for a long, long time. I'm out of that life, Leigh. Completely. What you see now is exactly what you get. John Gulliver, independent entrepreneur. Scarred, but not keeping any secrets."

She stiffened at the last word. Again, he thought he understood.

"How did you find me?" she questioned after a second or two, her voice tight.

"Those photographs I told you Marcy-Anne Gregg sent to Lucy Falco and Lucy sent on to me? You were in one of them. I called Marcy-Anne not because she's a valued customer but to find out where it had been taken."

"You hadn't been looking for me...before?"

John lifted his left hand and massaged his temple. His head was beginning to ache. "No," he said honestly. "But I spent part of every single day of the last five and a half years wondering about you. About where you were. What you were doing. Who you were with. Whether you were happy. When I saw you in that picture—"

"It was like seeing a ghost?"

The suggestion shocked him. "No, sweetheart. Oh, no. Never. You were alive for me."

A delicate tinge of color washed through Leigh's milk-pale cheeks. "You've been alive for me, too. My head kept saying you were dead. But sometimes my heart insisted you were still . . . That you couldn't be . . ."

"I understand." He took her hands in his, thinking about the internal battle he'd been waging. Which side had emerged victorious from the fray, he wasn't certain. He wasn't even sure whether what had occurred could be called a victory. "Believe me. I understand."

There was a pause. Finally Leigh withdrew her hands from his and pressed the critical issue by asking, "Why didn't you tell me who you were? If not that first day in the clinic, why not the next one when you came to visit?"

John expelled a weary breath, the ache in his skull escalating to a painful throb. "I came to Vermont to satisfy myself that you were all right, Leigh. That you'd gotten over me. Over . . . *Nick*. I needed to be sure that the new life Nordling and the Justice Department had given you was working out. I swore to myself that I wouldn't make any direct contact. I'd just look. One smile, I thought, and I'd know how you were."

"You think I'm that easy to read?" The anxiety he'd heard before was back in her voice.

"No." His response was quick and unconditional. "But Suzanne Whitney was."

"Oh."

He waited for a moment to see if she would say anything else. When it became clear that she had no intention of doing so, he went on.

"Whether I would've been able to make myself steer clear of you if what happened at the preschool hadn't happened, I don't know. I doubt it. But once the connection was made—once I found out about Andy—everything changed. Still, there was no way I could say what needed to be said that first day. You were too upset to listen. And I was, too...*God!* I don't know what I was. Then the next day when I came to visit, you seemed so damned skittish that I decided I had to back off and give you some time to get to know me.''

"To learn to...trust...you.'' Leigh's inflection was odd. So, too, the expression in her lovely blue eyes.

"Yes,'' he concurred, feeling his mouth twist. "I wanted you to learn to trust me enough to believe me when I confessed to having been a consummate liar.''

She studied him, seeming to ponder the perversity of the desire he'd just expressed. "And then what?''

"And then, I don't know. I can imagine Suzanne Whitney trusting. Believing. Forgiving. But Leigh McKay...''

"I've changed that much in five and a half years?''

Outwardly, no, John reflected. But inwardly, she'd been transformed. He scarcely knew how to define the differences he'd detected; much less how to explain how greatly they'd intensified the attraction he felt for her.

"You don't make me think of pale pink rosebuds anymore,'' he said finally. "You might have been well beyond the age of consent six years ago, but you were still a girl. Now...you're a woman.''

"I'm also a mother.'' There was a hint of challenge in the statement.

"That, too.'' John wondered if he would ever overcome the remorse he felt about the fact that she'd been forced to face maternity alone. He should have been there for her! For their son!

Leigh lifted her chin, her throat working. "About Andy—''

"It's all right,'' he interrupted, pressing a fingertip to her mouth, silencing the fear he was sure she was about to voice. "I'm not going to say anything to him about who I am. I won't...*ever*...say anything to him if that's what you think would be best.''

Her eyes widened with something that looked a lot like shock. John felt as though he'd been kicked in the stomach. Had she actually thought he would blurt out his claim of pa-

ternity in front of their little boy without consulting her? Didn't
she know him better than that?

Perhaps she did, he told himself with pang a second later.
Perhaps Leigh McKay knew him better than he knew himself.
Considering the debacle he'd precipitated in the kitchen, why
should she trust him to guard his tongue around Andy?

Indeed, when all was said and done, *why should she trust
him at all?*

"John."

The soft invocation of his name was accompanied by a tender
touch to his chest. His breath snagged at the contact, reaction
sizzling through his nervous system. Bleak brown eyes collided
with drowningly blue ones.

"What?" he managed.

"I believe you."

"You . . . believe . . . me?"

"I know you'd never hurt Andy."

She meant it. He could see it. Feel it. He waited a moment,
then asked very carefully, "Do you think I'd hurt *you,* Leigh?"

"No." She shook her head as though wanting to underscore
the reply, her fair hair rippling about her face. "Not . . .
intentionally."

Given all that had happened, John recognized that this was
a greater expression of faith than he had any right to expect.
But it was much, much less than he wanted. Still, the secret of
their shared past was finally out. And while Leigh had retreated from him because of it, she hadn't turned away. There
was hope for the future. There *had* to be!

Had she accepted what he'd told her about his stint as Nicholas Marchand? he asked himself. Did she have confidence in
his account of his conversation with Drake Nordling? Or did
she require more than his word about who had said what and
why?

If she did, he knew a way to give it to her. And even if she
didn't . . .

"Can you reach the marshal who's in charge of your case?"
he asked abruptly, coming to a decision.

Leigh blinked, clearly taken aback. "I . . . have a number for
him."

"Call it. Have him contact Drake Nordling and tell him to phone you here."

"Why?"

"Tell him to tell the deputy director you've got some questions about John Gulliver."

Nordling's call came through roughly thirty minutes after Leigh spoke with her relocation inspector. In the interim, she retreated upstairs to get dressed. She returned to the first floor carrying John's shoes, socks and wallet. He accepted the items with a quiet word of thanks.

They were sitting in the kitchen sipping Armagnac-laced tea and carrying on a very cautious conversation when the phone on the wall next to the refrigerator began to shrill. John waited to be certain that it was Nordling on the other end, then left the room.

How long Leigh talked with his former boss, he never knew. There were some situations in which the traditional methods of measuring time—seconds, minutes, hours—had no application. This was one of them.

His memory of what he did while he waited for the conversation to come to an end was equally uncertain. When awareness kicked back in, he found himself standing next to one of the living-room windows, staring out at Leigh's snow-covered front lawn. The amount of condensation on the inside of the glass indicated that he'd been keeping watch for quite a while.

Instinct told him to turn, and he did. Leigh was standing a few feet away. Whether she'd spoken to him to alert him to her presence, he couldn't say. But he'd definitely felt her approach.

He scoured her fine-boned features with his gaze. Her face was pale and her eyes were puffy from the weeping she'd done, but she seemed fully in control of herself. He marveled again at the strength she'd acquired during the past five and a half years. He also reaffirmed his belief that Andy McKay had been blessed with a remarkable mother.

"Are you all right?" he asked.

"Yes," Leigh answered steadily, closing most of the distance between them. Then, to his utter astonishment, she lifted her right hand and caressed the scarring on his temple and neck.

Although her touch was more soothing than sensual, it made his head start to spin.

"Leigh—"

Her fingers stoppered his lips. "Deputy Director Nordling's still on the line," she told him. "He wants to talk to you."

"I didn't know she was pregnant," Nordling said, the moment John picked up. "Not that day in the hospital."

John grimaced. There was no guilt in the other man's tone. He simply wanted to set the record straight. "So Leigh told me."

"You believe her?"

"Yes. Lucky for you."

"Is that a threat, Gulliver?"

"An observation."

There was a pause.

"She says you traced her through a photograph," Nordling eventually prompted.

"That's right."

"A snapshot some client of this travel agency of yours happened to take."

"Right again."

"So your finding her was purely a matter of chance."

"More like a miracle, Nordling, but I don't expect you to understand that."

Another pause.

"I warned her this was ill-advised."

"You mean you pushed for another relocation," John translated, his fingers tightening on the receiver. He shifted his position without really thinking about what he was doing, balancing his weight, instinctively readying himself to absorb a blow. "Another identity."

"I recommended it, yes."

"And?"

Nothing.

"And?"

"And she said no. She said . . . she trusted you."

John's knees nearly gave way. He sagged heavily against the side of the refrigerator. She trusted him! She'd told the son of a bitch she trusted him!

There was a third pause. It was longer than the previous two. Nordling finally ended it with an announcement that there was something he needed to know.

"Ask," John responded, bracing himself again. A change in the other man's voice had warned him that whatever was coming was the real reason he'd been summoned to the phone.

"Did you ever make a run at any of the department's data banks?"

"What?"

"I know you turned yourself into some kind of computer whiz while you were in the hospital. I also know you poked your nose into a lot of places it wasn't supposed to be while you were doing it."

John stayed silent. Cyberspace had become a refuge for him during his long and arduous recovery. A keyboard didn't care whether the hands that operated it were whole or maimed. A monitor didn't give a damn that the face reflected in it was badly scarred.

"I don't care about that," Nordling continued. "All I want to know is whether you've tried to hack into the system looking for information on Suzanne Whitney or any other individual in the Witness Security Program."

"No."

"Not once?"

"I've done some digging recently you could prosecute me for, but I've never gone near anything having to do with the witness program."

Nordling muttered something unintelligible.

"Has somebody gotten into the files?" John questioned.

"We ... don't know."

"Don't know or won't tell a civilian?"

"There were indications of an unauthorized entrance on an old password about three years ago."

John clenched and unclenched his free hand, thinking about Dee Bleeker and Wesley Warren. Their lives had first intersected with Leigh's within the time frame Nordling had just mentioned. Coincidence? Or something more sinister?

After a few seconds he asked, "Did there seem to be a specific target?"

"No. We're not even certain anybody did anything wrong. It could have been a systemic glitch. God knows, we've had enough of them."

"Any repercussions?"

"There was an incident with one protected witness, but he'd violated security guidelines so frequently he was basically walking around with a bull's-eye on his back."

"What did you do?"

"Cleaned up the mess."

John grimaced with distaste. "About the computer situation."

"Oh. That." The other man cleared his throat. "We brought in a specialist. He said the system was secure."

"Any problems since?"

"Nothing."

"*Nothing* nothing or the kind of 'nothing' you try to feed to Congress when you trot up to the Hill to testify?"

"Nothing, none of your business. You resigned, remember?" It was a retreat to the official line, a signal that Drake Nordling had gone as far as he was going to go. If truth be told, he'd gone a hell of a lot further than John would have predicted. Maybe he felt a little bit guilty, after all. "Leigh McKay and her son remain under the protection of the U.S. government. We don't intend to allow anything to happen to either one of them."

"Glad to hear it," John riposted in the same razor-rasp tone he'd used on Wes Warren during their encounter outside Leigh's home less than one week ago. "Because neither do I." Then he broke the connection.

He returned to the living room a minute or so later. Leigh had taken up his post by the window. She turned when he entered, her expression uncertain.

"I don't think I'm going to be asked to go back on the Justice Department's payroll anytime soon," he commented softly.

She gave him a crooked smile. "Were you hoping to be?"

"No." He crossed to her. They stood for several wordless seconds, staring deeply into each other's eyes. It seemed to him that the air began to vibrate.

Gently, he slid his arms around Leigh's slender waist. She stiffened slightly but didn't pull back. More gently still, he drew her to him. After giving her every chance to rebuff him, he dipped his head and brushed her lips with his own. She opened to him on a shaky sigh, her breath blending with his. The taste of peppermint teased his tongue.

"John . . ." she murmured.

The kiss deepened by mutual accord, building in intensity by honeyed, heated increments. They were both trembling when it finally came to an end.

"I want a chance with you and Andy, sweetheart," John confessed huskily as he lifted his mouth from hers. His body was throbbing with arousal but he warned himself against pressing for assuagement. "To make a family. A future. You know that, don't you?"

Leigh gazed up at him, her face soft with emotion, yet strangely shuttered. "Yes," she acknowledged after a moment or two.

"What do *you* want?"

Something flickered in the depths of her sapphire eyes. The muscles of John's belly clenched in a sudden pang of fear. What if what she wanted was for him to go?

Then he would, he told himself. Last time, *he'd* decided what was "best" for the woman he loved. This time, the choice had to be hers.

"Leigh?" he asked, willing his voice to remain steady. It was strange, he reflected fleetingly, how the name "Suzanne" no longer rose to his tongue.

"I want some time, John," came the quiet response. "The last five and a half years of my life have been predicated on lies. Lies about me. Lies about you. Lies about what we had together. I need time to face up to that. I need time to come to terms with the truth about the past. *Our* past. Or maybe I should say, Suzanne and Saint Nick's past. I don't know. That's part of what I have to get straight in my head. Because until I do that, I can't think about the future."

"Our . . . future?"

"Any future."

He inclined his head. "What can I do?"

"Leave me alone."

It hurt like hell, but he did.

"I didn't know you were going to *kill* them!"

Anthony Stone looked from the corpses of two U.S. marshals to the panicked face of the Justice Department computer expert who'd finessed his release from captivity. The same computer expert who'd hacked into government files to locate Suzanne Whitney for him and discovered she'd borne a son. *His* son.

"Of course, you did," he responded, showing his teeth. "You just didn't want to admit it to yourself."

"No!"

"Yes." Anthony Stone snagged the man's tie and yanked him off-balance. The synthetic feel of the tie's fabric offended his fingers. It should have been silk, he thought with contempt, given the amount of money he'd paid out.

"Please—"

"You probably don't want to admit you know I'm going to kill you, either." A second yank of the cheap tie. The man started to choke. And struggle. "Do you?"

Of course, he didn't.

But he died anyway.

Suzanne Whitney was going to die, too, former Federal Prisoner No. 00394756 told himself, staightening his cuffs and smoothing his hair. But before she did, she would admit to knowing what was about to happen to her . . . and why.

Chapter 12

Leigh brought her station wagon to a halt in front of Andy's preschool. Two weeks, she thought. It had been just *two weeks* since John Gulliver had entered—reentered, to be more accurate—her life.

It seemed longer. Much, much longer.

It seemed much longer than forty-eight hours since she'd asked John Gulliver to leave her alone, too. More like forty-eight years. Unfortunately, she was still struggling with the questions that had compelled her to make her heartfelt plea for solitude.

Leigh gripped the steering wheel and closed her eyes.

To tell or not to tell. That was the first question.

The second question revolved around how to deal with the consequences of her answer to the first. Because there would be consequences, whichever option she chose.

Consequences for the woman who'd been born Suzanne Whitney.

Consequences for the man who'd once claimed to be Saint Nick Marchand.

And consequences for Andy, who might or might not be—

"Mommy?"

Leigh opened her eyes with a start. Disciplining her expression, she turned toward her son. "What is it, sweetie?"

"Are you not feelin' good?"

"Not feeling—?" she echoed blankly, then shook her head. A moment later she wondered whether she'd fallen prey to the vagaries of preschool syntax and inadvertently confirmed her little boy's obvious concern. Summoning up a smile she said, "I'm just fine."

"Really?"

Her memory flashed back to the core of the conversation that had been resonating within her for nine days.

You telled *me to always tell the truth*, her son had reminded her.

And you always should, Andy, the man who believed himself to be her son's father had concurred. *But you have to be careful how you tell it . . . and to whom*.

"Yes, really," she replied.

Andy studied her for another few seconds, his lower lip jutting ominously. Then he dropped his gaze and began yanking at the buckle of his seat belt as though he couldn't wait to get away from her. Leigh felt a scalding surge of remorse, knowing she'd just been branded a liar.

"Andy—" she began unhappily, placing her hand on her little boy's snow-jacketed left shoulder.

He shrugged off her touch with an angry grunt, then raised his expressive eyes to meet hers once again. As he did, she caught a glimpse of the man he would one day become lurking beneath the soft contours of his unfledged features. If there was a clue to his paternity in what she saw, she couldn't decipher it. For good or ill, Andy remained uniquely himself.

"If you're fine, how come you cried last night?" he demanded, his treble voice vacillating between injury and accusation as the momentary illusion of maturity faded. "And don't pretend like you didn't, cuz you did. I heard you, Mommy. I got up cuz I didn't want to wet my bed again and I *heard* you. I was gonna come in and ask you what was the matter, only I got a-scared so I goed back to my room and put my fingers in my ears."

Oh, dear God, Leigh thought, appalled. She'd spent most of the weekend trying to recover from the tumult triggered within

her by John Gulliver's revelations about their shared past.
Stressed to the snapping point by the effort required to disguise her feelings in front of her son, she'd finally broken down
late Sunday night in what she'd thought was the privacy of her
bedroom. She'd never dreamed that Andy would be up and
about . . . and listening at the door.

"Did I do somethin' bad that maked you cry?"

"Oh, h-honey," she responded shakily. "Oh, Andy. No. *No.*
You didn't do anything bad."

But she had. Or so she'd believed in the darkest corner of her
soul for the past five and a half years. And the thought of con-
fessing her shame terrified her.

I love you, John had said to her over and over again Saturday morning. *I love you so much.*

And she loved him in return, although the burden of her
guilty secret had kept her from saying so. But how much would
her love count for if she admitted the truth about what had
happened the night Nicholas Marchand supposedly had been
killed? Would John still want that "chance" of which he'd
spoken so feelingly Saturday morning if he learned that the
child she'd borne might not be his?

"Did *John* do something bad?" Andy pursued with devastating single-mindedness.

Leigh bit her lip as her pulse performed an erratic hop-skip-
jump in reaction to this forthright inquiry.

Andy was aware that John had come to their home for dinner Friday night. The discovery had upset him at first, sparking a lot of indignant questions about why he'd been excluded
from the fun. He'd calmed down once she'd pointed out to him
that he'd had a previous engagement—specifically, attending
his first-ever sleepover birthday party.

Unfortunately, the restoration of tranquillity had been short-
lived. Andy had soon begun pestering her to let him phone his
grown-up buddy so he could tell him all about his exciting
overnight adventures. She'd fobbed him off as best she could,
hoping that he would lose interest in the idea. He hadn't. He'd
even repeated his request as he'd been getting ready for school
this morning.

"Did he, Mommy?" Andy pressed, clearly upset by the possibility. "Is that how come you telled me I couldn't call him up?"

Leigh drew a slow, steadying breath and met her son's distressed gaze. "No, honey," she answered. "John didn't do anying bad. The reason I said we had to wait to call him was that he told me Friday night he was going to be very, very busy with his work all weekend."

"Then why did you *cry?*"

They were back to square one.

"Sometimes mommies get sad, Andy," she hedged after a few moments, selecting her words with care. For once in her life, she regretted her son's perceptiveness. "It's not because anybody's done anything bad to them or because they're feeling sick. They just get in a blue mood and they cry. That's what happened to me last night. I'm sorry you heard. I'm sorry it scared you. And I'm especially sorry you went back to bed and put your fingers in your ears instead of coming in and talking to me."

Andy gnawed on his lower lip for several seconds, then asked very tentatively, "It would have been okay? My comin' in?"

"Yes."

"Really? Truly?"

"Really, truly."

There was more lower-lip chewing. Then finally, very quietly, he said, "I didn't want you to cry."

"I know that, sweetie," she responded, deeply touched by his compassion. "I didn't want to cry, either. But like I said—"

"Mommies get in blue moods."

"Exactly."

There was a long silence. The atmosphere in the car eased, at least on Andy's side. Finally he inquired, "Do mommies get in moods cuz they're . . . girls?"

Leigh caught a faint shimmer of mischief in her son's wide eyes as he uttered the final word of this inquiry. She said a swift prayer of thanks for the resilience of his innocent spirit.

"No, wiseguy," she retorted, reaching over and tweaking his lightly freckled nose. "It's not because they're *girls.*"

"Ladies, then."

"It's not because of that, either. Daddies get—" She broke off abruptly, wishing desperately that she could recall her last two words. Raising the subject of fathers with her son was not something she wanted to do.

"Daddies get in blue moods, too?" Andy sounded intrigued by the idea. "You mean, like, when Bryan's daddy makes his eyes go all buggy and yells dammit, dammit, dammit at the TV news?"

"Something like that," Leigh agreed with an awkward laugh. "Although going bug-eyed and yelling 'dammit' at the TV news sounds more like a *bad* mood than a blue one."

Andy mulled this over as he fiddled with the buckle on his seat belt. "Do you think John gets in moods?"

She caught her breath, trying not to remember the remarkable panoply of emotions that John Gulliver had revealed to her Friday night and Saturday morning. He'd been so open. While she— Lord! She could scarcely bear to contemplate what she'd been.

What she still was.

What she might be for the rest of her life unless she did something about it.

"You telled *me to always tell the truth."*

"And you always should, Andy. But you have to be careful how you tell it . . . and to whom."

"I think everybody gets in moods, honey."

"He's not a daddy, you know."

"H-he . . . told you that?"

"Uh-huh." Andy gave an emphatic nod. "At the doctor's office after I got my head owwie fixed. I asked him if he was and he said no. He's not married, either." The seat-belt buckle clicked open. "Do you think John likes me?"

Don't cry, Leigh ordered herself fiercely, blinking against the sudden sting of incipient tears. "Yes, Andy," she said. "I think he likes you very much."

Andy beamed at her. "I think so, too. And I like him back. A whole lot. And you know somethin'? I think maybe John wants to—"

A rapid knock-knock-knock on the driver's-side window interrupted his line of speculation. Leigh turned, her heart beating double time. Thalia Jenkins was standing outside the car.

"Time for class!" the older woman said, pointing toward the small brick building that housed the preschool.

"Yipes!" Andy exclaimed, shifting out of the reflective "gear" without missing a beat. Shrugging off his safety harness, he reached for the door handle. He was obviously eager to be off to join his classmates.

"Kiss?" Leigh's need for the comfort of their morning ritual seemed more acute than it had ever been.

To her everlasting surprise, her little boy flung himself into her arms and pressed his mouth against her cheek with a noisy smack. "I almost forgetted to tell you, Mommy," he confided, a giggle fizzing out of him. "I counted on the 'frigerator calendar again. And guess what? Only ten more days—"

"'Til Christmas. You mean you're planning to stay in Vermont indefinitely?"

"I don't know that 'indefinitely' is the correct word, Ms. Falco," the owner of Gulliver's Travels returned, massaging the nape of his neck. His temples throbbed with the residual effects of the headache that had erupted inside his skull following his departure from Leigh's home on Saturday morning. There was a part of him that thought he'd deserved the pain. Or worse. "And if I'm following a plan, I'm not aware of it. But to answer your question—no. I won't be back in Georgia for Christmas."

A dramatic pseudosigh greeted this statement. "There goes my brilliant scheme for persuading you to come to the agency's fabulously famous holiday party."

"I didn't realize Gulliver's Travels had a holiday party." If truth be told, he'd never thought to inquire about the possibility. It had been a long time since holidays had held any special significance for him.

He *had* nurtured a small, secret hope that he and Leigh and their son would celebrate the coming Christmas season as a family. But now—

It will happen, he told himself. *It has to. Just give Leigh the time she needs.*

"Oh, yes," Lucy affirmed breezily. "Everybody in the office is chipping in. It's going to be an annual thing."

"Going to be?"

"This is the first year we're having it."

"But the party's already—ah—'fabulously famous'?"

"It could have been if you'd agreed to show up. It would've been the equivalent of, mmm, Charlie paying a personal visit to the Angels."

"Excuse . . . me?"

"'Charlie's Angels.' You know. The old TV show with Farrah Fawcett, Kate Jackson and Jacqueline Smith? They played policewomen turned bikini-wearing private detectives who worked for this mysterious millionaire playboy named—"

"Charlie."

"Exactly."

"I'm sorry to disappoint you, Ms. Falco." And John genuinely was, which knocked him even more off-balance than he already was. Because as unpleasant as it was to contemplate, he recognized that it had been years since he'd cared about other people's judgments of him.

Except Leigh's.

And Andy's.

She'd said that she trusted him, he thought, clinging to the memory like a talisman. She'd admitted as much to Drake Nordling. She'd also said that she didn't believe he would hurt her or their son. At least . . . not intentionally.

What Leigh hadn't said was that she loved him. Although he'd confessed his own feelings repeatedly, she hadn't given him the words he wanted more than anything to hear.

She *had* given him her body. Overcoming a fear he still didn't understand the source of, she'd yielded to him at the most intimate level. If she'd held anything back at the crest of their mutual ecstasy, he hadn't been able to sense it.

But that had been before, he acknowledged grimly, his gut knotting. *Before* he'd told her the truth about who he was and what he'd once been. *Before* he'd peeled back the layers of deception that had shaped their relationship. Would Leigh McKay have surrendered herself to him with such heart-stopping generosity if she'd known—

"Not to worry," Lucy responded to his previous remark, her tone hinting that she'd had a fair amount of experience with disappointment. "Maybe next year."

John expelled a sigh. "Maybe."

There was a long pause. Then, in a voice shorn of its usual sassiness, the officer manager of Gulliver's Travels asked, "Did you find the woman in the photograph?"

He didn't bother to deny Lucy's assumption or to question how she'd come to make it. There wasn't much point. "Yes," he said simply.

"Problems?"

"It's a long story."

"Mmm."

There was another pause. Although John Gulliver knew himself to be an expert at manipulating the pressures inherent in certain kinds of silences, he found this particular conversational break extremely difficult to bear.

"Ms. Falco—" he finally began, intending to plead the press of other business and hang up.

"Look," the woman on the other end of the line interrupted simultaneously. "I realize I'm hardly qualified to give personal advice in this situation. My one and only marriage broke up after less than a year, for heaven's sake! But... well, if there *are* problems between you and this Leigh woman Marcy-Anne Gregg says is so wonderful, I admire you for sticking around and trying to solve them. It's a lot better than turning your back and running away."

"Is that what you did?" The question slipped out of its own accord.

A shaky little laugh jittered through the line. "That's a long story, too."

"I... see."

There was a third pause. Then, carefully, Lucy asked, "Is there anything I can do for you, Mr. Gulliver?"

The man who had once lived under the name Nicholas Marchand glanced at his wristwatch, calculating how long it had been since he'd left the woman he loved. Fifty hours and counting. It seemed longer. Much, much longer.

"Call me John, Lucy," he responded. "And forget about having the agency staff chip in to pay for the first annual 'fabulously famous' Gulliver's Travels holiday party. Send the bill to me."

* * *

"It's time to reorder that self-help book for people who are addicted to self-help books."

Leigh straightened with a jerk, nearly spilling a mug of long-gone-cold tea across the invoices she'd been pretending to review for the last half-hour. The documents could have been printed in hieroglyphics, for all the sense she'd made of them.

"Wh-what?" she stammered, looking up at her assistant.

"*Too Much Help Can Hurt You.* We need to reorder it as soon as possible. I just sold another copy. And I sold five on Saturday. I think the author went on 'Oprah Winfrey' last week and told people it would be the perfect Christmas present for people whose problem is thinking they have problems."

Leigh smoothed her hair back from her face. Her hands were shaking. "All right. I'll take care of it."

She looked around, trying to find a pen. Although her need for a writing implement was genuine, she recognized that her hunt was really prompted by a desire to evade Dee's gaze. She knew that the redhead had picked up on her turbulent mood as soon as she'd walked into the shop. So far, nothing had been said. She suspected her assistant was waiting for an opening. She did not intend to give her one if she could avoid it.

"Five copies on Saturday, you said?" she asked, continuing to shuffle papers.

"Uh-huh."

"Things must have been very busy."

"Not bad."

Leigh located a fine-point felt marker. She used it to scribble down the title Dee had mentioned, grimacing inwardly as she did so. She stalled for a few seconds more, then raised her eyes to her assistant's once again.

"I'm sorry I left you in the lurch," Leigh apologized, referring to the fact that Dee had ended up running the store all by herself on Saturday. In the aftermath of what had happened with John, she'd felt incapable of coping with with customers.

"That's my job." A shrug punctuated the demurral. "I'm glad I could help."

"You definitely did that."

There was an awkward pause in the conversation. Dee leaned against the edge of the desk and began fiddling with the hem of the moss-green sweater she had on. Although the garment was far too large for her, its richly verdant color complemented her pale complexion and flaming tresses. It was the most flattering thing Leigh had ever seen her wear.

"You're missing your program again," the younger woman said suddenly.

"My...program?"

Dee nodded at the TV on the corner of Leigh's paper-strewn desk. The flowers John had brought the previous week were arranged in a plain glass vase placed next to the set. Although the blossoms were a bit past their prime, they still exuded a luxuriously sweet perfume.

"Your favorite soap opera," Dee clarified. "It's on, but you're not watching it."

"Oh. That. I...guess I forgot."

"Or maybe you're not in the mood for evil twins and amnesiac brides, huh?"

Leigh manufactured a smile. It felt even phonier than the one she'd tried to use on Andy outside his preschool. "Not really, no."

The redhead studied her without speaking for several seconds, then quietly asked, "Do you want to talk about it?"

The phony smile fizzled. Leigh struggled to replace it with something more persuasive. "About what? My loss of interest in daytime drama?"

"Leigh."

The invocation of her name was a reproach. The expression that accompanied it revealed a great deal of hurt. Leigh bit her lower lip and averted her gaze.

"It's John Gulliver, isn't it?"

Leigh went rigid, her eyes slewing back to her assistant. She shifted onto the offensive before she fully realized what she was doing. "Look, I know you don't like him—"

"Actually," Dee interrupted, flushing, "I've kind of rethought that."

"You...have?"

"I still have the feeling he's got 'cop' in his background someplace." The redhead squirmed. "The funny thing is—well, not *funny,* ha-ha. Funny, kind of weird. Wes had just the opposite impression of him."

The opposite impression? What was that supposed to mean? "I don't understand."

"The first time Wes saw him was here, in the bookstore. It was two weeks ago. I, uh, told you—"

"I remember. It was the day Andy was hurt."

"Right. Well, he—Wes—took one look and figured John Gulliver for some kind of lowlife. He basically pegged him as a blast from my—" the redhead pulled a face "—nasty past."

Leigh said nothing. She wasn't certain she could.

"Wes knows about what I used to do," Dee continued doggedly. "I haven't exactly tried to keep it a secret. Not that I think I could have, given the way folks around this town talk."

"You've been . . . very honest." Although the sentiment was sincere, it was a struggle to get the words out.

The younger woman plucked at the bottom of her sweater again. "Self-defense," she confessed. "At least at first. I mean, I basically decided to get in people's faces with the bad stuff before they had the chance to stab me in the back with it."

"That doesn't make what you did any less honest."

"I . . . guess." She grimaced. "Wes and I—we're not *involved*, Leigh. I don't think I'm ready for that. But, like, we kind of started talking last Monday. Maybe you remember? Wes stuck around last Monday after he bought *Doctor Zhivago* and *Anna Karenina*. And, well . . . the bottom line for right now is that he knows. About me. About my . . . record. He doesn't like it, but he told me he admires the way I've been trying to turn everything around."

"He should."

Dee's face flamed anew. "I don't—I mean, that's not— Oh, never mind me and Wes, okay? To get back to my point about John Gulliver. I'm not going to say I've decided he's Mr. Warm-and-Fuzzy or anything like that, because I haven't. Frankly, the man intimidates the heck out of me. But I've seen how he is with you and Andy. And I've seen how you are with him. I'm not talking about that screwed up stuff I said to you last week. You and he . . . Well . . . you *care* about him, right?"

Leigh swallowed hard. "Yes, Dee," she admitted after a few moments, her heart beginning to thud. "I care about him. I care about him very much."

"You haven't told him about that other guy, though, have you? The one who was the, uh, criminal."

She didn't have to tell him, Leigh thought, choking back a wild little laugh. He'd *been* that other guy!

"It's a...complicated...situation, Dee," she responded, the adjective snagging briefly in her throat.

"Because of Andy?"

Yes, because of Andy. But also because of her. Because of her fear. And her shame.

Leigh closed her eyes for a moment. It *was* "funny," she reflected with a wrenching pang. Dee Bleeker had looked at John Gulliver and seen a cop, which he'd once been. Wesley Warren had looked at him and seen a criminal, which he'd once pretended to be. And she'd looked at him and seen . . .

What?

What had she seen?

The memory of the surge of connection she'd experienced two weeks ago in the examining room rushed back, filling her head and her heart. Hard on its heels came a kaleidoscopic series of images culled from the past fourteen days.

She loved him, she thought. She loved him so much! Her feelings for John Gulliver were richer and deeper than the feelings Suzanne Whitney had had for Saint Nick Marchand.

They were feelings on which to base a future.

Feelings on which to build a family.

I trust John with my life, she'd told Drake Nordling, meaning every word. *I trust him with my son's life, too.*

Could she find the courage to trust him with a piece of her past?

"Leigh?"

She opened her eyes and looked at her assistant—and friend. "Would you mind watching the store again?"

Deirdre Bleeker smiled.

Anthony Stone flicked on the turn signal of the pricey imported sedan he'd rented using the driver's license and bank credit card his lawyer had arranged for him. His mood was foul and getting worse. He hated this lousy little town. He couldn't believe that anyone would actually want to live in such a place. It reminded him of a postcard!

He'd just wasted the better part of an hour parked outside his son's preschool. He hadn't been contemplating a snatch. Although he would have been completely within his rights to take his boy away, that hadn't been his plan. He'd simply wanted to get a firsthand look at him.

He would have known him if it hadn't been for that damned snow gear, Stone told himself bitterly, mentally replaying the moment when the preschool's front door had swung open and about two dozen little kids had come romping outside. Blood would have called to blood and he would have *known*. But the hats and mittens and down-filled jackets had made it just about impossible to tell male from female, much less identify a child he'd never seen.

Still. His son had definitely been one of the bulkily dressed bunch. He was certain of that. He'd felt it in his gut. He would confirm it later, when they came face-to-face.

"I saw you today," he would say, letting the boy know that he'd been watching over him. God knows what kind of lies Suzanne had been filling his head with.

"I saw you, too, Pop," he could hear the kid answering. "I always knew you'd come for me."

He smiled a little, spinning out the entire reunion scene. His son would take to him instantly. That was the natural order of things. He hoped that Suzanne would be there to witness the initial bonding between him and his boy. He liked the idea of her dying with the realization that she'd been supplanted.

In the meantime ...

The witch's little bookshop—the business she'd chosen over her maternal duties—was up ahead. Maybe he should take a few minutes to scope it out before he headed for her house.

Then again, maybe not. He didn't want to tip his hand.

Still, the notion appealed to him. Going in. Giving the place the eyeball. Buying a couple of things with his brand-new credit card.

Anthony Stone laughed to himself. Well, no. Not *his* credit card, exactly. He'd had his lawyer acquire it using the name Nicholas Marchand. The gutless weasel had opposed the idea, but Stone had insisted. It wasn't exactly the same as spitting on Saint Nick's grave, but it was a nice little touch.

A beat-up station wagon was easing away from the curb directly in front of the bookstore. Former Federal Prisoner No. 0394756 took that as a sign he could visit the shop without endangering himself.

He'd taken the pale silk nightgown Suzanne Whitney had worn for him the night he'd come calling on her as a sign, too, he recalled suddenly. She'd pretended otherwise, of course, but he'd known. She'd wanted him.

He always knew everything. After all, he had the power.

John Gulliver stared at his computer screen without really registering what was on it.

You promised you'd leave Leigh alone, he reminded himself. *You've got to keep your word and let her work things through for herself. She's trusting you to do that.*

He would do his damnedest to live up to that trust. But it was hard. God, it was so hard!

Plowing his fingers through his hair, he expelled a weary sigh. He wondered fleetingly if this was what Lucy Falco had had in mind when she'd spoken of admiring his decision to "stick around" rather than run away. He seriously doubted it. Instinct told him that his office manager wasn't a big fan of passivity.

He sighed again. Maybe he could phone the bookstore. He wouldn't say anything. He would hang up as soon as he heard Leigh's voice. Or maybe he could drive by and—

Someone knocked on his door. John stiffened, catching his breath.

"Who is it?" he called after a moment, telling himself it had to be Edith from housekeeping.

"It's me," a soft female voice answered.

He was on his feet after the first syllable and across the room a second later. It took him a few frantic moments to unlock the door and yank it open. His pulse had kicked into a full gallop by the time that was accomplished, sending his blood stampeding through his veins.

"Leigh," he breathed, devouring the woman standing on the threshold of his room with his eyes. He wanted to reach out and touch her, to make certain that she was really there, but something about her expression warned him against it.

"John," came the quiet reply. While she looked as weary as he felt, she exuded an air of determination. It was obvious she'd come to a decision about her future.

Pray heaven, that decision included him.

"Come in." He gestured awkwardly with his disfigured hand. "Please."

She did so. He caught the scent of her hair and skin as she moved by him. Clamping down on his immediate and inevitable physical response, he shut the door behind her.

He turned. So did she. They faced each other without speaking for what seemed like an eternity.

"This is . . . hard . . . for me," Leigh finally said, meeting his eyes squarely for an instant then glancing down toward the floor. She began worrying her lower lip with the edge of her upper front teeth.

"It's Nick, isn't it," he blurted out, finally voicing the fear that had been building within him since he'd left her on Saturday.

"*N-Nick?*" She looked up at him once again, clearly shocked.

He nodded, thinking of the scarred visage he'd seen reflected in the bathroom mirror that morning when he'd shaved. He'd confronted a few truths as he'd done so. A few ugly truths. "You've realized that while you trust me, **you** love . . . him."

Leigh opened and shut her mouth several times, her sky-blue eyes very wide. Under different—very different—circumstances, her expression might have struck him as comic.

"*No,*" she said at last, her voice raw with emotion. The color in her cheeks fluctuated wildly as she shook her head back and forth. "Oh, no. Whatever Suzanne Whitney felt for Nicholas Marchand, it's nothing compared to what I feel for John Gulliver. I love you, John. I love you with all my heart."

"You . . . do?"

"I think I've always loved you. The real you, I mean. I never believed Nick was what people said he was. What . . . you . . . said he was. There were times when I—when Suzanne—would look at him and . . . Oh, God, I can't explain it—"

"Leigh." He moved to close the space between them. To sweep her into his arms. He was dizzy with relief. Intoxicated with expectation. She loved him. She loved him! "Oh, sweetheart—"

"No!" Leigh held him off with one hand. "John, please. Stop."

He did, but it wasn't easy. He yearned for her to the marrow of his bones. "Why?"

"I need to tell you s-something!"

"You've already told me you love me. Nothing else matters."

"This does." Leigh took a deep, desperate breath, then said, "It's about Andy."

John went cold inside. A dozen hideous possibilities sleeted through his mind. "Andy?"

"He may not be your son."

Chapter 13

At first, the words didn't seem to register with John. He stared at Leigh as though she'd addressed him in some alien tongue. She stared back, her heart racing, her body trembling.

Having played out this scene a dozen different ways during the drive from the bookstore, she'd believed herself to be ready to cope with just about any kind of reaction to her disclosure about the uncertainty surrounding Andy's paternity. She'd been wrong. In no way had she prepared herself to be on the receiving end of such . . . *blankness*.

"Of course, Andy's mine," John finally asserted. His tone struck Leigh as irrationally rational, given the circumstances. She could not say the same about the sudden flash of emotion in his eyes.

"I want him to be," she returned, fighting to keep her voice steady. "But I can't be . . . sure."

John's brow furrowed, the scarred skin on his temple puckering. "There was—" he swallowed "—someone else?"

She flinched from the question, both inwardly and outwardly. She tried to speak. She found she couldn't.

Most of the color drained from her companion's angular face. He started to reach out toward her, but apparently thought better of the gesture and aborted it. Leigh was thankful for this. For all that she loved him, she honestly didn't know whether she could have tolerated John's touch.

"Tell me what happened," he said quietly, his dark gaze very intent. "Whatever it is. Please. Sweetheart. *Tell me.*"

The endearment almost undid her. Holding herself together by sheer force of will she asked, "How much do you remember about the night you—Saint Nick—supposedly died?"

"Bits and pieces."

"Do you remember having a phone conversation with Suzanne?"

"I . . . think so."

"It was around lunchtime. You—*Nick*—told her he'd be over that evening."

John nodded slowly. "She promised to be waiting," he recalled, his voice much more certain than it had been a moment before. "She also promised to be wearing the nightgown he'd given her."

Leigh moistened her lips. "She . . . was."

"Was—?"

"Waiting. And w-wearing the nightgown."

"But Nick never showed up."

"No."

"Who did?"

Again, her voice failed her.

"*Who,* Leigh?" John took a half step forward, then checked himself, the price of his restraint clearly visible in the leanly powerful lines of his body.

She had to say the name, she told herself. She had no choice.

"Anthony Stone."

John looked sick. "Oh, no."

"He said he had a message from you. From Nick. I—Suzanne—knew you were friends—"

"*Not friends.*" The interruption was vehement, underscored by a shake of the head. "Never friends. I got close to Stone because of who he was. What he did. It was part of the job. But there were moments when it was hard to stomach being in the same room with him."

Leigh gestured this information aside. It didn't really matter, unless John intended to blame her for not having discerned the true nature of his relationship with Anthony Stone. And if that were the case . . .

"It was late," she continued, the scene unreeling in her mind like a film. "Nick was more than two hours overdue. Suzanne was getting worried. Very worried. Nick had been in a strange mood all week—"

"The Justice Department was getting ready to move in, Leigh. Eighteen months of surviving undercover was either going to pay off in a major way or blow up in my face."

"Suzanne didn't know that. She was afraid when Stone came to the door. She didn't like him. But since she thought he and Nick were—were—"

"Two of a kind?"

The suggestion stunned her. So did the expression on John's face. He looked as though he were being ripped apart from the inside. That he suspected where her recitation was headed was obvious. For a moment she considered cutting straight to the bottom line. But she knew she couldn't. She had to tell him the whole story of what had happened. Of *how* it had happened. She had to let him judge her culpability for himself.

"No," she denied rawly. "Oh, God, John. *No.* I told you before. She never believed that you were—that Nick was— I— *I never believed it!* Still, when Stone showed up saying he had a message—"

"Suzanne let him in." John's voice was hushed, half suffocated.

Leigh averted her eyes, a bitterly familiar sense of shame burning through her. When she resumed speaking, it was strictly in the first person. Somewhere in the back of her mind she remembered how John Gulliver had shifted into the first person Saturday morning when he'd explained why Nicholas Marchand had tried—and failed—to leave Suzanne Whitney alone nearly six years ago.

"Yes," she affirmed. "I told him to give me the message through the door but he said he'd promised Nick he'd deliver it personally. I asked him to wait for a minute. I was wearing the nightgown and something made me— I'm not sure how to describe it, but I didn't want him to see me in Nick's present. So I put on a robe over it. And then...I let Anthony Stone in."

"Leigh. Please. You don't have to—"

"Yes, I do," she disputed fiercely, forcing herself to meet his gaze once again. Her throat constricted. The bridge of her nose congested with the pressure of unshed tears. She told herself she couldn't weep. Not yet. "I let him in. I asked him what the message from Nick was. He said...he said it was that Nick wasn't going to be able to keep our date. That he wasn't going to be able to keep *any* d-dates, ever again. And then he said that was okay because he was there to keep me company instead. He said he knew I l-liked him. That he'd seen me looking at him. That he could tell I . . . wanted him."

"Sweetheart—"

"He grabbed me," she continued, the words coming faster and faster as the memories grew more and more vivid. "He kissed me. I pulled away. I tried to slap him. He caught my hands. He ripped open the robe. He . . . he *smiled* when he saw the nightgown underneath. Like he recognized it. Or had expected to see it. I started to scream but he covered my mouth. He kept saying I didn't have to pretend. That he knew he was the one I really w-wanted. That he'd always known. That he knew *everything* because he had the power. And then he tore the nightgown straight down the front." She mimed the action with shaking hands, her stomach roiling. "It was one of the ugliest sounds I've ever heard. That . . . ripping."

"*Leigh—*"

"I tried to fight him." She was completely locked into it now, reexperiencing the horror she'd tried to repress for five and a half years. "I kicked. I bit. I scratched. Only he . . . Oh, God, he started *laughing*, as though he enjoyed my fighting him. He was so much b-bigger than I was. So much . . . stronger. His hands seemed to be everywhere. And his m-m-mouth. But I tried, John. I *tried*. Then he hit me. Once. Twice. Nobody'd ever hit me before. My parents never ever spanked me! He knocked me down. I tasted b-blood on my tongue. My blood. And he was still laughing. Still saying he knew I wanted him. Calling me slut and all kinds of filthy names."

"He raped you."

Blue eyes stared deeply into brown ones. "I let him." Leigh made the admission without inflection. "I couldn't stop him. I tried, but I couldn't. In the end, I just...gave up. Gave in."

"He might have killed you if you hadn't."

"There have been times when I wished he had."

"No!"

"Yes." She drew a shuddery breath, hugging herself with her arms. She felt so cold. "Nick Marchand always wore a condom. Anthony Stone didn't use anything. Andy was born n-nine months after that night."

"That doesn't mean—"

"I want him to be y-your son more than anything in the world, John," she concluded, rejecting what she knew was likely to be a scenario predicated on the possibility of prophylactic failure. She understood the odds. "But the truth is... *I don't know who fathered my little boy.*"

Although picking the lock on the back door of Suzanne Whitney's house would have been a cinch, Anthony Stone chose to smash it open instead. He was in no mood to be subtle.

The redhead in the bookstore had really ticked him off. Who the hell did she think she was, asking him to wait while she finished ordering some damn book? Where did she get off refusing to answer his questions about the woman who called herself "Leigh McKay?" If that grease monkey with the Yankee accent hadn't shown up, he would have let her have it.

Reaching into the pocket of his jacket, former Federal Prisoner No. 00394756 fondled the black matte butt of the SIG-Sauer he'd taken off one of the dead marshals. The nine-millimeter automatic pistol fit comfortably in his hand. Yeah, he thought. He would have stuck it to that skinny little slut, but good. He might still stick it to her.

But first things first.

"Hi, son," he whispered as he stepped into Suzanne's snug little house. He absorbed the stillness, letting his mind fill with visions of the reunion scene to come. "Daddy's home."

He should have guessed, John told himself, torn between anger and anguish. All the clues had been there. The odd disconnect between Leigh's inherent sensuality and her overt behavior. The mixed-up combination of emotions he'd sensed when he'd kissed her for the first time in five and a half years. The fear she'd shown Friday night while they'd made love. Above all, her off-kilter response when he'd spoken of Andy after finally coming clean about Nicholas Marchand.

I should have figured it out!

"I'm sorry, Leigh," he said, damning the inadequacy of the words. "I'm so...so sorry."

"Why?" She looked at him, her sky-colored eyes very dark and distant. The skin beneath them appeared bruised. "You didn't do anything."

It was then that John Gulliver fully understood why Leigh McKay had held back the truth for so long. He also comprehended why she'd insisted on detailing what had happened to Suzanne Whitney the night Saint Nick had died.

He'd thought she'd been driven by a need to punish him. To make him face up to the price she'd paid for his inability to leave her alone nearly six years ago. But rather than blaming him—

"*I* didn't do anything?" he echoed, his soul aching. *"Dear God in heaven, Leigh! Neither did you!"*

"I let him in," she contradicted. "I didn't stop him. Maybe—maybe I did give off some kind of s-signal that made him think—"

John closed the small distance between them and caught her by the shoulders.

"No," he said, infusing his voice with every bit of conviction he had. "No. You did nothing wrong. *Nothing.* Anthony Stone is, was and always will be a sick bastard and if I could get my hands on him, I'd castrate him and then I'd kill him. But you... Oh, sweetheart ... Oh, my love..."

His vocabulary failed him. He drew her against him, his senses attuned to detect even the slightest hint of resistance. She stiffened for an instant, but yielded to his embrace before he could begin to release her.

"J-John..." she whispered tremulously, her arms sliding around his waist.

He tightened his hold, nuzzling his mouth against the top of her head as he repeated her name over and over again. The silken strands of her hair teased the underside of his jaw. He breathed in her warm, womanly scent.

"You never told anyone?" he finally asked, massaging the hollow at the base of her spine.

"I couldn't." Her tone was stark, a testament to the isolation she'd suffered for the last five and a half years. John swore to himself then and there that he would spend the rest of his life making up for what she'd endured. "I think Dee's guessed what happened. Not the specific details. But...enough."

"What did you do when you found out you were pregnant?"

"I considered getting an abortion. But in the end, I couldn't." Leigh eased back a bit, tilting her face up toward his. Her fair hair rippled back, brushing her shoulders. "I decided to give the baby up for adoption. I was afraid I'd be a bad mother to him. Because of the rape. And the not knowing. I was afraid I wouldn't be able to...love him. That I might look at him someday and see—"

"It's all right," he assured her quickly, stroking up and down her back. "It's all right."

"I would have," she continued doggedly, her eyes filling with tears. "I would have given him away. But someone put him in my arms in the delivery room and—" the tears overflowed her lower lids and began trickling down her pale cheeks "—suddenly everything changed. I knew I had to keep h-him, John. I knew I loved him and that I would do everything in my power to be the best mother I could. Above all, I knew he was *mine*. What I didn't know—*what I still don't know*—is whether he's y-yours."

There were ways to find out, John reflected. A blood test could prove his paternity. Or disprove it, as the case might be. The thing was—

"It doesn't matter," he said abruptly.

Leigh blinked, watching him with wide, wary eyes. "Wh-what?"

"*It doesn't matter,*" he repeated, meaning every syllable. "I'm not talking about what Stone did to you. That matters a lot. It matters that you were...hurt. It matters that you had no one to help you." He paused, renewing his vow of atonement. He pledged himself to protect her from this moment forward, too. He was ready to give anything, including his life, to safeguard her from further harm. "But Andy is Andy, Leigh. He's *your* son. I love you. I want to be a husband to you. And I want to be a father to your little boy. A real father. Biology be damned."

"Oh...John..."

"I'd like to help give him the baby brother he wants," he continued, astonishing himself more than a little. "And maybe a baby sister, too. That chance I talked about Saturday morning—"

Leigh silenced him by lifting her right hand and pressing her fingertips against his lips. Despite the shadows beneath her eyes and the tearstains on her cheeks, she had never looked more beautiful.

"It's yours, John," she told him in a dulcet voice. A soft flush stole up into her face, tinting her skin the same delicate shade of pink as the bouquet of roses Suzanne Whitney had once received from Nicholas Marchand. "Now and forever. It's yours."

The burden of the past seemed to fall away. The future opened, fresh and whole.

"No, sweetheart," the man who'd once been known as Saint Nick whispered to the only woman he'd ever loved, brushing his mouth against her cheek and tasting the salt of her tears. "It's ours."

And then he kissed her.

Anthony Stone snapped the plastic tomahawk in half and dropped the pieces to the floor. Lifting his foot, he stepped down on one of the strings of beads that clung to the broken handle. He ground the garish ornaments beneath the heel of his shoe until they shattered into powder.

"You think you can bribe my boy with your cheap presents?" he muttered angrily. He knew all about the tomahawk. And about the man who had given it. His source had been extremely informative on the subject.

He kicked the plaything aside with a vicious swipe of his foot. His son wouldn't want it anymore, he told himself. And even if he did...

Screw that. He wouldn't.

Anthony Stone walked out of the toy-strewn room and stalked down the hallway. He booted open the door to Suzanne Whitney's bedroom.

He stood on the threshold for several moments, surveying the pale, pristine decor. He snorted contemptuously, his ire rising in reaction to what he viewed as yet another indication of the inbred deceptiveness of the opposite sex.

Touch me not, the room said.

Saint Nick's blond, blue-eyed ladyfriend had said much the same thing the night he'd finally taken her, five and a half years ago. Pleading, she'd been. And crying. Trying to persuade him that she didn't want what he damned well knew she wanted. What they all wanted.

Touch me not.

He *had* touched her, he remembered with lewd satisfaction, his body stirring. Hard. Soft. Nasty. Nice. And he was going to touch her again. He would make her touch him, too. In any way—in every way—that pleased him.

Maybe he would do it in here, in this nice, clean room.

There was an old-fashioned looking glass standing in the far corner of the room. The sight of it made Stone smile. He could imagine watching himself in it as he had Suzanne again. He would order her to watch, as well. She would act as though she didn't want to, but she would come around. Her kind always did.

He'd given her a chance, he reminded himself with a sneer, crossing to a chest of drawers set against the wall opposite the foot of the bed. He'd been willing to forgive her for her past once she'd borne his son. All she'd had to do was keep herself pure. To keep herself exclusively for him.

She'd done so for a time, or so his source had assured him. But in the end, she'd succumbed to her own weak nature and betrayed him.

He pulled open the top drawer. It contained lingerie. He rummaged through the undergarments, comparing their chaste simplicity with the slinky nightgown Suzanne had been wearing the night he'd come to her. He'd known she would have it on. He'd overheard Nick talking to her about it on the phone.

She probably had the sexy stuff hidden away, he decided, lifting a pair of cotton panties from the drawer. He would make her take it out and show it to him, just like he'd made her show him the sleek, ivory silk nightgown.

No, he corrected, a sly smile tugging at his lips. It wouldn't be exactly the same as it had been five and a half years ago. It would be better. Because this time around he would get to watch Suzanne put on the garments before she took them off.

He would make her do it slowly, he promised himself with an anticipatory snicker. Real slowly. Both the putting on and the taking off.

He rubbed the panties against his cheek for a few seconds, fantasizing about the looming moment of reckoning, then tossed them carelessly aside. He did the same with a nylon bra. Finally he simply grabbed a fistful of the flimsy garments and flung them around the room.

He slammed the top drawer shut and opened the others. Their seemingly prim and proper contents infuriated him. Frustration exploded within him. He yanked the bottom drawer completely out of the bureau, upended it with an expletive, then dropped it to the floor with a crash.

He whirled around, facing the bed. His breath sawed in and out in rapid pants. That was where she'd done it, he told himself furiously. Suzanne had lain there on that creamy-looking quilt and she'd opened her legs for another man. Or men. She'd let others have what was supposed to be his and his alone. He could *see* her doing it.

He stalked over to the bed and sat down on the edge of it, rubbing the palms of his hands against the smooth surface of the coverlet. A moment later he flopped back on the mattress.

His source had believed that he would be glad to hear that Suzanne Whitney was moving on with her life. That he would be pleased to learn that she'd found a ''good man'' to ease her loneliness. His source had believed this for the same reasons that she'd believed he regretted his so-called crimes.

One of those reasons was that he'd told her so.

As for the other . . .

"Mmm." Leigh sighed as the man she was going to marry lifted his mouth from hers after a long, lingering kiss. The kiss was part of what had turned into a very protracted—but extremely pleasurable—process of bidding John Gulliver a temporary adieu.

They'd gotten out of bed.

They'd more or less put their clothes back on.

They'd finally managed to cross to the door of John's hotel room. Eventually, one or the other of them would open said door and she would walk out of it.

"Are you sure you don't want me to come with you now?" John asked, smoothing her hair back from her brow with gentle fingers.

She smiled up at him, knowing her heart was in her eyes. The kiss he'd bestowed in response to her declaration that the chance he wanted was his had flowered into an incandescent passion. The result had been several sweetly searing hours of lovemaking. Her body still throbbed with the echoes of sensual bliss.

Their joining had been an exorcism of all that had been wrong in their pasts and a celebration of all that would be right about their future. Every touch had been an affirmation of shared intentions. Every sound, a pledge of trust and truth. It had been the most overwhelmingly wonderful experience of Leigh's life and she could hardly wait to repeat it.

But first she had to get home to her little boy. To . . . *their* little boy. To the child they would nurture together as husband and wife.

"I'd like some time to talk with Andy first," she told him, caressing the angle of her lover's lean cheek. A hint of new beard growth sandpapered her fingertips, sending a thrilling little tingle dancing down her arm. "As I said before, he and I have a little unfinished business from this morning. But we'll be waiting for you at seven."

"And the pizza I'll be bringing."

"That, too," she agreed with a throaty laugh. "I suppose I'm doomed to eating pepperoni from here on out?"

"Majority rules in pizza toppings, sweetheart."

Leigh pretended to pout. She felt deliciously giddy. Innocent as an infant in some ways. Profoundly adult in others.

"I am open to... persuasion." John slid his hands slowly down her arms as he spoke. His dark eyes glinted provocatively.

"Oh?" she challenged as strong fingers encircled her wrists.

"Think of me as a member of Congress."

She let herself be drawn into another embrace. The acutely sensitized tips of her breasts brushed against his chest. She felt them tighten against the stretchy fabric of her bra. The sensation triggered a liquid fluttering between her thighs.

"You're suggesting I bribe you into changing your position on the pepperoni issue?" she queried a bit breathlessly.

"Something like that."

"I thought—" she went up on tiptoe and feathered her lips back and forth across his "—bribes were illegal."

"Not if you call them—" tongues touched and teased for a heady second or two "—campaign contributions."

"So, how much would I have to... contribute... to persuade you to switch to the anchovies-and-black-olives point of view?"

"A lot." John showed his teeth in a roguish smile that did nothing for the stability of her pulse. "Black olives are marginally tolerable. But anchovies are disgusting."

"This, from a man who encourages a preschooler to put *pickle relish* on pancakes?"

"Well..."

They both laughed. Then kissed. And kissed again. By the time they broke apart, they were both snatching air into their lungs in shallow, unsteady pants.

"Oh... my..." Leigh managed, leaning back against the door. She was a little surprised she didn't collapse to the floor. Her legs felt wobblier than gelatin.

"Oh, my... indeed," John raspily concurred, nuzzling the side of her throat.

She closed her eyes for a few seconds, a heated delight ravishing her senses. When she finally forced her lids open again, she found herself focusing for the first time on the bed they'd recently vacated.

"Oh, *Lord,*" she gasped, genuinely shocked by what she saw. There was no shame in the untrammeled ecstasy she and John had given each other, but... Well, she hadn't realized that the two of them had left so much physical evidence of what they'd done underneath—

Er, make that on top of—

Uh, no, more like tucked between and rolling around in—

"Leigh?" her partner in passion asked, lifting his head. "What is it?"

She felt herself blush from collarbone to hairline. In a small, stifled voice she replied, "The b-bed."

"The...*bed?*" John frowned at her for an instant, then glanced over his shoulder. He looked back at her, clearly perplexed. "What's wrong with the bed, sweetheart? Aside from the fact that we're not in it, of course."

"It's a mess, John!"

"Don't worry," he soothed. "I'll call Edith in housekeeping."

The implications of this proposal were nothing short of appalling. "I can just imagine what *she'll* say."

"Why imagine?" The riposte was wryly knowing. "Wait a couple days and I'm sure you'll be able to find out, verbatim."

Leigh groaned, the heat in her cheeks racheting up a degree or two. He was right. News of their tryst would be all over town before the end of the week. Possibly before the end of the day.

"Don't worry, love." John dropped a quick kiss on the tip of her nose. "I'll tidy things up myself. Better yet, I'll smuggle the sheets out when I come to your house tonight. You can wash them while Andy and I have a guy-to-guy discussion."

"A guy-to-guy discussion?" She decided to let his outrageous suggestion about the bed linen pass. If John Gulliver actually thought she was going to spend this very special evening doing laundry, he had another think coming. Maybe two. "About what?"

"You and me." The expression in John's eyes turned tender. Leigh's heart did a long, slow swoon in response. "Getting married."

You and me. Getting married.

Heavens, that had a marvelous sound to it!

"John—"

"Actually, I thought I'd ask his permission."

"You . . . *what?*"

"How do you think Andy would react if I requested his mom's hand in holy matrimony?"

Leigh blinked several times, then startled herself by giving the inquiry some genuine consideration. The notion of John seeking a nuptial okay from a preschooler was funny, of course. Yet, inherent in the humorous scenario was a touching concern for a little boy's feelings.

"Leaving aside the possibility that you may have to explain to him that 'matrimony' isn't some kind of pasta product?" she asked after a few seconds.

"And the issue of why in the world I'd volunteer to spend the rest of my life with a . . . *girl.*"

"Yes, well, there is that," Leigh acknowledged with a quirky giggle, admiring the dead-on invocation of her son's disdain for members of the opposite sex. "But to get back to the original question. I think Andy's main response if you ask him for my hand in marriage will be rampant curiosity about why you don't want the rest of me."

"Oh, I do, sweetheart." John's voice was husky. A distinctly masculine hunger flared in his dark gaze. "But I think it's going to be a few years before Andy and I get around to a guy-to-guy discussion on that particular subject. I plan to do a lot of research in the interim. As for a *man-to-woman* discussion of the matter . . ."

Anthony Stone had just finished prying open the lock on the gunmetal-gray box he'd discovered in the drawer of the nightstand next to Suzanne's bed when he heard a gasp from the doorway.

He turned.

He smiled.

"Hi, Ma," he said to Donatella Pietra. "Surprised to see me?"

Chapter 14

Leigh drove home under the influence of unalloyed joy. Fortunately, her emotional intoxication didn't impair her skill behind the wheel. She did, however, find herself grinning like a loon at nothing in particular. Likewise, singing along with a golden oldies station on the car radio in a voice that she freely admitted fell less than musically on the ear.

This wasn't to say that she couldn't croon on key. She would argue vehemently that she could.

The problem was, her key of choice tended to be...oh, somewhere in the neighborhood of a dissonant Q-flat—very flat! unbelievably flat!—minor.

Flicking on the station wagon's turn signal, she swung onto the tree-lined street on which her modest, two-story house was located. There was an expensive-looking sedan parked on the right-hand side of the road about fifty yards before her driveway. The vehicle was a tad pricey for the area. It also had out-of-state license plates.

Somebody must have a visitor, Leigh decided.

Which, very naturally, steered her thoughts back to the guest who would be calling on her and her son in—she darted an eager glance at the dashboard clock—a little more than two hours. She could imagine Andy's response when she informed him that John was coming over with dinner. His favorite grown-up hero *and* a pepperoni pizza? He would be in seventh heaven!

As for his reaction when he heard the rest of the news... Well, she had to believe that Andy would be thrilled. He'd bonded with John Gulliver the moment they'd met and his affection had never wavered. And if John carried through with the idea of asking his "permission"...

A happy laugh bubbled out of her as she envisioned the scene. Maybe she should coach Andy a bit in preparation for it, she considered mischievously. Give him a few tips on how to grill an erstwhile suitor about his intentions.

Leigh laughed again. She felt as buoyant as a helium-filled balloon. Freer than she'd ever felt in her life. The future was unfolding before her, beckoning her onward like the legendary Yellow Brick Road to Oz, and it looked absolutely beautiful.

Sharing the truth about what had happened to her five and a half years ago had been the key to her liberation. She'd shed her shame. She'd finally let go of her fears. And in exchange, she'd been given more than she'd ever dreamed possible.

John's words echoed through her brain as she turned the station wagon into her drive.

Andy is Andy, Leigh, the man she loved had told her after she'd confessed to the uncertainty that had racked her for so long. *He's your son. I love you. I want to be a husband to you. And I want to be a father to your little boy. A real father. Biology be damned.*

Her heart was full to the point of overflowing.

I'd like to help give him the baby brother he wants, he'd gone on. There had been a hint of wonderment in his eyes as he'd spoken, as though he'd only just begun to gauge the depth of his paternal impulses. *And maybe a baby sister, too.*

She would love to have a little girl, Leigh decided dreamily as she pulled up behind Nonna P.'s brown car. And she would bet Andy would love it, too, even though he professed to believe that all members of the opposite sex were— Now, what was that charming phrase she'd heard him and Bryan use last Thursday in the bookstore after story hour?

Ah, yes. Doodoo heads. As in, "Sisters are doodoo heads cuz they're . . . *girls.*"

Leigh laughed a third time and reached for the car's ignition keys.

"We've got lots more sounds of the seventies coming up," the announcer on the radio promised ebulliently. "Including a special salute to disco! But first, the headlines. Topping the news right now, a multistate search for a convicted killer. We go live to—"

Leigh turned off the engine, silencing the announcer in mid-sentence. She definitely wasn't in the mood to hear about a manhunt for a murderer. She understood with bitter clarity that the world could be a cruel and dangerous place. But tonight she was going to shove that comprehension far, far to the back of her mind and revel in the security of loving and being loved.

Unbuckling her seat belt, she gathered up her purse with her right hand while fluffing her pale hair with her left. Although she'd done her best to restore her appearance before she'd finally managed to tear herself away from John, a quick glance in the rearview mirror told her that she'd only been partially successful. Despite her efforts, she still had a rather. . . uh . . . *ravished* look.

Andy was still too young to notice such things, thank heavens. His beloved baby-sitter was a different story. Leigh just hoped that the stamp of approval Nonna P. had seemed to bestow upon her relationship with John Gulliver had not been revoked.

She got out of the station wagon and shut the door. Squaring her shoulders, she inhaled deeply. The early-evening air was crisp and cold and carried the faint scent of woodsmoke. She expelled the breath she'd taken, then inhaled again. As she did so, her memory replayed a small piece of the Friday-night conversation she'd had with Donatella Pietra.

You've been alone for a long time, the older woman had observed.

I've had Andy, she'd responded, well aware of the blessing her little boy had been.

Nonna P. had smiled then, her homely features temporarily transfigured. A few moments later, her expression had changed. The light had faded from her face, taking with it the illusion of beauty. The imprint of age and an inarticulated grief had become brutally obvious.

Sometimes children aren't enough, she'd said with painful simplicity.

Had Nonna's comment been based on personal experience? Leigh wondered as she followed the snow-dusted walk that led from the driveway to the front door. She didn't know. But if it had been, why had the older woman never spoken about being a mother? There had been dozens of opportunities for her to do so during the past two-plus years.

It was strange, she thought with a fleeting frown, opening her purse and fishing out her keys. Now that she stopped and looked back, she could recall at least a dozen instances when Donatella Pietra had sidestepped inquiries about her past. Her ploys seemed so obvious in retrospect. Yet, at the time . . .

All right! All right! Until this moment, she'd never paid much attention to the way Andy's baby-sitter tended to pull back when a conversation turned intimate. Was it any wonder? She had trouble enough keeping track of her own evasions without adding the task of trying to catalog someone else's.

She'd checked out Nonna's references very thoroughly before hiring her, of course. She'd had no intention of entrusting her son to an unvetted stranger. But when it came to personal questions, she'd never pressed. It hadn't seemed . . . right.

And the older woman had never pressed *her,* either. Friday's conversation aside, she'd never been anything but the soul of discretion. She hadn't even asked about Andy's father!

Which was very odd, Leigh realized with a twinge of uneasiness, sliding her front-door key into the lock and turning it. Because Nonna was intensely curious about everything else in Andy's young life. Witness her endless stream of questions about the accident at the preschool playground. So why had she never broached the issue of Andy's paternity?

Leigh opened the front door and stepped inside. "Andy?"

No response.

"Nonna?" she tried again, the skin on the nape of her neck starting to prickle.

Still no response. The house seemed ominously still.

A game, she told herself firmly. Andy was playing some kind of game and he'd gotten his baby-sitter to go along with him. Any second now, he would pop out from behind a piece of furniture and yell "boo!" The more rattled she seemed in re-action, the more delighted he would be. He would probably suggest playing the same trick on John once he learned of his impending arrival.

"Andy?" she called, walking down the foyer. "It's Mommy. I've got something to tell you, sweetie."

She reached the entrance to the living room. The lights were off. She felt for the wall switch by the door and clicked them on. Then she gasped. Her purse fell from nerveless fingers, hitting the hardwood floor with a thud.

Her son was sprawled on the sofa like a rag doll. He wasn't moving. From where she stood, he didn't even appear to be breathing.

"A-Andy," she choked out, rushing forward. She collapsed beside the sofa, feeling frantically for a pulse. "Oh, God. Andy."

She found what she was searching for an unmercifully long second later. Although he seemed to be deeply—*unnatu-rally*—unconscious, her son was definitely alive.

And then it happened. An atavastic sense of horror swept through her. Her skin went clammy. Her blood threatened to clot in her veins while her breath congealed at the top of her throat.

There was someone else in the room.

She could feel it through her pores.

She could . . . smell it.

Please, God, she prayed silently. Please. Whatever this is. Whoever this is. Protect my little boy.

Still on her knees, Leigh McKay shifted around to confront the embodiment of a waking nightmare.

"We've been waiting for you, Suzanne," said Anthony Stone, and leveled a handgun at the middle of her forehead.

* * *

John was halfway out the door when the phone on the nightstand started to ring. He was more than a little tempted to ignore the shrilling summons. He had a pizza to pick up!

Two pizzas, actually. One large with double pepperoni. One small with black olives and—ugh!—anchovies.

The possibility that the caller might be Leigh lured him back across the room. He snagged the receiver with his scarred right hand, raking the fingers of his left through his shower-dampened hair. He'd decided it behooved him to be all scrubbed up when he petitioned for permission to marry Andy's mother.

"Hello?"

"Gulliver?"

"Nordling?" Every instinct he had went on red alert in the space of a single heartbeat. "What's wrong?"

"Anthony Stone's escaped."

John went rigid. He spat out a curse. "When? How?"

"Late yesterday. We're still attempting to sort out exactly what happened. Two U.S. marshals and a, uh, member of my staff are missing."

"A member of your staff?"

"The computer specialist I mentioned Saturday morning."

Oh, Lord, John thought. Oh, sweet Lord in heaven.

"You mean the one who told you your damned data system was secure?" he demanded harshly. "The one who's probably been poking around in every confidential file you've got?"

"Look, John, we haven't been able to contact Ms. McKay—"

The man who'd once gone by the name Nicholas Marchand hung up. He knew what he had to do. He also knew he couldn't accomplish it yammering on the phone.

Leigh moistened her swollen lower lip, watching her captor assessingly from beneath her lashes as he paced back and forth in front of her. She was in the eye of an emotional storm, possessed of a terrible kind of calm. Although she was nearly naked and bound hand and foot, she was beyond being afraid for herself. What fear she felt was for the little boy who was lying

drugged on the sofa a scant ten feet away and for the man who
might come stumbling in on this horror show at any moment.

John, she thought. Oh, God, John.

Whether Anthony Stone had been sane when he'd raped her
five and a half years ago, she didn't know. But he certainly was
not sane now. To look into his eyes was to see a snake pit rather
than a human soul.

He'd already admitted to having killed Saint Nick Marchand. He'd boasted with almost-salacious relish of having
tampered with his car. He'd repeated in sickening detail from
some accident report that he'd apparently committed to memory.

"Wh-why?" she'd asked, trying to disguise the revulsion
she'd felt.

"Because I hated him," was all he'd said.

She took a deep breath, telling herself that she had to keep
the insane dialogue she'd initiated going. She had to keep this
monster...occupied.

"So...Donatella Pietra is your mother?" she questioned
carefully, knowing that she was dealing with the human equivalent of nitroglycerin.

"She gave birth to me." The tone of his response did not
bode well for the fate of the woman he'd earlier claimed to have
safely stashed somewhere upstairs.

"But she didn't raise you."

"She gave me away to some alcoholic second cousin and his
slut of a wife. Then she went off on her own."

"And your...father?"

Stone checked his stride, his gaze careering from her to Andy
and back again. "Who the hell knows and who the hell cares?"
he snarled, then resumed his predatory pacing.

Leigh breathed a silent prayer of thanks, realizing she'd come
very close to touching off an explosion. After a second or two
she shifted in her seat, testing the bonds that held her wrists.
She thought there was a teeny more give than she'd felt the last
time. She flexed her hands to keep the circulation going.

They were still in the living room. Stone had ordered her to
strip down to her bra and panties, then lashed her to a chair
with a combination of rope and duct tape. He'd hit her twice,

raising a welt on her cheek the first time and splitting her bottom lip open the second. He'd seemed to savor the sight of her blood. He'd even dipped his head and tasted it.

He was determined to kill her. That much he'd made chillingly clear. And he'd been equally explicit about what he intended to do before he took her life.

Whether he would be able to follow through with his graphic plans for sexually abusing her—for "giving her what he knew she wanted," in his twisted parlance—was a question mark. Although he'd rubbed against her body for several minutes after the second time he'd hit her, his flesh had remained flaccid.

Remembering the perverted pleasure he'd appeared to take in her struggles five and a half years ago, Leigh had forced herself to stay passive through the entire nauseating ordeal. And when it was over, she'd reverted to what seemed the only strategy open to her: *getting him to talk.*

It had been less difficult than she'd expected. So far, at least. Anthony Stone liked to run off at the mouth, especially about himself. What's more, her five-plus years in the Witness Security Program had imbued her with a singular skill for priming other people's verbal pumps.

She filled her lungs with a slow, cleansing breath, then released the air through her lips in a silent, steady stream. Eventually she asked, "How did you find me?

Stone smiled, plainly proud of his cleverness. "A computer nerd in the Justice Department had a little money problem a few years back. I helped him solve it. He asked how he could pay me back. I told him I wanted his bosses to think someone from the outside was messing with their confidential data files. No one was, of course. Not really. But people got worried anyway. So they called in a specialist."

"Your...nerd."

"Uh-huh. He tapped into everything I needed to locate you. He also found out I had a son."

"And you sent Nonna to spy on me."

Again, her captor stopped. His nostrils flared. His eyes flashed. "I sent her to watch over what's mine."

"Yes," Leigh quickly concurred. "Of course."

It wasn't sufficient. He moved to her in three swift, savage strides, grabbed her shoulders in a bruising grip and shoved his face to within inches of her own.

"What's *mine!*" he repeated, spraying spittle.

"Y-yes," she managed. Bile rose in her throat; she swallowed it. "I . . . understand."

A split second later his mood changed. He straightened, chuckling. The sound of his amusement made Leigh's flesh crawl. Her stomach roiled.

"No, you don't, Suzanne," he contradicted, fingering the right strap of her bra, then slowly pulling it off her shoulder. The cup on that side sagged forward. She bit the inside of her cheek, willing herself to stay absolutely still as he began to trace the delicate upper swell of her breast. "But you sure as hell will."

He punctuated this threat with a cruel pinch of her right nipple. Then he went back to pacing, chuckling to himself every few moments. Leigh watched him, gauging his mood, blanking out her anger and disgust as best she could.

After about a minute she resumed her line of questioning. "Why did she agree to do it?"

Stone gestured with the gun he was still holding. Leigh had recognized the model as soon as she'd seen it. A 9-mm automatic. It was very similar to the firearm she had locked away upstairs.

"Because I'm her bastard son," he answered. "Because a few years back she got religion and decided she had to atone for the wrongs she'd done me. She read about me in the newspaper, you see. About my trial and all the awful things I supposedly did. She got in touch with my lawyer. I had him string her along. I figured she'd be useful."

"I . . . see."

"I played her the way I play everybody else. I told her I knew I was going to be in prison for the rest of my life. I told her I knew I deserved it. That I'd done wrong and I was sorry for it. She really ate that part up. My lawyer said she cried when she heard it and claimed she'd been sure I couldn't be as bad as all the news stories made out. That's when I snapped the trap. I told her I had a son. A son nobody knew about except me and his mother. I swore I could handle the time as long as somebody I trusted was out making sure my woman and my boy were all right. I swore I wanted them to have a good life without me." His face contorted. "The stupid idiot bought it all. Every word of it. She *believed* me, Suzanne. She believed me so much, she actually thought I'd be happy to hear that you were screwing another man."

John eased open the back door of Leigh's home. He knew that Anthony Stone was inside. He *knew* it. He'd sensed the bastard's presence the moment he'd spotted that pricey sedan parked down the road from the McKays' driveway. The smashed lock on the door had simply confirmed his instincts.

Stone liked to break things. According to the records, he always had.

John moved noiselessly across the threshold and into the airy cream-and-yellow kitchen where the web of lies about his and Suzanne's shared past had begun to unravel a little more than two days ago. His gut twisted as he heard the sound of an angry male voice coming from the front of the house. Although the words being said were impossible to make out, their tone was unmistakable.

A cold, killing rage settled like a cloak over him. He wished he'd brought a gun. Unfortunately, he'd turned his back on such things the day he'd quit the Justice Department.

He thought fleetingly of the firearm he'd been told was upstairs in Leigh's bedroom. Maybe—

No, he decided. Too risky. Even assuming he could reach the second floor undetected, Andy had said the gun was in a locked box.

He looked around. His gaze settled on something that made him bare his teeth like a wolf. He moved to the counter to the left of the sink. Reaching across it, he plucked a knife from a magnetized rack on the wall.

It was the same knife Leigh had turned on him when he'd slipped and called her Suzanne.

"You brought this on yourself," her captor said huskily, stroking the barrel of his pistol up and down Leigh's throat. He jabbed it into the tender flesh beneath her chin, forcing her face up toward his. "You know that, don't you?"

"I never . . . meant . . ."

"Never meant *what?*" Another jab. "Never meant to open your legs to other men?"

"I was l-lonely."

"Lonely?" He withdrew the gun, his expression contemptuous. "You were a dog in heat, Suzanne. Anytime. Anywhere. Anybody."

"No!"

He backhanded her, snapping her head to the right. Agony detonated inside Leigh's skull. She whimpered, struggling not to lose consciousness.

Stone leaned in close. He was smiling. "The first time I saw you in the dance club with Saint Nick, I had you pegged. And that night I gave you what you had coming—"

What alerted him, Leigh never knew. Maybe it was something she did. Because a heartbeat before he broke off his vicious recitation and whirled around, she shifted the focus of her pain-blurred gaze to a spot behind him.

She thought she must be hallucinating; that in the terror of the last few moments she'd lost her mind. Because what she saw was John Gulliver. He was holding a knife. The expression on his scarred face was implacable to the point of inhumanity.

Stone turned, the handgun coming up, his finger tightening on the trigger.

Leigh screamed. At the same time, she pitched her body to one side, somehow managing to rock the chair she was tied to up on two legs. She leaned hard, straining against her bonds.

The chair tipped over, knocking into Stone. He staggered. The handgun went off, missing its intended target. A moment later, John was on him.

It was a fight to the death. Angry. Animalistic. Leigh couldn't see much of it. But she could hear every blow. Every curse. Every grunt of pain.

Stone's gun fell to the floor, sliding to within a few feet of her. She struggled wildly against the rope that restrained her wrists. If she could get just one hand . . .

She would grab the gun and kill him. Without hesitation. Without mercy.

John gave a cry of agony. A split second later Leigh heard the clatter of metal hitting wood. The knife, she thought despairingly. Oh, God. *He'd lost the knife!*

The battle went on. And on. Leigh wriggled and squirmed, trying frantically to free herself. The two men crashed into her. The combatants toppled over, grappling for advantage.

What happened next was never entirely clear to her. She thought she heard John say something about people returning from the dead. Whatever it was, it provoked a gibbered string of obscenities from Stone. He went completely mad.

And then, hideously, the struggle was over. The monster who'd raped Suzanne Whitney and plotted the murder of Nicholas Marchand staggered to his feet, triumphant. John lay on the floor, alive but apparently unconscious.

Stone wove an unsteady path over to the gun. He bent to retrieve it, giving Leigh a wink as he did so. "You're next," he said in a feral rasp, then started to laugh.

Blinking back tears of mortal dread, Leigh watched as he walked back to his prey's prone body. He uncorked a savage kick to John's ribs. Then he lifted the gun.

He took his time about aiming.

The head.

The heart.

The head.

The—

John groaned and twitched.

Stone pulled the trigger.

Nothing happened.

Stone pulled the trigger again.

Still, nothing happened.

It's jammed, Leigh thought, perilously close to screaming. *My God, the gun is jammed!*

"*Anthony!*" It was Donatella Pietra's voice, coming from the doorway of the living room.

Stone jerked like a man who'd been poked with an electrified prod. He turned. "*Ma!*" he cried. "*No!*"

"*I gave you life. Now I take it away.*"

A shot rang out.

Anthony Stone crumpled to the floor, the gun dropping from his lifeless fingers. A moment later Leigh heard another gun clatter against the hardwood, followed by what sounded like the collapse of a second body.

"L-Leigh—?" It was John, stirring on the floor.

"M-M-Mommy—?" It was Andy, struggling to sit up on the sofa.

"Freeze!" somebody yelled. *"This is the police!"*

For the second time in her life, Leigh McKay fainted.

Chapter 15

While people in small towns may be willing to tell all to each other, they tend to clam up in the presence of outsiders. Or so members of the national press corps discovered when they descended on a picturesque village in Vermont to uncover the "real" story behind the death of the murderous fugitive, Anthony Stone.

It didn't matter who they were. Be they well-heeled network correspondents accompanied by multiperson crews and satellite trucks or semistarving stringers from third-rate grocery-store tabloids who could barely afford to use a pay phone, local folks regarded them with flinty Yankee stares when the subject of what had occurred at Leigh McKay's house ten days before Christmas was raised.

"Dunno much about that" was the standard comment.

That Deputy Drake Nordling knew a whole hell of a lot about what had happened, and why, was obvious to everybody in the media horde. Getting him to go one syllable beyond the official story sent out in an obliquely-worded statement to the press was an entirely different matter.

Under normal circumstances, such stonewalling would have produced a journalistic firestorm complete with front-page accusations of a government cover-up and demands for a congressional investigation. A couple of factors mitigated against that in this case.

First, it was the holiday season and a lot of assignment editors were complaining that the public was clamoring for "uplifting" stories, not true crime.

Second, one of the juiciest sex scandals in American history erupted a day and a half after Stone's death. It was a bicoastal thing, involving three Hollywood superstars, two hotshot players from the National Football League, a member of the U.S. Supreme Court and a boa constrictor. Not only was everyone associated with the story spilling their guts, they were peddling videotapes to back up their stories, as well!

The media circus moved on without ever having a chance to speak to Leigh McKay or John Gulliver, much less a not-yet-five-year-old named Andy. Nor did they happen to discover that it had been an ex-junkie/hooker-turned-bookstore-clerk named Deirdre Bleeker who had summoned police to her employer's aid. It seemed she'd flipped on the TV in the back office of the shop as she'd been going over the day's receipts and caught a spot news story about the manhunt for an escaped convict. She'd recognized the man in the mug shot flashed up on the screen as the customer who had come into the store several hours earlier asking questions about her employer.

Most of what Anthony Stone had told Leigh during her captivity had turned out to be true in a twisted kind of way. His lawyer had confirmed a majority of the details as part of a plea bargain.

The bodies of the two U.S. Marshals were recovered and interred with the honor befitting their line-of-duty deaths. The corpse of the computer nerd was claimed by an ex-wife who apparently thought she was due some insurance money. It was cremated on the same day a team of specialists whose bona fides had been checked, rechecked and re-rechecked began a security overhaul of the Justice Department's entire data-storage system.

Anthony Stone was buried in a pauper's grave. Unmourned. Food for worms and maggots. He'd been shot through the head by the handgun that had been kept in the metal box he'd failed to open after prying off its lock.

His mother, Donatella, was laid to rest in the cemetery of the church she'd attended—with Dee Bleeker, Thalia Jenkins and Edith from housekeeping—for more than two years. She was eulogized with kind words and genuine tears.

"Massive cardiac failure," had been the medical examiner's verdict about the cause of her death. But Leigh was inclined to believe that Andy's explanation was closer to the mark.

"The bad man breaked her heart," he'd said. "And nobody could fix it."

Andy seemed to be handling the trauma he'd endured pretty well. Drugged into unconsciousness as he had been, he'd missed the worst of what had occurred. A counselor had told Leigh that time, TLC and a stable environment in which he could talk openly about what had taken place were crucial to his emotional recovery. Leigh had assured the woman that she—and her husband-to-be—would see that Andy never lacked for any of those things.

As for her own recovery and John's... Well, perhaps the best indicator of that was their decision to pledge themselves as husband and wife on Christmas Eve.

And after celebrating their marriage with a small group of very fond friends, the blissfully happy couple and their beaming little boy went home to the house the groom had purchased as a gift for his new family just two days before.

"You know what?" Andy asked as he bounded into his brand-new bedroom in his same old bunny slippers and baggy pajamas. He was clutching a tomahawk. A rather classy-looking tomahawk. It had been a gift from Drake Nordling, of all people.

"No, buddy," John responded, briefly debating whether his night-night duties included informing his son that he'd put his pajama top on backward and inside out. He decided there was no point in being picky. "What?"

"I'm really, truly glad you married Mommy."

"I'm really, truly glad, too. Thank you for giving me permission."

Andy giggled. "D'you think Mommy b'lieved me when I pretended like maybe I wouldn't?"

"She looked a little worried for a minute."

"Yeah. But she looked beautiful today, huh?"

"She certainly did."

"She put some girl stuff on her face so her owwie didn't show at all."

John's stomach clenched for a moment as memory assailed him. He took a deep breath, forcing himself to relax. It was over, he told himself. It was over and the two people he loved most in the world were safe.

"Miss Bleeker looked pretty, too," Andy continued, plunking himself down on his bed. "I almost didn't know who she was at first!"

John smiled crookedly. If truth be told, he'd been rather stunned by Dee's transformation himself. "I hope you didn't tell her that."

"Naw. I just said she looked very, very nice. She got red when I did and for a minute I was a-scared she was gonna cry. Cuz girls do stuff like that at weddings, you know. Only then she looked at Mr. Warren from the garage and he got kind of red, too. Then they started smilin' really funny."

"Well, uh—"

"I think he likes her."

"Do you?"

"Uh-huh. And I think she likes him, too."

"Could be."

"If they get married, will he have to show her his secret card tricks?"

Whoa. He'd definitely missed something. "Excuse me?"

"His secret card tricks," Andy repeated with a trace of impatience. "Mr. Warren knows lots of 'em. He showed me some the other day when him and Miss Bleeker stayed with me. 'Member? When you and Mommy had to go meet with that Mr. Nordling guy?"

"Yeah . . ."

"He's really good at cards. Miss Bleeker said he won lots of money playin' 'em when he was in the army. That's how come he could 'vest in his garage."

It took a moment or two for the full implications of these remarks to sink in. Then John started laugh. So much for his paranoid theories about money laundering and smuggling, he thought. Wesley Warren was a cardsharp!

"I . . . had . . . no idea," he said, sinking down on the bed.

"What's so funny?" Andy demanded.

John got himself under control. "A grown-up joke, buddy. On me."

"Oh."

There was a pause. John reached out and ruffled Andy's toffee-brown hair, hoping he hadn't offended him. Unfortunately, there was just no way he could explain why he'd been laughing without coming off like a . . .

Well, leave it that there was just no way he could explain it.

Andy frowned suddenly, looking down at his chest. "Uh-oh."

"What?" John stiffened.

Rueful blue-gray eyes lifted to anxious brown ones. "I think I put my jammies on wrong."

"Oh." Phew. "That."

Andy got up off the bed. "Yeah," he said with a sigh, starting to pull the garment up and off. "The tag thing is s'posed to be on the inside. And the picture of Simba from *The Lion King* is s'posed to be on the outside in the front."

John didn't respond to this artless recitation. He couldn't. He was transfixed by the sight of a crescent-shaped birthmark located to the right of the base of Andy's bumpy spine.

"*Help!*" The squawk was muffled by the fabric of the pajama top.

John returned to full awareness with a jolt, realizing that Andy had gotten himself all tangled up. He staggered to his feet, coming to the little boy's aid with shaking hands. The urge to brush the birthmark with his fingers to make certain that it was real was very strong, but he fought it down.

"Is somethin' wrong?" Andy asked when his jammies were restored to their proper order.

"No." John shook his head. He was having trouble breathing. "It's just that . . . I, uh, hadn't seen the mark on your back before."

"Oh, yeah." Andy sat back down on the edge of the bed and kicked off his bunny slippers. "The one from when I was borned. I telled you about it."

"You . . . did?"

"Uh-huh. The very first day I meeted you. I said Mommy said—"

"That you'd been kissed by an angel." The words surfaced from the depths of John's memory and slid out his mouth.

"Right!" Andy concurred with an approving smile. The smile gave way to a jaw-cracking yawn. He sagged a little, suddenly looking very weary.

"Time for bed, buddy," John declared huskily. "Santa can't show up until you're asleep."

Andy rubbed his eyes, then stretched out on the bed. John drew the covers up, tucking him in.

"Will Santa know our new house?" the little boy asked through another yawn.

"Absolutely," John replied, bending down and kissing his son on the forehead. His control almost broke when Andy lifted his arms for a hug. "Sleep tight," he managed to whisper as he eased out of the childish embrace.

He had the light switched off and was about to step out the door when Andy's voice stopped him.

"John?"

"Yes, buddy?"

"Can I be Andy Gul'ver now?"

He swallowed convulsively, tears blurring his vision. "You can be anything you want to."

"Really?" The word was spiced with wonder.

"Really. Truly."

"And . . . can I maybe call you Daddy sometimes?"

John took a deep breath then said what was in his heart. "Yes, son. Oh, yes. You can call me Daddy."

Leigh Gulliver blotted her eyes with the sleeve of the exquisite silk peignoir that had been a wedding gift from Deirdre. She was sitting on the king-size bed in the master suite of her new home, awaiting the return of her new husband.

Spread around her were two-dozen travel brochures, each one more incredible than the next. They'd been contained in a beautifully gift-wrapped box the man she loved with all her heart and soul had handed her before he'd gone to tuck their son in for the night.

"From the former Saint Nick to his beloved bride," the card accompanying the box had read. "Where do you want to honeymoon?"

"I hope those are tears of happiness, sweetheart," a resonant male voice said.

She looked up and held out her arms. "How could they be anything else?"

John went to her. They embraced—kissing, caressing.

"You've given me so much," Leigh whispered, stroking her husband's compellingly imperfect face. The ring finger of the hand she used was banded with gold.

"No more than you've given me," he avowed with passionate conviction. "You've given me a life in the light. You've given me your love. You've given me . . . a *s-son.*"

Something inside her went very still at the way he inflected the final word of this litany. She eased back, her heart beating very rapidly. She stared at him for several moments. Then she started to tremble.

"J-John?" she faltered. "What . . . what do you know?"

He took her hands in his, enfolding them tenderly between his warm palms. "I meant what I said about damning biology," he told her, gazing deeply into her eyes. "I love Andy unconditionally because he's your son. But he's mine, as well, Leigh. Mine, in every sense of the word."

"How—?"

His lips curved. "Because I was kissed by an angel, too."

She shook her head, bewitched by the sensuality of her husband's smile but bewildered by the words that accompanied them. "I d-don't—"

John rose to his feet in a lithe movement, tugging the bottom of the dark turtleneck he was wearing free of the waistband of an equally dark pair of pants. Then he unzipped his fly.

"At the risk of reminding you of our appendix-scar exhibitionist Bryan—" he said wryly, easing down his trousers and turning his back to her.

Leigh gasped as she focused on a crescent-shaped birthmark that was identical in size and positioning to the one she'd seen on her little boy hundreds of times.

John pivoted back to face her, his eyes ablaze with tender joy. "My father had one. His father had one."

"Oh . . . *John!*"

Then he was back in her arms. They kissed again. And again.

"Sweetheart," the father of her son murmured, pleasuring her with nuzzling licks and teasing nips. "Oh . . . Leigh . . ."

"But why didn't I *know?*" she asked, tugging at his clothing with greedy fingers. Her blood was fizzing in her veins like electrified champagne.

"Because—" he laughed throatily, his own hands busy with the tiny pearl buttons on her peignoir "—Suzanne Whitney was too shy to look at Nicholas Marchand when he was naked."

She stopped for an instant, drawing back so she could see his face. A unique feminine sense of power suffused her. She watched his eyes flicker and his nostrils flare in response to it.

"Leigh McKay isn't shy," she finally asserted, her voice lush with erotic promise.

John smiled. It was a slow, searing smile that threatened to fuse every synapse in her nervous system. "That's one of many, many reasons I'm madly in love with her."

Leigh took his hands and pressed them against her breasts. His palms curved, caressing and claiming at the same time. Her lungs emptied in a rush of air. She swayed forward.

"I have a wonderful idea," she said at last. "Let's have our Christmas honeymoon . . . right here."

* * * * *

*Look for RESOLVED TO (RE)MARRY—the next
book in the HOLIDAY HONEYMOONS series,
coming January 1997 from Silhouette Desire.*

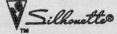

Your very favorite Silhouette miniseries
characters now have a BRAND-NEW story in

Brought to you by:

LINDA
HOWARD

DEBBIE
MACOMBER

LINDA
TURNER

LINDA HOWARD celebrates the holidays with a **Mackenzie**
wedding—once Maris regains her memory, that is....

DEBBIE MACOMBER brings **Those Manning Men** and
The Manning Sisters home for a mistletoe marriage as
a single dad finally says "I do."

LINDA TURNER brings **The Wild West** alive as
Priscilla Rawlings ties the knot at the Double R Ranch.

Three BRAND-NEW holiday love stories...by romance fiction's
most beloved authors.

Available in November at your favorite retail outlet.

The collection of the year!
NEW YORK TIMES BESTSELLING AUTHORS

Linda Lael Miller
Wild About Harry

Janet Dailey
Sweet Promise

Elizabeth Lowell
Reckless Love

Penny Jordan
Love's Choices

and featuring
Nora Roberts
The Calhoun Women

This special trade-size edition features four of the wildly
popular titles in the Calhoun miniseries together in
one volume—a true collector's item!

Pick up these great authors and a chance to win
a weekend for two in New York City at the
Marriott Marquis Hotel on Broadway! We'll pay
for your flight, your hotel—even a Broadway show!

Available in December at your favorite retail outlet.

NEW YORK
Marriott®
MARQUIS

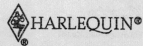 

Add a double dash of romance to your
festivities this holiday season
with two great stories in

Christmas Celebration

Featuring full-length stories by bestselling authors

**Kasey Michaels
Anne McAllister**

These heartwarming stories of love triumphing
against the odds are sure to add some extra
Christmas cheer to your holiday season. And this
distinctive collection features <u>two full-length novels,</u>
making it the perfect gift at great value—for
yourself or a friend!

Available this December at your favorite retail outlet.

In February, Silhouette Books is proud
to present the sweeping, sensual new novel
by bestselling author

CAIT LONDON

about her unforgettable family—*The Tallchiefs*.

TALLCHIEF FOR KEEPS

Everyone in Amen Flats, Wyoming, was talking about
Elspeth Tallchief. How she wasn't a thirty-three-year-old
virgin, after all. How she'd been keeping herself warm at
night all these years with a couple of secrets. And now one
of those secrets had walked right into town, sending
everyone into a frenzy. But Elspeth knew he'd come for
the *other* secret....

"Cait London is an irresistible storyteller..."

—*Romantic Times*

Don't miss TALLCHIEF FOR KEEPS by Cait London, available
at your favorite retail outlet in February from

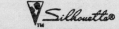

CLST

COMING NEXT MONTH

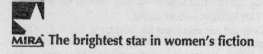